DOUGLAS WATT is a historian, poet and novelist who lives in Linlithgow with his wife Julie and their three children. He won the Hume Brown Senior Prize in Scottish History in 2008 for *The Price of Scotland: Darien, Union and the Wealth of Nations* (2007). *Testament of a Witch* is the second in his series of ingenious murder mysteries set in seventeenth century Scotland featuring lawyers John MacKenzie and David Scougall.

By the same author:

Fiction
Death of a Chief (2009)

History
The Price of Scotland: Darien, Union and the Wealth of Nations (2007)

Poetry
A History of Moments (2005)

Testament of a Witch

DOUGLAS WATT

Luath Press Limited

EDINBURGH

www.luath.co.uk

First published 2011

ISBN: 978-1-906817-79-4

The author's right to be identified as author of this book
under the Copyright, Designs and Patents Act 1988 has been asserted.

The publisher acknowledges the support of

ALBA | CHRUTHACHAIL

towards the publication of this volume.

The paper used in this book is recyclable. It is made from
low-chlorine pulps produced in a low-energy, low-emissions
manner from renewable forests.

Printed and bound by CPI Antony Rowe, Chippenham

Typeset in 11 point Sabon

© Douglas Watt 2011

To Robbie

Nam, ut vere loquamur, superstitio fusa per gentis oppressit omnium fere animos atque hominum imbecillitatem occupavit.
Cicero, *De Divinatione*, Book 2, Chapter 72.

Speaking frankly, superstition, which is widespread among the nations, has taken advantage of human weakness to cast its spell over the mind of almost every man.

Acknowledgements

I would like to thank my wife Julie for her continuing love and support. Her belief in the characters John MacKenzie and Davie Scougall has kept me writing about their journey through late seventeenth century Scotland. Thanks to my children, Jamie, Robbie and Katie, for keeping me firmly grounded in the twenty-first century. I apologise to them for spending too many hours in the seventeenth century. Thanks also to everyone at Luath and to Jennie Renton for editing the text.

List of Main Characters

John MacKenzie, advocate in Edinburgh, Clerk of the
Court of Session

Davie Scougall, writer in Edinburgh

Elizabeth MacKenzie, daughter of John MacKenzie

Sir George MacKenzie of Rosehaugh, advocate, ex-Lord
Advocate

Grissell Hay, Lady Lammersheugh

Andrew Cant, minister of Lammersheugh

Janet Cornfoot, servant of Lady Lammersheugh

Euphame Hay, daughter of Lady Lammersheugh

Rosina Hay, daughter of Lady Lammersheugh

Archibald Muschet, merchant in Lammersheugh

Theophilus Rankine, session clerk of Lammersheugh

Marion Rankine, sister of Theophilus Rankine

Adam Cockburn, Laird of Woodlawheid

Helen Cockburn, Lady Woodlawheid

George Cockburn, son of Adam Cockburn

Colonel Robert Dewar, Laird of Clachdean

Lillias Hay, Lady Girnington

Gideon Purse, lawyer in Haddington

George Sinclair, author on witchcraft

John Murdoch, servant of Lady Lammersheugh

Elizabeth Murdoch, wife of John Murdoch

Margaret Rammage, confessing witch

Helen Rammage, sister of Margaret Rammage

John Kincaid, pricker of witches

PRELUDE

A Sermon on Witchcraft

October 1687

'THIS PARISH IS enthralled to the Devil,' the minister began his sermon, carefully articulating each word. He was a young man in his thirties dressed in black gowns, standing in a large wooden pulpit elevated above the congregation. On the canopy above his head, a board was carved with the text: 'Fear the Lord and honour his house.' His eyes darted round the packed church, moving from face to face.

'This parish is enthralled to the Devil,' he repeated, before turning over an hourglass at the side of the lectern. 'Satan walks amongst us.' He waited through an intense silence.

'We begin,' he continued, 'with Exodus Chapter 22, Verse 18.' The people knew what was coming. They had heard the verse on countless Sabbaths. He raised the volume of his voice: 'Thou shalt not suffer a witch to live.' Then shouting: 'Thou shalt not suffer a witch to live!'

His eyes came to rest on two penitents, a man and woman wearing sackcloth, sitting on stools at the front. Cards tied to their shoulders allowed those behind to read the words scrolled in capitals on their backs:

'FORNICATOR, FILTHY WHORE'.

'We have in this verse a precept of the Law of God, a precept of law given to the judges of the people of Israel, a precept given to those to whom the power of the sword is committed. They shall not suffer a witch to live.' Again silence.

'But what is a witch?' He glared across the worshippers before looking down at his notes. Some gazed longingly back at him. Others were so terrified they could not raise their eyes lest he see into their black hearts.

'By a witch is understood to be a person that hath immediate converse with the Devil. So Leviticus Chapter 20, Verse 27 tells us: "A man also or woman that hath a familiar spirit, or that is a wizard, shall surely be put to death: they shall stone them with stones: their blood shall be upon them." The spirit of God doth expressly mention either man or woman.'

His eyes shone with the ecstasy of power. 'And Deuteronomy Chapter 18, Verses 10 to 13, says: "There shall not be found among you any one that maketh his son or his daughter to pass through the fire, or that useth divination, or an observer of times, or an enchanter, or a witch, or a charmer, or a consulter with familiar spirits, or a wizard, or a necromancer. For all that do these things are an abomination unto the Lord."'

He snatched a look at the hourglass. There was still plenty of time. He repeated with more vigour: 'An abomination unto the Lord!'

Raising his eyes, he continued: 'There are some sins so gross in nature that every single act of them deserves death by the law of God.' He slowed his delivery to emphasise what followed: 'Such sins are bestiality, incest and sodomy. And so I take an act of witchcraft to be such a gross sin. Every act deserves death by the law of God.' The expression on his face was suffused with such earnestness, no one could have doubted that he believed what he said.

'What constitutes a person to be a witch? I speak now of both men and women, as from scripture. It requires a real compact between Satan and that person. They receive the Devil's Mark upon their flesh. Or the parent offers their child unto Satan.'

He addressed a line of older children in the second pew on the left side of the congregation: 'The parent offers their child to him. They receive his mark just as the children of professing parents receiving baptism will be in covenant with God. A witch shall worship Satan as their God. They shall follow him as their guide. They are constituted to be worshippers of Satan. They sell themselves in body and soul to do wickedness. They follow the Devil who is the prince of the power of the air.' He lowered his head, briefly pausing.

'Why do God's creatures turn from him? It flows from the blindness and perverseness that have fallen upon us by the fall of Man. It flows from people who undervalue, slight and condemn the Gospel of Jesus Christ. It flows from the prevalence of lust and corruption among the people in the visible church. It flows from covetousness, pride and malice.' He raised his head: 'Turn you away from Satan.' Then, after another longer pause, lifting his voice: 'Turn you away from Satan!', then shouting: 'Turn you away from Satan!'

He stared again at the penitents. The woman looked down at her bare feet in humiliation. The man gazed at the whitewashed wall behind the minister.

'Men and women are led by Satan to carry out deeds of depravity and evil whether by ordinary means, such as using a cord or napkin to strangle with, or by putting pins in a picture or clay figure, roasting it on a fire and flaming it with vinegar and brandy. This is done to put an innocent person to torment. Witches are called to meetings by Satan where all manner of debauchery and perversity is manifest, such as dancing, drinking strong liquor and singing. All kinds of sin are indulged in, including,' he paused to emphasise what was coming, 'the gravest sin of all, the grossest sin imaginable –

carnal dealings with Satan. It is so opposite to that natural moral honesty which dignifies the marriage of man and woman. It flows from that blindness and perverseness that have fallen upon us by the fall of Man.

'Witches are the greatest hypocrites under the sun. Witchcraft is one of those evil deeds that the spirit of God enjoins death upon. There are today witches in our midst who pollute the parish of Lammersheugh, bringing discord and immorality. We desire that God will bring their works of darkness to light so that His enemies may be punished. Satan blinds the mind of those that despise the Gospel. Show us, oh God – show us who they are.'

The silence was unbearable. It was broken by a finely dressed middle-aged woman rising from her pew. With head bowed, she walked to a side door and left the kirk. She was followed by an old woman, shuffling behind.

The movement distracted the minister, breaking the dramatic momentum of his sermon. Although he was angered by the interruption, he quickly gathered his thoughts.

'Satan blinds the mind of those who despise the Gospel. Let this humble us all. Let us bewail it as a great evil that such a place as Scotland, where the gospel of Christ has been purely preached, should have so many under suspicion of the crime of witchcraft. You that are free, bless God that hath kept you from the wicked one, and pray out of zeal to God and his Glory that he shall bring these works of darkness to light that mar our solemnities and are fearful spots in our feasts. I beseech you, be vigilant. Watch your neighbours. Watch your children. Watch your mother and your father. Watch your master and your servant. None are free from the stain that darkens the nation. Satan walks and smiles in our parish. He spreads evil amongst us. Let us pray...'

Placing a hand on the Bible in the lectern, he closed his eyes, raising the other above his head, palm outwards. At last he appeared to relax. A smile was on his face. It was the smile of a man communing with God, the smile of a man who knew God, a man who knew he was right in what he did, a man who knew that he was saved, chosen from the beginning of time to be one of God's Elect. The congregation lowered their heads and followed the prayer.

'Let all the congregation say Amen. Let all the saints in heaven and earth praise him. Let all the congregation say Amen. Let sun and moon praise him. Let fire, hailstorms, winds and vapours praise him. Let all the congregation say Amen. Let men and women praise him. Let all the congregation say Amen.'

CHAPTER I

Lammer Law

THE WOMAN WAS a streak of black against the browns and greens of the broad rounded hilltop. She stood under a heavy sky beside a small copse of birch. Staring northwards, she listened to the wind in the leaves. It was their last song before autumn cast them into the universe.

When she removed her bonnet, dark auburn hair flecked with grey fell down onto her shoulders. She let the breeze enliven her pallid face as she watched a small boat miles away on the Firth, far beneath her to the north. It was bound for Leith, having crossed the German Sea with a cargo from Amsterdam, she supposed. In her mind she saw a sailor on board thinking of his sweetheart in the Indies, a world away. She felt his loneliness as he stared on the grey sky and brown hills of Scotland. Her own daughters had always loved her stories. Their two faces came to her as they were when young girls. They had lived inside her body once, also. She had been able to protect them, then.

She looked over to the Bass Rock, a dark tooth protruding from the sea. It was where the conventiclers were imprisoned; rigid, self-righteous men. Her eyes moved to the cone-shaped Berwick Law where they burned witches long ago. In the far distance to the west was the sleeping lion of Arthur's Seat and the town of Edinburgh. She had not been there for years, not since before Alexander's death. Her eyes focused on a castle in the foreground, perhaps two miles to the north-east of where she stood, but a thousand feet beneath her. It was a fine structure, perhaps more of a great house than a fortified dwelling, for it had been substantially altered by the Earl during her lifetime. Tweeddale was the head of her husband's family, the Hays. But she did not think that he would be able to help her.

A few miles from the castle were the lineaments of her own world. How still and peaceful it appeared from here – the spire of a kirk, a few dwelling houses between the trees, the gables of Lammersheugh House where she had lived since her marriage, all those years before. The House was surrounded by gardens which they had planted together. It seemed like another world, or someone else's life. She saw him as she always did when she thought of him, or when someone spoke of him, walking in the garden in summer. The image of his body sent a wave of excitement through her. The girls are playing at his feet. He takes one of them by the arms, Euphame, and lifts her off the ground. There are screams of delight. Then the image fades. His arm is round her waist in the lengthening shadows. The memory of the feel of him returns, the memory of happiness – real love, not just desire. They had known each other since they were children, although he was two years older. There had always been something between them. She had watched him standing beside his tall sister in the kirk. But she had not expected that he would choose her. She was the daughter of a decaying house. When he had gone to college in Edinburgh the heart was ripped from her life. The two long years he was in Europe were empty ones when she imagined he had found a rich foreign heiress. But he came back to her, as he had said he would.

She closed her eyes, luxuriating in the bliss of bygone years. It was as if they had lived in a storybook which was not real, a dream maybe. This was real life. She opened her eyes. Pain engulfed her like the tide on a lonely shore.

The vision of the garden was gone. She saw him lying in his winding sheet; pale, cold, but still beautiful. Now he would never return from across the water. And would she ever see him again? In her heart she believed that the minister and elders were wrong. There was still a chance that they might be reunited. She must believe that.

'Grissell.'

For a moment she thought that he was calling her name, that he had come back to her. But in an instant despair returned. The voice was familiar. But it was not his. She did not turn in the direction it came from. The realisation of the present cut deep. She did not hate the voice, only the thought that it was not his. She imagined the small red heart beating inside her.

CHAPTER 2
A Round on Leith Links

SCOUGALL WAS SUFFERING from a cold. As he lowered his head to address the ball, his nose dripped onto the ground between his feet. He sniffed loudly before swinging the club. The ball shot off at a terrific speed, but was sliced. Following it in the air, he watched it bounce on the fairway about two hundred yards away, move violently to the right and come to rest in the rough.

'Confound this cold!' He had almost cursed. He chided himself. It was only a game, after all, the pursuit of leisure. It should not be taken too seriously, unlike work. He asked God for forgiveness. But he did love golf so much, the feeling he got from striking a good shot. Despite his diminutive stature, he could drive further than most men. He loved the sense of satisfaction it gave him, similar to completing a long instrument in the office. But, although he found it hard to admit, it was even more enjoyable to win.

Scougall was dressed in black breeches and jacket. The short white periwig on his head was a fashion accessory he had only recently added to his wardrobe and to which he was not yet accustomed. His pale face looked disconcerted as he stood back to let his partner play.

MacKenzie was a foot taller and a generation older than Scougall. Bending over to tee up his ball on the best spot, he smiled. 'I may have a chance today, Davie. Only a slight one, but a chance.' As he straightened his back, he groaned. An image of himself lying flat, unable to walk for a week, flashed through his mind. Like most tall men he suffered from bouts of back pain. He must try not to hit the ball too hard.

As he concentrated, his expression became deeply serious. Touching his periwig with his right hand, a golfing mannerism, he placed it beside his left on the handle. At the apex, the club stopped for just too long to give the swing fluency; it presented a staccato appearance which lacked the natural elegance of his young companion's. MacKenzie was not a natural golfer like Scougall. Despite having played the game for fifty years he had never managed to improve a swing moulded as a child. Indeed he often joked that he had played his best golf as a twelve-year-old student in Aberdeen in 1643, the year the Scots signed the National League and Covenant, a foolish document if there ever was one. Interfering in the affairs of another nation was always a bad idea, leading to nothing but trouble.

The result on this occasion was a pleasing one. He made sound contact, launching the ball into a perfect parabola. It landed about a hundred and eighty yards away in the middle of the fairway.

The two men gathered their clubs. The weather was fine, the day possessing the freshness of autumn, the sky a glorious blue, the grass of Leith Links a lush green.

'Is this not a day to treasure, Davie?'

'It is a grand one, sir. I might appreciate it better if this cold would lift.'

'Now, before I forget. I have been asked by Sir John Foulis of Ravelston and the Lord Clerk Register to make up a party,' said MacKenzie. 'I have told Sir John that I will bring a partner. I mentioned your name.'

'I would be most honoured, sir.' Scougall was thrilled to

hear of an opportunity to show off his golfing skills in such exalted company.

'Excellent. I may wager a pound or two on the result.'

'I do not gamble, sir,' Scougall said seriously.

'I did not expect that you would, Davie. But you would not deny another man his pleasure?'

The conversation stopped when they reached MacKenzie's ball. He addressed it with an iron, swung inelegantly and threw a large divot into the air. The ball came to rest about thirty yards away.

He swore angrily in Gaelic, before continuing in English: 'The frustrations of golf! Always raising expectations only to crush them the next moment!' He walked forward to play his third shot. 'Have you received your invitation?' he asked casually.

MacKenzie's question lowered Scougall's flagging spirits further. It was three months since he had heard the news of Elizabeth's engagement to Seaforth's brother, but it still caused a sinking feeling. He knew he had no right to feel jealous. After all, he was only her father's clerk and of lower standing in society. She was the great-grand-daughter of MacKenzie of Kintail. But he had fantasised about a future with her.

'I am most honoured, sir. I look forward to it very much,' he lied. 'How do preparations proceed?'

'They go well, Davie. Of course Elizabeth takes great care with everything. The Earl and I are still negotiating about the tocher.'

Scougall was now addressing his ball, which was snugly encased in thick grass. It would be a challenging shot. He put Elizabeth to the back of his mind. After a couple of practice swings he played, but made heavy contact. The ball landed on the fairway a dozen yards away. He closed his eyes. This was most unlike him. He had not played so badly in years.

Before MacKenzie could return to the subject of his daughter's marriage, Scougall moved the conversation in another direction. 'I hear the execution is to take place tomorrow, sir.'

'Poor creature,' replied MacKenzie.

'But she is a witch. She has confessed to her crimes.'

'She is just an ignorant woman, Davie.'

'She has sold herself to Satan!' Scougall grew animated, forgetting his cold. 'Three confessing witches saw her at meetings with the Devil. Her magic caused the deaths of two women and a child. And...' he hesitated as his face reddened, 'she confessed to copulation with Satan.'

'Copulation with Satan!' MacKenzie replied mockingly. 'Well, well. I do not believe she is a witch, Davie.'

'But Satan, sir...'

'I have grave doubts about the crime of witchcraft. I believe it is nothing more than superstition. There are also a number of legal concerns. I assume you have read Rosehaugh's *Criminal Law* on the subject.'

'I have not, sir.'

'The Lord Advocate, or should I say ex-Lord Advocate, may be of a gloomy disposition, but he is a perceptive lawyer...'

'These are dangerous times for Scotland,' Scougall interrupted. 'The Devil is amongst us. He seeks to lead us astray.'

Noticing Scougall's morose mood, MacKenzie decided to say no more on the subject for the moment. The young lawyer's words had brought back dark memories. He saw himself standing at the edge of a crowd in Edinburgh in 1658, almost thirty years before. He could still hear the screams as she was dragged to the stake, recanting her sins, begging to be saved. For the alleged crime of changing herself into a great dog, meeting with the Devil and fornicating with him, she was burned to ashes. MacKenzie shook his head. That same year a hermaphrodite had been executed for lying with a mare, and two young boys burnt on the Castle Hill for buggery. The superstitious nonsense that was believed in Scotland! The witch-hunt following the Restoration of Charles in 1660 had been, if anything, even more vicious. The words of Cicero came to him, as they often did: 'Nam, ut vere loquamur, superstitio fusa per gentis oppressit omnium fere animos atque hominum imbecillitatem occupavit.' He looked at Scougall and shook his head. The young man had much to learn.

CHAPTER 3
The Devil's Pool

THE YOUNG BOY smashed a clump of nettles with a stick as he reached the pool. It was a place he visited often. The other children were too scared. They believed that it was where the Devil washed his feet. They believed that it was his pool and the woods were haunted by fairies. But he liked the place. It was a world away from his dominie's dreary Latin and sharp tawse, from his father's moods and his mother's sadness. Here he could play with toads, fish with his line or watch the birds.

He made for a huge boulder which stood over the pool like a squat tower. It was a base from which to fish for minnows, or defend against the English army. In summer it was where he lay, letting the sun caress his face, enjoying the wanderings of clouds. Today he realised that it was no longer summer. There was a sharpness in the air, a different odour, the smell of change. His eyes followed a murder of crows in a sky pregnant with rain. The birds knew when the seasons changed.

It was only when he sat on the rock, dangled his legs over the edge, boots an inch or two above the surface, taken an apple from a pocket and bitten into it, that he saw the shape under a large birch tree about thirty yards across the still water. The realisation that there was something different came as a shock. He had been to the pool most days during the summer, sometimes in the afternoon, but more often in the gloaming when the place came alive with insects, black flecks of life, wee beasties, as he called them. He loved the birds that haunted the pool at that time, mesmerising him with their acrobatic flight.

From his position he could not tell what it was. It looked as if a cloak had been thrown onto the water. He felt a pang of annoyance – he had thought that he was the only one brave enough to come here. The rock was his tower which he defended with his life. He grabbed a stone from a small hole where he stored them and rose to his feet. He had a good arm. It flew across the pool, hitting the cloak, making a dull thud like a chuckie striking a bag of corn.

Clambering back the way he had come, he crossed the boulders in front of a small waterfall and made his way down the eastern side, moving northwards. Descending beyond a narrow channel where the burn left the pool, he was able to cross the dark brown water by jumping over a few smaller rocks. He knew the easiest way.

Once over, he moved up the western fringe of the pool towards the woods, the large birch and the cloak. He passed through smaller trees, pushing pliant branches back to make his way, before jumping down onto a thin strand of sand.

Only then, when he was a few feet away, did he see that it was a body, face-down in the water, floating in the shallows. He could make out a head with long tangled hair, a cloak, a dark skirt – a woman was drowned. Comprehending all this in a moment he looked around, fearing that he was being watched.

Then a sound came from the woods which sent a pulse of fear through him, a pulse so strong that he had felt nothing like it before in his life. It was not like a whipping from his teacher. It was not a pain like that. It was a deep feeling of desolation. It was the presence of evil. He recalled the words of the minister in the kirk on Sunday.

Glancing over his shoulder, he looked into the woods. They were full of swaying shadows.

A figure appeared, a human shape, a black presence – like a man, but not a man – far back in the woods, its eyes on him. It raised a hand, palm towards him. He heard it speak his name. He heard his own name – his name! 'Geordie, Geordie.' He was being called into the woods, called into the shadows, to come quickly – to obey.

He leapt along the edge of the pool and down to the crossing point. When he reached the other bank he had a compulsion to look back at the creature that was calling him. Something was telling him to stop, to turn. He heard a voice inside his head, whispering his name – 'Geordie, Geordie. Come into the woods – come, boy. Come, join me in the woods, boy.' But he resisted. He ran from the pool, away from the rock, away from the dead woman – away from the thing that called him.

He knew who was beckoning him. He knew it in the pit of his stomach with the certainty of a knife. The minister's words echoed in his head: 'This parish is enthralled to the Devil. Satan walks amongst us.' It was him. It was his pool. It was named after him. Satan had called him.

CHAPTER 4
A Letter in the Library

23 October 1687

MACKENZIE WAS ASLEEP in a chair by the fire in his library, snoring gently. On his lap was the first volume of *Principia Mathematica* by Isaac Newton. A dog lay at his feet in a similar state of slumber, the reverberations from the animal in perfect synchrony with his master's. Rain lashed against the sash windows.

There was a knock at the door. Elizabeth MacKenzie began to speak as she entered, not realising that her father was asleep: 'Father, Archie has come with the mail.'

MacKenzie woke with a startled look, his eyes bulging slightly as he took deep breaths, trying to remember if he was in Edinburgh or at The Hawthorns. Sadness enveloped him when he recalled where he was, who he was. He asked himself, as he had done countless times before, why the feeling always returned. He had a beautiful daughter, success in his profession, a fine house, a library full of books, friends. The same answer came back to him: because of the past. We can change the future, but the past is set in stone.

'Father, I am sorry to have startled you.' Elizabeth approached him with a worried expression.

'It's all right, my dear. As I grow older, my dreams become more vivid. The shock of returning to this body is great.' He smiled at his daughter. 'There is nothing to be concerned about. There, I am awake. Philosophers have commented on the halfway house between sleep and wakefulness. I am fine now.'

Panic dissipated but melancholy remained. The feelings had been worse over the last few months, rising and falling like waves in the ocean. There for a couple of days, then gone for a week. He looked at his daughter standing before him. She was the image of her beautiful mother, the woman he had killed, or that was how he always felt. He tried to think of something else. But the mind was driven by its own master. It was only when fully distracted that such feelings were banished completely.

The dog was also awake, sitting on its haunches, bending its head down to clean its tail, nibbling the end of it, before shaking and letting out a squealing yawn.

MacKenzie pulled himself up in his chair and patted it on the head. 'There, Macrae. What thoughts drift through your mind as you awake?' He often reflected on the canine life. It was interesting how often dogs appeared in the sayings of his people – *Cho leisg ri seana chù* – As lazy as an old dog. He chuckled to himself. The proverbs that he had learned in his youth still brought him amusement.

Elizabeth was standing over him. She kissed him on the forehead. 'Too much work, Father. You need some rest.'

'Perhaps we should visit London before your marriage,' he suggested.

Her young face brightened. 'Really, do you mean it? It would bring me great happiness. We could visit the shops and go to the theatre. Order silk for my wedding gown.'

'I will think about it, my dear. New scenes might rouse me from my lethargy.'

He took his daughter's hand and kissed it.

'Here is your mail.'

Handing him a leather pouch, she withdrew from the

room, the old dog following, hindquarters waddling. MacKenzie emptied the contents onto his lap – a collection of documents and letters. A bundle of instruments from Scougall were tied together by a white ribbon. He placed them on the table beside the chair, putting other legal documents on top.

Two letters remained. He recognised the writing on one. It was from his old friend Archibald Stirling, the Crown Officer. He broke the seal. Stirling was writing to remind him that he had promised to provide his recollections of Montrose's arrival at Inverness in May 1650. MacKenzie smiled. Stirling was still labouring over his history of the Great Rebellion and the nation at the time of the Covenant; an attempt to explain how a country at peace under a lawful king fell into discord and how the Scots, in opposing their king, brought disaster on Scotland, England and Ireland. It was a mighty task to put so much into words. He recalled their conversation by the fireside in Glenshieldaig Castle the previous year at the time of the affair of Sir Lachlan MacLean. As far as history was concerned, Stirling never forgot.

He must write those recollections down for him. There was no excuse. Perhaps it was time to compose an account of his own life. He had witnessed many important events. He was in Edinburgh in the aftermath of the Battle of Dunbar in 1650 and in London for the Restoration of King Charles in 1660. He was present there in the year of the great fire. He had known many of the outstanding figures of his time – Argyll, Lauderdale and Monck. He had spoken with Cromwell and kissed the hand of King Charles himself. A full memoir might be of interest to his grandchildren or generations to come. He could employ Scougall on the research. It would be excellent training and might induce in him a love of history, or at least deflect him from the religious works that he studied so assiduously.

The thought lifted MacKenzie's mood. It would be a new

project, perhaps for his retirement. He would begin with the description Stirling requested. He closed his eyes and tried to recall the scene – the colour, smells and noise of the past – the town of Inverness thirty-seven years before, at a vitally important moment in the history of Scotland. Montrose, on his way to be executed in Edinburgh. How was he to convey in words what it felt like to be there? Phrases came to him first in Gaelic, his native tongue. He would have to translate them into English for Stirling.

Paradoxically, MacKenzie remembered the 1650s as a happy time, despite the bloody war which had ripped the heart out of the Highlands, devastating his clan. The signs were not good for the present time. He was a loyal supporter of the King, although James was an open Catholic. But the King's recent policies were misguided and would only cause trouble, despite their intention of toleration. The conversions of Perth and Melfort were fodder for the extremists, as was giving command of Edinburgh Castle to the Papist Duke of Gordon. The King was bent on promoting Popery in a land which had no appetite for it. It was a policy of the utmost folly. Better to be canny in politics, to promise little and do less.

MacKenzie opened his eyes. The past had a strange flavour. You could have a longing for it, a bitter-sweet feeling, almost a pain for its passing. He could not recall the word in Gaelic to describe it. He did not know an English one that was quite right.

Putting Stirling's letter down, he took up the other. He did not recognise the graceful hand.

To Mr John MacKenzie
Clerk of the Session
Libberton's Wynd
Edinburgh

Peering closely at the small red wax seal, he identified the coat of arms of the Hays of Lammersheugh, an East Lothian family who were clients.

Lammersheugh House
20 October 1687

Dear John,
If you are reading these words set down with my own hand, I am no longer in this world but have joined my beloved husband.

The opening sentence brought MacKenzie forward in his chair. He straightened his back, lowering his eyebrows. Thoughts of history were gone. He rose, taking the letter to the windows overlooking the garden, where leaves were falling from the trees into the sandstone fountain. Rain was pouring down the panes. The infusion of natural light allowed him to read on.

I have ordered my servant Janet to send you this letter if anything should happen to me, as now it surely has. Dark forces have overwhelmed my poor family. It is not for my own sake that I write to you but for my daughters, Euphame and Rosina. They are young women without a mother or father to guide them through this valley of tears. I fear they are in great danger.
I am not able to write openly to you of all matters, lest this letter should be intercepted by my enemies. So I ask you to seek out Janet Cornfoot, my oldest servant, whom I have known since I was a girl. She is the only one I trust in the parish. Believe all that she tells you, even if it runs counter to your rational thoughts. She can

be found in her cottage in the Blinkbonny Woods where she is settled in old age.

I know my dear husband held you in the highest regard, as do I. I have no one else to turn to. I beg you to protect my children. But do not tell anyone that I have made this request of you. When you come to Lammersheugh, follow the role of family lawyer.

I ask that you have particular regard to my latterwill which I have recently altered. You will find much in it if you read deeply, as I know you will. Only a man of experience and wisdom can unpick the tangled threads which have led to this calamity.

Please keep my daughters at the front of your thoughts. The future may bring happier times for the House of Lammersheugh.

Your most humble friend,
Grissell Hay, Lady Lammersheugh

MacKenzie looked solemnly out of the window. The wind was whipping leaves widdershins around the fountain. He wondered what dreadful events had overwhelmed Grissell. The last time they had met, about two years ago, she was in mourning for her husband Alexander, who had died of the flux. A Gaelic proverb came to him – *Chan eil fhios air an uair seach a' mhionaid*. He translated, speaking the words aloud as if explaining them to Davie Scougall – The hour of death is as unknown as the minute. It was over forty years since his father died, five since he had buried his mother. And now this fine woman had been taken in the most terrible circumstances.

Clouds rolled in. The sky darkened. There was a slight hint of something remembered, the familiar feeling of nausea. But he knew he could dispel it. Despite the disturbing news, he felt his mind opening, turning away from itself. There was something more to be done than dull work at the Session. Life had been uneventful since the escapade with the evil rogue Glenbeg and the chameleon Primrose.

He adjusted his periwig in a small mirror, noticing that he was almost an old man. Almost, he thought, but not quite. His memoirs must wait. There was work to be done.

His daughter was in the kitchen overseeing the preparation of dinner, chatting to Meg, the cook. 'Beth.' He always used the diminutive when he thought she might be displeased with what he was about to say. She smiled, relieved to see his good humour had returned. 'I have news from Edinburgh. I must go back tonight.'

Her smile disappeared. 'But father... a storm is on the way. You cannot travel on such a night!'

MacKenzie took his daughter's hand and kissed it.

CHAPTER 5

Death on the Castle Hill

SCOUGALL CHECKED THE time on his new clock, completed the clause he was writing, and returned his quill to the stand. With great care he placed the document in a small chest, which he then locked. As he pulled on his black cloak, he ruefully thought of Elizabeth MacKenzie, smiling to himself as he recalled the painful shyness of his first visit to The Hawthorns. He had imagined that they had become good friends and had allowed his imagination to create a future for them. But what could an advocate's daughter, and a pretty one at that, see in a dull notary public who brought neither wealth nor looks? He caught his reflection in the window. He was a small plain man with a ridiculous wig on his head. As self-loathing rose within him, his face coloured. He was no catch, of that he was sure. The company which Elizabeth kept was miles above him; sons and daughters of advocates and lairds, even the nobility, a world of which he was not a part of. It was only natural that she should seek to marry as high as possible. He knew in his heart that MacKenzie would not approve of a match to a man like him.

But on opening the door of his small office, his feelings of inadequacy disappeared. The view of the crown-shaped steeple of St Giles against the sky always cheered him. He could offer other things, if not looks or wealth – affection, security, love. He would have to lower his sights somewhat. Perhaps the daughter of a Musselburgh merchant. His mother could secure him a list of candidates as she knew everyone in the parish. He must visit home soon and begin proceedings. But the prospect of a local girl did not excite him much. There was also Edinburgh – a daughter of a fellow notary public. He could ask MacKenzie to keep his ear to the ground. He thought of the wry smile appearing on his face as he broached the subject. But after a laugh he might provide some sound advice.

His parents had been on at him for years to marry. For some reason he kept putting it off. He was now twenty-five with savings of 500 pounds Scots, more than 40 pounds sterling, a healthy sum for a man of his age. Paying only a lodging fee to Mrs Baird, he was able to put away a little each month. And he had prospects. MacKenzie held his work in high regard. When he retired he was likely to recommend him to his clients. But would a Musselburgh lass or an Edinburgh one make the better match? That was a question for MacKenzie's philosophers!

He closed the door, locked it and climbed a few steps. The High Street was much busier than usual. All kinds of folk came to town to see a witch burn.

He picked his way through the crowd drifting up towards the castle. Crossing the road to the Luckenbooths, he began to browse in the shops surrounding the ancient kirk, looking for a bargain, perhaps a collection of sonnets to impress a prospective wife. He found himself, as he often did, at Mr Shields' booth – a bookseller who dealt in golf clubs, the perfect combination!

Scougall had begun to collect books, influenced by MacKenzie's large library at The Hawthorns. He had purchased a bookcase which took pride of place in his lodgings and was now filled with a hundred books. A year before he had only possessed half a dozen texts. A new purchase would bring him much pleasure.

He rummaged through the books, broadsheets and pamphlets on the table, before catching sight of a work he had not seen before. Taking the small book in his hands, he read the title with growing interest: *Satan's Invisible World Discovered; or, A choice Collection of Modern Relations, proving evidently against the Saducees and Atheists of this present Age, that there are Devils, Spirits, Witches, and Apparitions, from Authentick Records, Attestations of Famous Witnesses, and undoubted Verity by Mr George Sinclair late Professor of Philosophy in the Colledge of Glasgow.*

The old bookseller addressed him enthusiastically, revealing a cavern of decaying teeth: 'A recent publication, Mr Scougall – a work of fine scholarship. The author was a professor at the college of Glasgow.' He lowered his voice, looking around furtively to make sure no one was listening. 'He is a man of the Covenant. Our time comes, our time comes.' Shields knew that Scougall shared his preference for the Presbyterian form of Protestant worship.

Putting religious politics aside, he continued his sales pitch. 'He proves beyond doubt the ignorance of atheism.' The bookseller shook his head. 'We must be vigilant, Mr Scougall, always vigilant. Satan is at work in Scotland. He ploughs in fertile fields. We are all sinners.' Then lowering his voice again: 'Our King is an agent of Antichrist, is he not?'

Scougall ignored the question. Weighing the book in his hands, he experienced a slither of excitement. The subject matter was intoxicating.

'How much are you asking, Mr Shields?'

The young lawyer attempted to conceal his interest, but the bookseller knew he had a sale.

'A fine read, Mr Scougall. A fine read. You will learn much

from it.' He looked up in the direction of the castle. 'I must close up soon, sir. It is almost time. Five shillings.'

It was more than he had expected to pay, but Scougall was too eager to barter. 'I will take it.' Removing some coins from his pocket, he handed them to the old man.

Engrossed with his purchase, he had not noticed the crowd swelling around the Luckenbooths, drifting slowly up the High Street towards the Castle. As he thanked Shields, a hush descended. All eyes turned in the direction of the Canongate. Scougall slipped the book into a pocket of his cloak.

A small procession was just visible coming from the direction of Holyrood House. At first he could only discern a horse drawing a cart, but as it came closer he saw that a tall figure walked in front. The realisation that this was the public hangman gave him a jolt. A minister and four town guards followed behind. As they approached, he noticed another person sitting in the cart; a small bareheaded woman dressed in sackcloth. Her head was cast down. She was a tiny, crumpled thing.

The cart seemed to take forever to reach him. When it did, the wheels stopped suddenly, directly across the road. He was shocked when the woman raised her head, for he had expected to see the ugly countenance of an old hag. Instead he looked on a young woman with a desperate look on her pale face. Although she was emaciated and exhausted, her eyes still burned with life. For an instant they fixed on him. Out of the whole crowd she had chosen him! The gaze of a witch was upon him! Fear danced across his chest. He was terrified that she was about to accuse him of complicity in her crimes. He looked down at his boots, counting the seconds. At last the wheels turned.

She did not look capable of harming anyone, but Satan could trick the unwary. He closed his eyes, beseeching God to protect him, recalling the words of Exodus: 'Thou shalt not suffer a witch to live'. The Devil was surely at work in Scotland, as Mr Shields said.

Scougall joined the throng behind the cart, drawn by the invisible pull of a public execution. They plodded their way in a silence broken intermittently by angry shouts, words of bitter hatred launched at the witch.

They were soon in the Lawnmarket, the part of the High Street nearest Edinburgh Castle, where tenements rose steeply on either side to six storeys. The windows were all open. Another crowd was witnessing events from the stone walls above. By the time they reached the Castle Hill it was growing dark. Scougall looked around him at the morbid procession of flickering torchlit faces: men and woman, young and old, rich and poor, nobles, lairds, lawyers, clerks, craftsmen and beggars. Cloaks pulled in tight against the cold.

The sun set behind the black mass of the Castle, transforming the hill into an amphitheatre of darkness. The cart came to rest in an open area lit by torches. The woman was dragged down by the hangman and pushed towards a wooden stake about six feet in height. Scougall noticed that she was shaking. A whimpering sound came from her lips. But he was too far away to hear the prayer she uttered. He did not catch her words of recantation, begging God for forgiveness.

The executioner tied her to the stake. Recalling the list of sins that she had committed, Scougall wondered what path had led her to such a death. The minister offered a brief prayer, but his words were lost in the wind, blown into the black emptiness. As he moved back into the shadows, she looked down, unable to meet the eyes of the tall figure who was approaching.

Scougall had expected more ceremony, but the hangman's hands were round her neck, crushing the life out of her as if strangling a goose. She was dead in a couple of minutes.

Scougall prayed for her soul. The executioner set light to the faggots around the stake. The body was quickly engulfed in flames, the reek of roasting flesh drifting across the night.

Satan is diminished, God is victorious, Scougall told himself. He experienced a mixture of emotions; relief for his country and his own soul – a witch was dead; but also an aching hatred of the Devil for corrupting such a pitiful creature.

CHAPTER 6
A Portrait of Lady Girnington

LOOKING AT THE portrait of the young woman, she tried to remember what it was like not to be afflicted by grossness. It had been painted just after her marriage in 1656, when the great Oliver Cromwell was Lord Protector of England, Scotland and Ireland. She was sixteen and her husband sixty-four. She had returned to Scotland after a torrid six months in London, having delivered an ugly little child which was taken from her a few minutes after the birth. She recalled the baby's startled bastard face as it was presented to her after a day's agony. When fever took hold of her, the doctors had thought that she would not live to see the dawn. But somehow, against the odds, she had rallied. When she woke, childless, she felt transformed herself; no longer the young maid seeking excitement in the south. Perhaps the Devil had taken her soul.

Her time in London was a frivolous sequence of dinners and receptions among the great and good who surrounded Cromwell; a court of a kind. Oliver was king in all but name and would have made a glorious one. She recalled the lightness and dizziness of her youth. She was beautiful and courted by all, even the great man himself had praised her beauty. Elizabeth Murray, who was now Duchess of Lauderdale, was a jealous rival. It had seemed that anything was possible.

Then she met him, a young kinsman of the Earl of Fairfax. He lured her with his fine looks and wit, writing sonnets in praise of her, expressing his love, the urgency of his desire, telling her they should seize the moment, not tarry, for who knew what the future might hold. And he was proved right. Two years later he was dead from plague.

She looked at the image of herself from that time. She was lean with soft white skin, dark curls of hair on her shoulders, sparkling eyes. She was struck by her body's fecundity. The artist, whose name now escaped her, had done a good job. But the man in London had taken everything from her, disappearing like a spirit when he learned she was with child, seeking out another virgin to deflower.

The birth had changed her. She looked again at the image of the young woman recently married to the Laird of Girnington. She knew that behind those eyes was furious resentment at the way she had been treated. When she emerged from the fever she had vowed that she would live thereafter on her own terms, and had done so during the thirty years since, although she had paid a price. A twinge of guilt was banished by anger; for her treatment by the courtier, the poet, the liar; but also for her treatment by her father who had banished her, to the small estate of Girnington not far from where she was born, and to the little laird whom she had married, and whom she literally and metaphorically looked down on; a man she had regarded as old, even as a young girl when he had played with her in the gardens of Lammersheugh.

She had removed every portrait of him from Girnington when he died. There were no close relatives to complain about their disappearance, so she had gathered them up, thought about consigning them to the cellar, but instead carried them herself to a quiet spot in the gardens and burned them. She had hated the little creature so much that she had rejoiced when he was struck down by palsy two years after their marriage. She had hastened his end, taken the eiderdown pillow from his bed and smothered him with it. He was so weak there was barely any struggle. She told herself that she did not want him to linger in pain. And there he lay, peacefully. She wondered if she was destined for Hell, but somehow she could not believe in such a place. How could there be a Hell if there was no God? There was only human power, hard and brutal, the sole absolute in the universe.

The image of the little man on her wedding day still brought colour to her cheeks, even after thirty years. She had hoped to marry an English earl's son. Negotiations between her father and the Earl of Moltonfield were well advanced. Her father's service for Cromwell's regime had propelled him from Lothian laird to political figure of importance. They had met on a number of occasions, but were never left alone. He was tall and handsome, a real catch. But she had been weak. Desire had tortured her. She could not wait. She had let lust transport her.

A vision of her wedding night came back to her with all its humiliations. The withered cock in her hands, like a lifeless sparrow starved of blood; her vain attempts to bring life to it, the words she had used to rouse him. She could recall each one as if spoken yesterday. No girl should have to suffer in that way. She had demanded her own bed and he had obliged readily enough. She could not sleep with such a creature. She was voluptuous. She had a body which men were captivated by. He was unmoved by her full breasts. She called him 'sodomite' in her anger, remembering something of the stories he told of his youth in Italy.

She had sought refuge in food and lovers. She had exalted in both pleasures, eating men like dishes, devouring dishes like men. She hoped that one would make her pregnant. A child would be some return for her misfortune, a replacement for the one she had been forced to give up. Her first lover was the artist who had painted the portrait she looked upon. She remembered with pleasure the shocked expression on his face as she took the brush from his hand, placed it on the easel and held his young hand to her breast. He was good; they had fucked each time he painted her. After a couple of sessions she lost her inhibitions, uncaring of whether she was interrupted by the servants. On one occasion her husband himself came into the chamber as she straddled her lover. He left as if he had witnessed nothing and never mentioned it. She threatened the servants that if they spread rumours they would be dismissed. Anyway, she did not care. It conquered her despair for a little while. But there was no child.

The painter was soon gone and she took others, sucking the seed from them, hoping that they might impregnate her. She chose them judiciously, seeking satisfaction only in those over whom she had power and whose silence could be bought, so that none might control her; virile servants, indebted lairds, doctors with pregnant wives. Only one had caused trouble. A lawyer, who went to swear before the kirk session that she had spoken lewdly to him when ostensibly seeking legal advice, but she denied everything and preserved her reputation for rectitude within the parish. Sometimes she travelled to Edinburgh or London, where she could more easily obtain young men. She never loved another after the poet. As she became more gross in body and her beauty faded, she felt her power grow.

The years passed, but she did not fall pregnant. The desires of the flesh faded, but not her appetite for food. Her life became more serene and she spent time improving her house and estates. In politics she placed herself with those who opposed the King and his Catholic brother, looking back to the days of the Commonwealth with affection, although in private she viewed that time as a mistake. She supported the exclusion of the Duke of York and gave succour, secretly, to Presbyterians who came out in the rebellions of 1666 and 1679.

She would make sure that her nieces did not make the same mistakes she had. They would inherit Girnington when she died. If only her beloved brother had not passed away so prematurely. The estates of Girnington and Lammersheugh joined together would make a powerful patrimony. But she must proceed with caution.

There was a knock on the door. She turned from the view out of the window of the Lammermuir Hills. A servant entered. She had never made an advance on Leitch during his twenty-five years' service. She smiled to herself. Even as a young man he was repulsively ugly. But he was loyal. He stood in front of her with his usual imperturbable look.

'They have found a body at the Devil's Pool, my lady.'

'What do you mean, Leitch?' The news was interesting.

'A woman's body is found at the Devil's Pool. She is drowned.'

'Who is she?'

'Lady Lammersheugh. The body is taken back to the house.'

She turned to the hills, a smile on her fat face. 'Thank you Leitch. Keep me informed. I will have dinner in my chambers tonight.'

CHAPTER 7
Coffee in Edinburgh

24 October 1687

THE ROYAL COFFEE HOUSE was full by the time Scougall arrived, the air thick with tobacco smoke and the smell of coffee – a drink which he had no liking for, but which was much praised by MacKenzie. He spotted him at the back of the room, reading a book.

'Here, sit down, you look tired, Davie.' MacKenzie smiled at his young assistant. 'Some coffee will revive you.' He signalled to the boy that he wanted two more cups.

'I did not sleep well last night, sir. The execution left me in a state of... agitation. After dinner I read a book which I had bought from Mr Shields, a most engrossing, but disturbing work – *Satan's Invisible World Discovered*.'

'I have a copy, Davie. It was published by Reid in 1685.'

Scougall ignored MacKenzie's comment. 'Once I began reading, I could not put it down. By the time I sought sleep, it would not come. My mind kept returning to certain passages, especially relating to the troubles Sir George Maxwell of Pollock met from the Devil and his hags.'

'I would have advised you not to attend such a spectacle, nor to read such a book after witnessing it. You have watched the death of an innocent woman,' said MacKenzie sternly.

'Witches are infecting the kingdom, sir!' exclaimed Scougall, suddenly invigorated. 'There is news this morning of delations in Ayr, Dumfries and Fife. A witch-hunt is started!'

The waiter arrived with two steaming cups of coffee. MacKenzie took a sip from his. Scougall let a small amount into his mouth, swallowing reluctantly. It was, perhaps, an acquired taste.

'Our countrymen lose their wits,' MacKenzie observed. 'The kingdom is supposedly threatened by the charms of old women. Most are accused by their neighbours out of spite.'

'Then you do not believe we are in danger?'

'A fever takes hold of us, a frenzy of our senses. We seek to explain our ills by blaming others. It is a malady which has only afflicted us for a hundred years or so, Davie. Our histories have little to say of witchcraft before the great change of religion in 1560. Witches are the spawn of our reformation! The witch-hunt is a cancer which robs all of reason, whipped up by men of God!'

'Are you saying there are not any witches? Sinclair warns of Sadducism.' Scougall was troubled.

MacKenzie recognised that Scougall would have difficulty accepting his sceptical views on the subject. A debate could wait for another occasion. 'I simply ask you to lay aside your prejudices. Apply reason to these cases. Do not accept what you read in the pamphlets of fanatics or what you are told by ministers. Think for yourself, Davie. Rosehaugh calls into question the legal basis by which many of these poor wretches are convicted.' He took another sip of his coffee before continuing. 'I accept that the parishes of Scotland are full of men and women who believe in witches, or who believe they are witches. But it is a delusion. It is superstition. The kingdom is in as much danger from the smoke from his pipe.' MacKenzie nodded towards a man at the next table.

Scougall reflected on what MacKenzie had said. But his acceptance of witches was as firm as his belief in the existence of his own mother and father. The name of Rosehaugh did not sway him in any way. The man was a cruel persecutor of conventiclers, brave men and women who risked everything to worship God in the way they chose. MacKenzie was wrong. The kingdom was in danger. Satan was present in Scotland. An image from his childhood came to him. The face of a woman accused of witchcraft in Musselburgh. She was known to his father as she had worked as the servant of a burgess. His parents' conversations were full of nothing else for weeks. And he had met the woman! She had even been civil to him, greeting him warmly in the street, seeming little different from the other women in the burgh. He had never seen her again. She was tried in Edinburgh, found guilty and executed. Her children and grandchildren were shunned, left to fend for themselves. Most of them died in poverty. Satan could destroy lives, innocent lives. He summoned up the courage to pursue the point.

'I can only praise the ministers who root out such Devilry.'

'May I suggest you leave aside the study of witchcraft. There are enough zealots in Scotland. It is a crime which masks others, revealing the very worst of humanity.' Anger flashed in MacKenzie's eyes.

Scougall yawned. He could not deny that the subject was interrupting his sleep. He knew the word of God on the subject. Witches should be put to death. The Bible said so.

MacKenzie sensed that it would take more than a conversation in a coffee house to overturn a lifetime's belief. And the Presbyterians accused the Papists of superstition!

'Let us change the subject, Davie, and turn to the reason I have asked you to meet me this morning.' MacKenzie withdrew the letter from his leather case and passed it to Scougall. 'Yesterday I received this from Lady Lammersheugh. She lives, or I should say, lived near Haddington. I have represented the family for years.'

After reading it, Scougall raised a perplexed face.

'This morning I have word that Grissell Hay is dead, drowned in the Lammer Burn. She is to be buried two days hence. What do you make of that?'

'She has foretold her own death, sir. Or at least she had suspicions that her life was in danger.'

'I must follow her instructions. Her husband, Alexander Hay, died a couple of years ago. He was a client and friend. I travel to Lammersheugh tomorrow for the funeral. I will have little work for you over the next few days. You may rest your quill and practise your golf swing.'

'Then I will leave town also, sir. I had intended to visit my parents. Now I have the time to do so,' Scougall said enthusiastically before taking another sip of coffee. 'We could ride together to Musselburgh. Take a meal with my family before you travel on to Haddington.'

'That is a fine idea, Davie. It would give me great pleasure to meet them. Let us leave tomorrow at dawn.'

CHAPTER 8

An Evening by the Fireside

SHE SAT BY the fire, sharing the warmth with her dog. The cottage was a single room lit by a candle on a table beside the solitary chair. Humming a gentle melody, she gazed into the flames, tapping her foot on the dog's side. She remembered her granny singin the same air in a bustlin cottage fu o bairns, nae alane as she wis now. Aw gane – her brithers an sisters, mither an faither; her man tane ten year ago, her son lost. The thought brought a tear to her eye. Naethin heard o him fir twenty year since he left in a ship fir Jamaica. Aw her ither bairns stillborn or short-lived.

And now Grissell tane as weel, bonnie Grissell, who wis like a dochter tae her. She had nursed her as a girl, loved her as her ain. She saw her as a bairn playing in the gairdens at Aikwood in the year the Scottish army was routed at Dunbar by Cromwell. The daft ministers had cawed fir a spiritual army. Her memory wis still shairp fir lang ago. It wisnae sae guid fir the present, like whaur she had put her scissors.

She thought again o Grissell, her body lyin in the hoose, tae be buried the morrow, set beneath the cauld earth wi Alexander. Her twa bairns left withoot a faither or mither. She had thought that they had done enough. Grissell seemed content, at last. Anger replaced grief in her heart. They were aw aifter the lands of Lammersheugh. But nane wid hae the saft body o Grissell now! At least there wis that – the only guid tae come o it. But how were the girls tae survive? They were young women, vulnerable tae a corrupt wirld which devoured aw that wis guid.

She wid look aifter them as she had looked aifter thir mither. She kenned not how lang she had afore being cawed by the Lord, but she wid devote aw tae them. Though it wis nae really her place, she wid counsel them. She had power. She had wirds o power. Her chairms wid protect them. She must speak tae the girls the morrow. Tears were on her cheeks. She felt a need to take Grissell in her arms.

The dog was suddenly awake, ears cocked, the hair on his back erect. He growled at the door. The growl became a snarling bark. No like him, she thought.

'There lad, hush, hush.'

There was a tapping sound on the window shutter. Taking a shawl from the back of the chair, Janet placed it over her shoulders, rising painfully with her candle.

She walked slowly to the door, opened it and stared into the blackness. The dog stopped barking. 'There, ye see, laddie. Only the wind.'

As her eyes adjusted to the darkness, she noticed a hanging shape. There was a sound: a drip, drip, dripping on the stone floor. The dog ran forward and began to lick at the dark pool. She raised her candle and screamed. The body of a black cat loomed in front of her. It had been garrotted with a thin cord and nailed to the lintel.

CHAPTER 9
Spiritual Exercises

'COME IN MR CANT. Please be seated.' The young woman spoke in a commanding tone. Turning to her servant, an old stooping man, she snapped, 'We are not to be disturbed, Murdoch.'

Cant took a seat by the window, placing the Bible on the table. He removed his hat to reveal a prematurely bald head. He was not wearing a periwig today, the only indication that he did not consider this to be a formal occasion.

She followed the servant to the door. Watching him make his way down the corridor, she closed it carefully before speaking to the minister. 'Now, Mr Cant. Where were we?' She was dressed in a fine blue velvet gown. Her hair fell loose over her shoulders, a single pearl necklace gracing her neck.

'I must again pass on my condolences for the loss of your mother, Rosina.'

She felt tears welling up within her. But she would conquer her emotions.

The minister hesitated for a moment, peering closely at her. 'Are you well, Rosina?' As she did not reply at once, he began to leaf through the Bible, searching for the chapter they had discussed at their last meeting.

'I am as well as can be expected, Mr Cant.' The minister raised his head to observe her. She did not look like a girl who had just lost her mother. She seemed almost cheerful. 'You must realise that we had no choice. We had to act on the accusations made against her. Our souls are in danger, Rosina.'

'I do not want to talk about her, Mr Cant,' she said emphatically, before sitting down.

He had watched her change from a child into a woman. Although initially reluctant, believing that the instruction of the female sex was beneath him, he had come to enjoy their weekly meetings, which were so different from his preaching or the labours of the kirk session. The spiritual wellbeing of a soul was such a responsibility. As directed by Lady Girnington, his aim was to guide Rosina towards the Presbyterian form of worship, counteracting the Episcopalian tendencies of her mother. But he had to admit that after three years of instruction he had no idea whether she tended towards bishop or presbytery. All he could say was that she had a sharp mind, often posing questions that he found difficult to answer, sending him back to his theology books in the manse. Sometimes he had suspicions that she was playing a game, acting out a role. There were parts of her which she would not open up to him. But he hoped that in time she would come to see the importance of the Presbyterian form of worship.

There was another reason the sessions were becoming challenging. He found himself increasingly deflected from his purpose of instilling godliness into her. He had begun to notice her eyes, the texture of her hair, her smile, the shape of her shoulders, the comeliness of her figure. At first he was annoyed with himself for being unable to control the feelings of lust which were kindled within him. The flame grew with each visit and as the weeks passed he became more and more intoxicated. He told himself that lust within marriage was not a sin. It was something to be exalted. But she was a laird's daughter. Marriage was out of the question. However, he might be considered if no one else would take her. The accusations against her mother might put off other suitors. His desire to touch her was overpowering. He imagined reaching out his hand. He could not. He found the passage he was looking for.

'Here we are, Rosina – Chapter 6 of the Book of Esther.'

She knew she had power over him. She knew by the way that he looked at her. His instruction was irksome in the beginning, but as she noticed how he was with her – his devouring eyes and pious comments – she sensed an inner turmoil and gained enjoyment from observing it. She felt sure that he could be manipulated. She moved her hand forward, resting it for a moment on the back of his.

CHAPTER 10
A Meal in Musselburgh

25 October 1687

'DAVIE!' A SMALL woman shrieked from the far side of the room. She dropped her kitchen knife on the cutting board and rushed to the door, flinging her arms round Scougall's neck. 'Come awa. Come awa in.'

'Mother, this is Mr MacKenzie,' said Scougall, embarrassed by the welcome.

The older lawyer ducked as he entered, for the door was only about five feet above the floor. The dark feelings of the last months were gone. The pit was vanquished. Life was rushing back to him full of interest. Here he was in a new affair of some kind, and where better to begin than in the house of a Musselburgh merchant!

'Come awa in Mr MacKenzie, come awa in.' Taking his hand, she shook it warmly, beaming up at him as if towards a giant. She was a dumpy woman in late middle age in the dark attire of a burgess's wife. Her sleeves were rolled up to reveal flabby but powerful arms. MacKenzie reflected on the length of Scougall's drives on the golf course. This was perhaps where his prowess with a club came from.

'It is a pleasure, Mr MacKenzie, a rare pleasure for aw the family. We've heard muckle aboot ye in Davie's letters. An here ye are in the flesh in oor ain hame. It is a great honour, sir. Ye dae us a great honour, tho,' turning to Scougall who was wishing the floor would eat him up, 'he disnae write much, Mr MacKenzie, nor did he tell us ye were sic a distinguished gentleman. And sae tall. He never telt us that!' She burst into laughter.

'Why was I to tell you Mr MacKenzie's height, mither?'

Ignoring her son, she continued: 'It has brocht us baith, masel and ma husband, much content, much content, tae see Davie sae weel settled in yer service, sir, and doing sae weel in the law and sae muckle esteemed by ye.'

'Mother!' Scougall switched back into English to emphasise his annoyance. He had forgotten how she could humiliate him.

'Your mother is quite right, Davie. You do great service to me and to the profession of writer. He has the most accurate pen in Edinburgh, Mrs Scougall. His work is praised by all the lawyers I know. He is also, I must add, a very agreeable companion and a master on the Links!'

Mrs Scougall was delighted to hear her son so highly praised. 'He was aye swinging a club, ivver since he was a bairn.' But her joviality suddenly disappeared. 'As lang as he doesnae spend too much time on the course and still seeks tae serve God.'

As soon as she said this, however, she broke again into bright laughter. MacKenzie found himself laughing too, although he was not sure why. Scougall did not see the joke.

'Please sit by the fire. There's a cauld wind the day. Tak Mr MacKenzie's cloak, Davie. Fetch him a cup o ale. Ye will hae tae excuse me, sir. Davie's note only arrived yestreen. I must prepare oor meal.'

'Please do not go to any trouble, Mrs Scougall.'

She looked as if she had just been insulted. 'Nae advocate will cross ma threshold and no savour the delights o ma kitchen. Certainly nane as tall as you, Mr MacKenzie.' Again her earnest expression gave way to a broad beam. She shuffled off to the other side of the room and took up her knife.

Scougall filled two wooden cups from a keg and returned to the fireside. As was often the case, he could not think of anything in particular to say. He thought about raising the subject of the burning on the Castle Hill, but decided against it. He did not want to spoil the convivial atmosphere. Anyway, MacKenzie seemed happy enough sipping his ale and watching the fire. He sat back and closed his eyes, remembering the reason for his visit, wondering how he might broach the subject with his parents. Should he have a word with his father or his mother first? The image of a faceless wife filled his thoughts as he pictured himself returning home from work to a bonnie companion – sharing the rest of the evening together, and then the mysterious joys of the marriage bed.

MacKenzie was woken by the sound of the door opening. He had fallen into a delicious nap after finishing his ale. A small man entered who bore a striking resemblance to Scougall; the dark shadow caused by vigorous growth of facial hair, small eyes. Behind him were two soberly dressed young women. They must be Davie's twin sisters.

Scougall rose to make the introductions. 'Father, Janet, Jean. I am delighted to introduce Mr John MacKenzie.'

The merchant shook hands with MacKenzie. The girls curtsied: 'Here is oor ain Davie back hame wi the famous John MacKenzie,' said Mr Scougall. 'This is a great pleasure, sir.'

The twins smiled shyly as MacKenzie bowed his head.

'The food is ready. Tak a seat, Mr MacKenzie,' called Mrs Scougall from the other side of the room.

The table was set for a small feast. There was a dish of marrow-bones, a leg of mutton, a loin of veal, two capons and an assortment of vegetables. They took their seats around the wooden table. Before eating Mr Scougall said grace.

MacKenzie lowered his head out of respect to his hosts.

He opened the conversation. 'How is business, Mr Scougall?'

'It is brisk, sir. We cannae complain.'

'What do you trade in?'

'I deal mainly in fish, sir. I buy frae the men here in Musselburgh and sell tae the merchants in Edinburgh. Ma faither followed the same trade. It is a fairly regular one.' Scougall's father passed round the dish of vegetables before continuing: 'Are ye spending the nicht in Musselburgh, Mr MacKenzie?'

'No. I head for the Bell in Haddington tonight. Tomorrow I must attend the funeral of Lady Lammersheugh.'

The merchant's face dropped. He stopped munching on his mouthful of mutton.

'What is it, Father?' Scougall asked.

'Only what I hae heard in the toon.' Mr Scougall lowered his voice. 'Lady Lammersheugh was accused of witchcraft by a confessin witch, Margaret Rammage, and questioned by the Lammersheugh session last week. Three days later her body was found in a pool in the Lammermuirs. Folk are sayin she's tain her ain life to escape the stake.'

Scougall's face whitened. The twins lost their playfulness. Mrs Scougall's laughter drained away.

'I did not know this, Mr Scougall. It is most distressing news,' said MacKenzie. 'I received word that she was dead two days ago. I had not expected such a development. I have known Lady Lammersheugh for many years. I can assure you that such accusations are ill-founded and must be motivated by malice.'

His mind was racing back through the letter. This news placed everything in a very different light, especially the wellbeing of the girls. The words came to him: *only a man of experience and wisdom can unpick the tangled threads which have led to this calamity. Have particular regard to my latterwill which I have recently altered.*

Scougall's father continued in a respectful but determined tone. 'There is evidence, sir – the delation o a confessin witch. Lady Lammersheugh must hae selt hersel tae Satan. Some say she used witchcraft tae hairm Lady Girnington, her sister-in-law.'

'These are dark times, Mr MacKenzie,' Mrs Scougall interjected, 'dark times for oor land. Satan walks among us. God help us. I fear for ma dochters. He can trick a young girl. Tak her as his ain. Appear as a handsome gentleman dressed in black. Turn her heid wi promises.' She spoke directly to her daughters. 'Ca canny, girls. Dinnae linger wi ony strangers.'

The girls nodded seriously.

'I am sure there is a rational explanation for what has happened,' said MacKenzie.

But Scougall knew in his bones that his mother was right. There was great danger in the parish of Lammersheugh.

CHAPTER 11

The Burial of a Gentlewoman

26 October 1687

MACKENZIE STOOD A few yards behind the mourners in Lammersheugh kirkyard, a cold wind blowing in his face, leaves spinning round his feet. He recalled the words of Genesis, Chapter 3: 'for dust thou art, and unto dust shalt thou return.' It had been a similar day all those years before when he had buried Elizabeth, although there were hundreds packed around the graveside then, despite the cold. There had been something else too. Perhaps it was the vibrant colours of the plaids or the sparkle of the Gaelic, or the consolation of family and friends – the presence of the clan.

The image of his wife's dead body came to him, lying in a winding sheet of white linen on the bed where she had conceived, given birth and died. He remembered the tumult of emotions following her death – anger, grief, guilt. He had tried to be rational, applying the lessons of stoic philosophers like Marcus Aurelius. But he could not. He felt a knot in his stomach. He knew that unless he acted to loosen it, it would grow until it formed a pit, bottomless and black. And there was the face of the midwife. He had not seen her for twenty years, blaming her, although there was no reason. Women died in childbirth. It was always thus. Why, then, the guilt he carried, the sense that, ultimately, it was he who was responsible? By an act of will, like the prising open of a trap, he forced himself to think outwards, away from himself, away from the past, away from pain, away from the knot.

He watched the minister consumed by piety in prayer. MacKenzie held no affection for such men, whether Protestant or Papist, Presbyterian or Episcopalian. 'Priests of all religions are the same,' as Dryden said in *Absalom and Achitophel*. He had no time for those who told others what they should believe, what was a sin and what was not. The hypocrisy of the priesthood of all believers, the self-righteousness of men of God, putting themselves between the people and the higher power, if one existed; snuffing out joy; killjoys literally. He hoped that one day Man would be free from such bleak masters.

Although, not all churchmen were from the same mould, he reflected. There was wisdom and tolerance in Bishop Leighton's sermons. He was always telling Davie to lay aside his prejudices. But the thought of Archbishop Sharp's demise came to him; hacked to death on Magus Muir by fanatics. He sensed a similar faith smouldering in the soul of the young minister. He was perhaps thirty-five. He looked fervent, holy, emotional – a fatal combination. He was no doubt sceptical of the present church government and a supporter of the exiles. Many of his more eager colleagues were in the United Provinces, waiting to return. Some were already in Scotland following the last Indulgence. A man, perhaps, after Davie's heart? But Scougall was a creature of a confined upbringing. His parents were good folk, but rigid in their beliefs. They had little experience of the outside world. Mrs Scougall had never left Musselburgh. There was still hope that Davie might begin to question the dogma of his faith. He was a bright young man.

The minister articulated each word in a cloying manner, as if to remind the mourners that he was not a Scots speaker, that he had command of English, the language of the Bible. MacKenzie had never met him, but already held strong feelings about him. He must challenge himself more. After all, the stain of witchcraft might have kept other preachers away. Burial was being allowed within the churchyard.

MacKenzie's eyes moved round the mourners who stood beside a large stone obelisk, the elaborately carved tomb of the Hays of Lammersheugh. He recognised the two young women as Grissell's daughters, Euphame and Rosina. If he remembered correctly they would be eighteen and sixteen years old. He knew little of their characters. They had always appeared as shy girls on previous visits. There were two other women, the older one presumably Janet Cornfoot, to whom Grissell had referred to in her letter, the other perhaps a maid or cook from the house.

There were only two men by the graveside. The people of the town had stayed away. The smear of witchcraft had a powerful effect. One was a lugubrious fellow he knew to be a long-standing servant of the House of Lammersheugh. He could not remember his name. The other was a finely-dressed laird in middle age. A young boy was at his side.

MacKenzie's thoughts gravitated towards Scougall. It might be useful to have him here in Lammersheugh. Talking to him stimulated his faculties. Scougall was most useful in that respect. He was also skilled with the pen and could keep accurate notes. His own memory was not as good as it used to be. He decided to send Scougall a message requesting he come to Haddington the next day.

CHAPTER 12

The Delation of Margaret Rammage

'PLEASE READ Margaret Rammage's confession, Mr Rankine,' said the minister from a wooden chair beneath the pulpit.

A thin man cleared his throat and began to read from a book lying on the small desk in front of him. Rankine had taken considerable care with the entries, which were based on a ream of notes written as Rammage was questioned over a number of occasions. She was now burned to dust, praise be to God. Satan was diminished. He had written a summary of what she had said, before copying it into the book in a neat hand. The work had given him great pleasure. He was serving God. He was assured of eternal bliss as one of the Elect. Satan had tempted him often. A vision of his sister as a sixteen-year-old girl came to him. He experienced a threatened hint of arousal. At least he was tempted less as the years passed. He had fought many battles with the Devil. Now he found her old body repulsive. His erection eased. A place was his in Heaven, despite his sinful life. He was assured of God's grace.

In a slow serious voice, he began: '"The following is the free and voluntary confession of Margaret Rammage, servant of Janet Cranstoun in Aikenshiels, written by Theophilus Rankine, session clerk of Lammersheugh."'

He waited for a moment to indicate that the words

following were not his, but those of the witch:

'"I declare that two years ago I was in bed in the house of my mistress, when she woke me and told me that I must speak to a gentleman. She brought me to the hall where I saw a man dressed in black. He was tall and handsome. He wore a hat with a black feather in it. He smiled when he saw me. He took me in his arms and kissed me. He had no breath. He was cold like stone. Nothing more happened that night.

'"The next night when I was going to bed the Devil came to me again. My mistress was not there. He brought me to the fireplace in the hall, where he forced me to lie with him. He told me that I must be his servant.

'"Two weeks later my mistress took me to the Blinkbonny Woods to a meeting with the Devil and other witches. We danced and sang and drank strong liquor. I renounced my baptism, putting one hand over the crown of my head and the other under the sole of my foot. I delivered all that was between my hands unto Satan. He gave me a new name, calling me Jenny. He lay with me in the woods, heavy as a horse on top of me, his penis cold within me like fresh well-water.

'"My mistress Janet Cranstoun was present at this meeting. There was also Marion Campbell, Helen Laing, Katherine Russell, Hugh Black, Margaret Bannatyne, Isobel Dodds, Jean Maxwell, Elspeth Dargie, Catherine Cass, Andrew Love, Bessie MacHimson, Janet Hastie, Marjorie Durie, Margaret Gourlay, Agnes Pride, James Breadhead, Barbara Moncrieff, Helen Deans, John Sinclair, Beatrix Leslie and Bessie Melrose. There was a lady in a green velvet dress wearing a mask. From her voice, I knew she was Lady Lammersheugh. Her daughter Euphame Hay, a thin girl in a fine scarlet dress, was also present."'

There was a sigh from an elder in the front pew. 'Euphame Hay was not mentioned in the previous confession,' said

Cant, shocked to hear her name.

'That is right, sir. Rammage told us that she had forgotten to give a full list of those in attendance the first time she was questioned. Katherine Russell, Margaret Bannatyne and Isobel Dodds were also missing from her first confession.'

'Are you certain that the name of Euphame Hay was provided by her, Mr Rankine?'

'I am, Mr Cant. I asked her the very same question. Did I not Mr Muschet?'

'You did, Mr Rankine,' replied another elder.

'Please continue,' said the minister.

'"There were other meetings with the Devil in the woods, and also at the Lint Hauch and the Weird Haugh. When we went to them, we were sometimes in the shape of crows and sometimes in the shape of magpies. Sometimes we went in our own shape. Sometimes the Devil appeared to us as a great dog.

'"I was with many witches at the contriving of the death of the child who was the daughter of Katherine Haliday and her husband William Hair. We made a painting of the bairn which we roasted over a fire. The next week the child fell ill and died.

'"On the night of 12 August in the year of God 1681 we dug up the body of an unbaptised bairn and cut off its arms and legs. Andrew Watson made a pie from it, so that we might eat it and by this means never confess to our witchcraft.

'"I went three times widdershins naked about Andrew Thomson's house. We cut one of the legs off a mole, put it in a box and buried it outside the threshold of Agnes Pogavie's home.

'"We fashioned a clay figure of a child to kill the Laird of Wedderlaw's eldest son. We stuck pins into it. The boy died a month later.

"'I am guilty of divination, of looking into the years to come, which is contrary to the law of God.

"'At our meetings the woman in the green dress sat next to the Devil, serving him as we ate. He was like a stallion after mares with us and sometimes like a man, very eager for carnal copulation at all times, and we desirous of him. We called him Black John.

"'On one occasion he commanded us to open three graves in the kirkyard of Lammersheugh and cut the joints of fingers, toes and knees from the corpses. We divided them amongst us. He told us to keep the joints and to make a powder of them to do evil with.

"'I confess to carnal relations with the Devil in many places throughout the parish. I did fly in the sky. I changed my form into that of a cat.'"

Rankine was briefly silent, allowing what he had read to sink in.

"'The Devil turned towards us and we went unto him. We did worship him lasciviously, touching him with our hands as he bid us. We took his manhood within our mouths. His discharge was blood. Two women held back; one was dressed in a fine green gown with a mask over her eyes. She had authority over the rest of the witches and warlocks. The green gentlewoman was Lady Lammersheugh. The other was her daughter Euphame Hay. Vile words came from their lips, ordering us to do things to Satan. She told us that we should lie with him in the position of beasts...'"

One of the elders rose, eyes burning feverishly: 'Shame on the witch. Shame on her!'

Rankine was exhilarated as he read the last extract from the minute book:

"'We made a painting in the likeness of Lady Girnington at the bidding of Lady Lammersheugh and roasted it with brandy over a fire in the Blinkbonny Woods.'"

He indicated with a slight nod of his head that he was finished. The minister rose to his feet. 'Thank you, Mr Rankine. Our parish is infected with much evil. As minister I am obliged to do all I can to root out such vile sin. There is clearly enough evidence to take Euphame Hay into custody for questioning.'

Trying to restrain his excitement, Rankine added, 'I have heard that Kincaid is back from the West. His services can be secured for a small fee.'

The minister hesitated. He had not anticipated the use of such a man.

'It may supply the final piece of evidence, Mr Cant. Provide a watertight case for the High Court. Kincaid is well known for his skills. He will seek out the Devil's Mark.'

'So be it, Mr Rankine. Let it be put in the minutes that a vote was taken on whether to employ Kincaid to prick Euphame Hay.'

'All those in favour?' The hands of Muschet and Rankine rose. The minister reluctantly followed suit. He had doubts about the use of such a man. They always appeared as a witch-hunt began, sniffing out the prospect of easy money. But what troubled him particularly was that Kincaid was beneath him. He was not a man of God.

CHAPTER 13
A Conversation with Janet Cornfoot

THE MOURNERS DISPERSED, leaving the old woman alone at the graveside. As MacKenzie approached her, he realised that she was speaking in a slow melodic voice. The rhythm reminded him of the Gaelic charms he had heard in his boyhood. The poetry was the same.

She turned as his footsteps announced his presence behind her. A dark face was lined by age, eyes milky white. She did not appear to be devastated by grief, but seemed at ease. It was as if she had expected him to arrive at that very moment. 'I am glad you have come, Mr MacKenzie. I am Grissell's servant...'

'Janet Cornfoot,' he said, smiling. 'I remember you well, though it's been many years. I believe you are retired from the house?'

'I am, sir.' She dropped a handful of earth into the grave. 'I saw Grissell every day. She was like a dochter tae me, bonnie Grissell. Now her bairns are alane. But they still hae auld Janet Cornfoot. You received the letter?'

'I did, Janet. We must talk. The graveside is perhaps not the proper place.'

'Come tae ma hoose the nicht,' she said.

'Where do you live?'

'I bide in the Blinkbonny Wids. Walk thro the gairdens o

Lammersheugh, oot o the gate, across the muir, ower the Lammer Burn an intae the wids. Tak the path on the richt until ye come tae a glade. My cottage is there. Knock thrice so I ken it's you. Now, I hae work tae do.'

MacKenzie concentrated on retaining the directions. As she passed, she rested her hand on his arm. 'It cheers me tae see ye here to look aifter the bairns, Mr MacKenzie. I dinnae trust Gideon Purse, the lawyer in Haddington. There are others also who... we'll talk later.'

She disappeared into the mist that had descended over the graveyard. MacKenzie stood alone beside the tomb, looking down into the grave. A beautiful woman was in the coffin beneath his feet. He wondered exactly what evil was afoot in Lammersheugh. He must tread carefully. Emotions were running high. Many were eager to cast the finger of accusation. He remembered the dismal spectacle of 1661, the carnage following the Restoration. A strange hysteria took hold of Scotland, as day after day innocent men and women were garrotted and burned. He tried to remember if the Greeks hunted witches. They had tried Socrates, making him drink hemlock for corrupting the youth of Athens. And there was the cruelty of the Romans. The philosophers of old had much to teach us, but the lesson of history was that we repeated the same mistakes. Human nature was set in stone. Some were inclined to be good, others compelled to be evil.

At the church gate he mounted his horse and proceeded down the main street of Lammersheugh. The mist had reduced visibility to about fifty yards, exaggerating the sound of the hooves on the cobbles. It was like any other small Lothian town. On each side of the road were squat dwelling houses with red pantiled roofs. He recognised the tavern where he would take a room.

As he looked to the left he thought he glimpsed a woman through a window. But the next instant there was only dark

glass. The feeling of being watched was unsettling. He passed
the mercat cross and the weighing beam where the houses
were larger, a couple three storeys high, belonging to the
merchants of the town. He noted a small shop on the ground
floor of one; a sign read 'Muschet's Store'.

From another house on the left a noisy group of children
spilled onto the street, breaking the eerie silence. One of them
ran straight onto the road in front of him. Luckily he was
able to draw up his horse in time.

'You should be more careful, my boy,' said MacKenzie
sternly.

But the child did not reply. He stared up at him before
taking off across the road and running down the High Street.

CHAPTER 14

Lammersheugh House

MACKENZIE FOLLOWED THE servant up the stairs and across the hallway. They entered a room, much of which was in shadows. He could make out an elaborately carved fireplace, a painted ceiling and portraits on the walls. Sash windows looked onto the gardens. He was reminded of his library at The Hawthorns.

The grim servant spoke in a gruff voice: 'Mr John MacKenzie, Clerk o the Session.'

There were two figures in the room. His eyes were drawn first to the one standing by the window. 'Thank you, Murdoch,' she said, coming forward to greet him.

She was dressed in mourning, a billowing black skirt engulfing a slender body. MacKenzie noticed how pale her face was; the hint of bone beneath papery skin. Dark lines curved under eyes which reminded him of her mother, but her features were a mixture of both parents. She had not inherited Grissell's beauty. The chin of her father was too dominant; her mother's voluptuous lips diluted.

'Mr MacKenzie, welcome. I am Euphame. I must thank you for attending our mother's burial. She always spoke of you with great affection.'

'My dear, may I pass on my condolences. I was deeply shocked to hear of your mother's death and much regret we meet under such circumstances.'

There was a hint of a smile on Euphame's face: 'This is my sister, Rosina.'

The other figure moved towards him from the shadows around the fireplace. As no candles were lit, it was difficult to differentiate her black dress from the surrounding darkness. MacKenzie experienced the sense of a spirit drifting towards him. The image of a burning witch on the Castle Hill flashed through his mind – a body engulfed in fire.

The younger sister took his hand. 'I welcome you to our home, Mr MacKenzie.' She was smaller in height, more curvaceous in body. She had inherited Grissell's beauty.

'Please be seated. Murdoch will bring us some refreshments,' said Euphame, indicating a chair beside the fireside. The two sisters sat on the couch facing him.

'I am sorry to raise the subject of business at such a time, but there are a number of legal matters we must consider. The estate will have to be administered. I believe your mother has not employed a factor since your father's death?' MacKenzie began.

Euphame looked down at her hands. There were tears on her forlorn face. It struck MacKenzie how alone the girls were. Despite it being the day of their mother's burial, there was to be no solace from the Hay kin. Their father had been a fine man. Now his family was shunned by relatives and neighbours alike.

Euphame raised her head. 'What are we to do, Mr MacKenzie? You must help us!' Her voice was brittle.

'Of course, my dear. I will do all I can to keep the affairs of the estate in order.' He thought it best not to mention the letter.

'It is not the estate that concerns us.' Rosina seemed calmer. 'It is what has happened to our mother. I presume you have heard of the accusations made against her? Men who have benefited from their connection to the House – Cant, Muschet and Rankine were her accusers. Margaret Rammage delated her. Sir, our mother was no witch!'

MacKenzie inclined his head in assent. 'I will do all that I can to find out what has happened. But we must tread carefully. While I am in the parish I will follow the role of family lawyer. If it was thought I was here for other reasons it might make enquiries difficult. I do not want to draw attention to myself.'

'We understand, Mr MacKenzie. We are most grateful to you for we have no one else to turn to,' said Euphame.

'I will do everything I can. First, I will write to my assistant, Davie Scougall, asking him to join me. He is in Musselburgh visiting his parents. As we say in Gaelic, *Is e iomadaidh nan làmh a nì an obair aotrom* – many hands make light work.'

Euphame removed a handkerchief to dry her tears as Murdoch entered with a tray. He placed it on a small table beside them. 'Please join us, Mr MacKenzie.'

Euphame filled a glass with wine. MacKenzie took a sip, waiting until Murdoch left the room before continuing. 'What do you believe happened to your mother?'

She took a deep breath. 'She mourned deeply for our father. His death drained the life from her. And recently she has been afflicted by other concerns. We are not sure of their nature, exactly.' Euphame placed her hands on her lap. 'She did not share her cares with us. I think that pressure was being applied to her in some way. Archibald Muschet was calling in debts. She was sorely troubled by this. She feared that he would take her to court.'

'What kind of man is he?' asked MacKenzie, munching on a piece of bread.

'He is a merchant who has prospered by money-lending. He is a vile little man,' Rosina intervened. There was venom in her voice.

'Our mother was very worried by the financial position of the estates. She could not raise sufficient cash to pay him,' added Euphame.

'I will examine the finances as soon as I can. But why would Muschet want to kill your mother or have her accused of witchcraft? He will still have to follow legal process despite her death.'

'I believe he loved her,' blurted out Rosina.

'My sister speaks hastily, Mr MacKenzie. I can assure you, they were not lovers.' Euphame turned a sharp eye on Rosina.

'I never said they were. But I know the way he looked at her. I am sure that he had made an offer of marriage. Can you imagine it – a stepfather who was born in a hovel!' The younger sister held back none of her disgust.

'Many men looked at her in that way,' said Euphame. 'She did not seek their attention. Her beauty attracted it.'

'Are you saying that Muschet was a scorned lover?' asked MacKenzie.

'No. I do not believe that he was.'

'Do you have any evidence to suggest that he was involved in her death?'

'None,' said Euphame emphatically.

MacKenzie took another sip of wine. 'Who was the woman who delated her?'

'Margaret Rammage was a servant of Janet Cranstoun in Aikenshiels. She was executed last month with her mistress. Our mother never met her.' Euphame began to shake. She folded her arms across her chest, rubbing them. 'I cannot get warm, despite the fire.'

'You must eat, sister,' said Rosina.

'I cannot. I cannot keep a morsel down.'

'You will waste away. Then where will we be?'

MacKenzie watched the interaction between the girls. 'Are you sure that your mother did not know Margaret Rammage?'

'I do not think so,' replied Rosina.

He cut off a piece of cheese, placing it on a slice of bread. 'Tell me what happened on the day she died.'

Rosina took a deep breath. 'She ate breakfast with us, then dressed in her riding suit. We thought that she was bound for the hills. She left at about eight in the morning. The day passed without incident. But in the afternoon word came from Murdoch that a body had been found in the hills. In the evening the men brought her back. She was drowned in the Devil's Pool.'

Euphame closed her eyes, attempting to control herself. But the shaking continued. MacKenzie was reminded of a frightened bird.

'Where is the place?' he asked.

'About two miles from the town in the Lammermuirs. You follow the Lammer Burn. It is a place most of the people avoid. There are stories about it. We never go there,' said Rosina.

'Where were you during the day?'

'At the house and in the gardens,' said Euphame.

'And Janet?'

'Janet was with us the whole day.'

'Is there anything else you can think of that might help to explain what happened? As you know, those accused of witchcraft sometimes seek escape in this manner.'

'I do not believe she would kill herself, Mr MacKenzie. Her love for us was too strong. She would not abandon us,' said Rosina.

Euphame looked down at her skeletal hands. She moved a ring up and down her finger. She shook her head, but said nothing.

Rosina sat forward. 'Something is happening in the parish,' she said intently. 'We feel it. Janet has felt it.'

'What do you mean?'

'I do not know. But there is something.'

There was a knock on the door. Murdoch entered and began to light the candles on the wall brackets. MacKenzie waited until he had completed his task and left. 'Who are your neighbours?'

'Tweeddale has land to the west, but we have little to do with him,' said Euphame, who had recovered her composure. 'He is in London mostly, on political business. Our close neighbours are Lady Girnington, our father's sister, Colonel Robert Dewar of Clachdean and Adam Cockburn of Woodlawheid.'

'How would you describe them to me, Rosina?' MacKenzie had noticed the more direct replies of the younger sister. He addressed his question to her.

'Our aunt did not like our mother. We do not like our aunt. Woodlawheid is a good neighbour. He has helped us often. The colonel is a brute.'

'A brute?'

'A lecherous drunkard,' Rosina said contemptuously.

MacKenzie was aware of noises somewhere in the house. He could hear Murdoch's raised voice. The sounds were getting closer. Suddenly the door burst open.

'I am sorry, my lady.' The beleaguered servant was pushed back.

Leading the intruders was the minister, a grim expression on his face. MacKenzie counted six others enter the room.

'What is the meaning of this intrusion, Mr Cant?' Euphame summoned the authority of her social position.

'I am sorry. My task is of the utmost gravity,' replied Cant, short of breath.

MacKenzie saw the panic on Euphame's face. Clearly the message brought by the minister was not one of condolence.

'Grave accusations have been made. Margaret Rammage has delated...' Cant glanced at Rosina, hesitated, and then commenced: 'Euphame Hay of Lammersheugh, eldest daughter of Alexander Hay of Lammersheugh for the crime of witchcraft.'

The young woman sank back onto the couch from which she had just risen, whispering: 'God help me, God help me.'

'Margaret Rammage has delated Euphame Hay as a witch,' the minister continued. 'She is accused of meeting with the Devil in the Blinkbonny Woods and other places in the parish, of lying with him and other libidinous behaviour.' Cant spoke as if reading the minutes of a session meeting. He could not bring himself to look into Euphame's eyes.

'You are surely mistaken. She is an innocent girl,' MacKenzie gasped.

'I do not know who you are, sir. But we have evidence.'

'I am John MacKenzie. I act on behalf of the family as their legal agent in Edinburgh.'

'We must investigate the accusations. Satan walks in Lammersheugh!' exclaimed the minister.

'Surely you do not believe that this young woman could be involved?'

'Her mother was under suspicion at the time of her death. The parish is in much danger, Mr MacKenzie. As minister of Lammersheugh I must do all that is in my power to root out such evil, wherever it presents itself – in the byre or in the laird's house.'

'I cannot allow such madness to go unchallenged.' MacKenzie moved in front of Euphame. 'Such accusations are ridiculous. I ask you to calm yourselves, gentlemen. Look at this in a rational...'

A man standing beside Cant with a crazed look in his bulging eyes pointed at Euphame: 'We must take her!'

The minister stood back to let the others forward. MacKenzie was manhandled out of the way. Heavily outnumbered, he realised that resistance was pointless.

As Euphame looked up at him imploringly, a terrible thought passed through his mind. He wondered if her fate was sealed already. Was she to be garrotted and burned to dust on the Castle Hill like the poor creature witnessed by Scougall?

CHAPTER 15
A Cottage in the Woods

THE EVENTS OF the afternoon added urgency to MacKenzie's steps as he made his way through the gardens of Lammersheugh House in the gloaming. He would usually have taken time to examine the plants in the long border against the wall, but his horticultural interests were relegated to the back of his mind. The arrest of Euphame placed everything in a different light. He had no time to lose.

He found the gate at the end of the wall. A path led across the muir and over a small brig into the darkness of the woods. After about fifty yards it bifurcated. He took the right fork. The gurgling of a burn could be heard on the left, but he could see little in front of him beyond a few feet, so he kept his head down, fearing he might trip over a tree root. After about half a mile he came to a glade where a small cottage could be seen in the half light, a line of smoke drifting into the sky from the chimney. It was an old stone dwelling-place with a little garden surrounded by a low wall. A birch tree shimmered silver and two rowans stood like sentries at the gate. Light glimmered at one of the windows.

He knocked three times, as instructed. A dog barked. There was a short delay before the door opened and Janet peered out. 'Come awa in, Mr MacKenzie – come in. It's a cauld nicht.'

After sniffing his leg, the dog returned to the fire. 'Please be seated, sir.'

He sat on the chair, but realising it was the only one in the cottage, rose to his feet.

'No, sir, I insist. My auld body is a twisted root. I cannae sit at rest sometimes. I will pour us some ale.'

She disappeared into the shadows at the other side of the room. A candle on the table beside the chair was the only source of illumination. He noticed a box bed in a corner, a black cauldron by the fire and a long wooden table.

'You no longer live at the house, Janet?'

'No. I hae a wee annual rent granted in ma auld age. The cottage is ma ain until I dee. Ma family are gone, sir, deid or gone, at least fae roond here. I still hae some on ma mither's side in Perthshire. She was a Gaelic speaker like yoursel.'

'Where was she from?'

'A village near Blair. I hae never been there. She came sooth tae the Lowlands when she wis a girl. Ma faither widnae let me speak her tongue. He said it wis the language o beasts. So I hae only a few wirds o Gaelic. But she taught me much else besides. She had the second sight. I hae some o her skill.'

MacKenzie smiled. 'It is a shame you cannot speak Gaelic. What of the rest of your family?'

'Ma faither wis a servant o Tweeddale's at Yester. I served at Aikwood afore Grissell was born and stayed wi her. Ma man served the House of Lammersheugh. He died in the year the rebels rose against the King.'

'Was that in 1666 or 1679?' asked MacKenzie.

'It wis 1666. They were a bundle o grim craws. Oor parish still crawls wi em, wirms like Marion Rankine. Looking doon their noses at ye. Aye tellin folk what tae do. I hae nae time for 'em, Mr MacKenzie.'

'Then we will get on well, Janet. I have little liking for

fanatics. Who is Marion Rankine?'

'She is the sister o thon session clerk, Theophilus Rankine. Hae ye ever heard sic a name, Theophilus – lover o God I've been telt it means, but they are sic a joyless pair o crimmers. They are aw up tae somethin, mind, I'm sure o it.'

'What do you mean?'

'I've seen strangers in the parish. Folk oot at nicht up tae nae guid. I hae seen them wi my ain een. Only last week there were three cairts on the Haddington Road at midnight.'

'What were they carrying?'

'I dinnae ken. It wis somethin which was to be kept secret. But they couldnae hide it frae Janet Cornfoot. I often walk in the wids at nicht. And ither things, Mr MacKenzie – strange screams at nicht.'

'What kind of screams?'

'Wailin sounds, like spirits cryin fir release.'

MacKenzie wondered how reliable she was as a source of information. 'You have no one else, Janet?'

'Ma lad went aff tae sea twenty year ago an ne'er returned.'

'How old are you?' He saw that she enjoyed the chance to talk. It was an old lawyer's trick. Put a person at ease with a few questions about themselves, then down to work.

'I dinnae ken. I wis aye telt I wis born in the year guid King James came back tae Scotland aifter winning the English Croon. That wis in 1617, which wid mak me sixty-nine or seventy. What is certain is I'm an auld cailleach. Is that not what you say in Gaelic!' she chuckled.

'Your Gaelic is good, Janet.' MacKenzie felt that he could not withhold the events of the afternoon any longer. His expression became serious. 'I'm afraid I have bad news, very bad news. Euphame has been taken to the steeple, suspected as a witch, to be questioned by the session tonight.'

The old woman had to support herself against the chair

on which MacKenzie sat.

'Ma Phamie tain like pair Grissell!' she gasped. 'When will it end, Mr MacKenzie? Folk accuse each ither of onything under the sun.' She stood beside him trembling.

MacKenzie helped her into the chair. There were tears in her eyes. 'I should hae done mair. I promised Grissell I wid look aifter them...'

'I will do everything in my power to free her, Janet. This afternoon I wrote to my kinsman, Rosehaugh, who has much experience of such cases. I will appeal to Euphame's kin to stand caution for her, although I know she has few relatives alive.'

'Grissell's parents are baith deid. She had nae brithers or sisters. Nae close kin foreby Lady Girnington. And she will be of nae help.'

'I will appeal to her ladyship to intervene. Also to Tweeddale, although I understand he is in London.'

'It will be nae guid, sir. The girls hae naebody – nae kin tae come tae their aid. The end o the hoose o Lammersheugh has lang been prophesised.'

'I know that some put great store by prophecy and second sight Janet, including many in my own clan. I do not,' MacKenzie said firmly. 'We cannot know what is to come.'

The old woman said nothing.

'I realise the news is a great shock,' he continued, 'but I must ask you some questions about what has been happening in Lammersheugh. It is very important that you tell me everything you know. The slightest detail may help to secure Euphame's release.'

'Ye are richt, sir. I hae muckle tae tell, muckle indeed. Some of it I hae ne'er spoken of tae anither, as I promised Grissell. Where shall I begin?'

'Tell me first of the death of your mistress.'

'She drowned, Mr MacKenzie. It was nae accident. She

feared fir her life as ye ken frae the letter. She wis slain. I'm sure o it.'

'Tell me all you know.'

'Four days ago I attended her in the morning. Although I bide in ma cottage I spend maist days at the hoose. She ate naething for breakfast. She wisnae hersel. She asked Murdoch fir her horse tae be made ready and refused tae tell me whaur she wis bound. I was sure she had a meetin o some kind, a meetin of importance.'

'When did she leave?'

'Sometime in the early mornin, perhaps an hour aifter dawn. I settled tae ma knittin and spent the day leisurely, as they say. Little did I ken what wis happenin as I sat wi ma needles. In the late afternoon in comes John Murdoch sayin a body has been found at the Devil's Pool up on Lammer Law. I kenned richt awa it wis Grissell's. I saw her there, a bleak picture in ma mind. I blurted this out, but John says they didnae ken. Some men frae the toon had left tae fetch the body.

'She was brocht hame in the darkness. It was Grissell sure enough, drowned in the Devil's Pool, found by Woodlawheid's boy, who had wandered up there in the afternoon. He swore that he had seen Satan in the wids. But I ken it was a man whae killed her.'

'What man?'

'I dinnae ken, sir. I cannae see everythin clearly, nae yet. But I will.'

'What do you mean, Janet?'

The woman closed her eyes to concentrate. 'I see them at the pool. I cannae say whae's wi her. I cannae see his face. It is the curse o the gift. Sometimes it shows only hauf the truth. I see Grissell and a man.'

'Who is Woodlawheid?' enquired MacKenzie.

'Adam Cockburn is the Laird o Woodlawheid. He wis a

great friend of Lammersheugh. But he is married tae a puir creature whaes lost her mind. He was aye givin Grissell his counsel an I'm sure he would hae liked to gie her mair. His laddie, George, says that the Deil called tae him at the Pool aifter he found the body.'

'How old is the boy?'

'Aboot ten years auld, a guid laddie.'

'Did you notice anything about Grissell's body when it was brought back?'

'She wis ice cauld frae the water. There wis one thing – a mark on her temple, a small bruise about here.' The old woman indicated with her forefinger. 'Also, her pearl necklace wis missin, the yin gied tae her by Alexander which she aye wore.'

'Anything else?'

'No, sir. Only the saft body I had cared for since she was a bairn.' The old woman's voice began to break. 'They dinnae believe she was killed, Mr MacKenzie.'

'Who do you mean?'

'The sheriff-deputy says it was an accident. She slipped on a rock and fell intae the water – she couldnae swim.'

'Who is the sheriff-deputy?'

'Colonel Robert Dewar of Clachdean. A vile beast.'

'Why do you say that?'

'He's a cruel, hertless sodyer back frae the wars, a bottle licker wi little interest and nae siller, weel kent fir whoring whaurever and whaunever.'

'I am sorry, Janet, very sorry that I must keep asking questions at such a time. Do you know anyone who might want to harm her?'

'You have heard the accusations made by Margaret Rammage, that Grissell was at a meetin wi the Deil. Margaret was an ignorant dolt.'

'I am aware of the delation. How were relations between

Grissell and Lady Girnington?'

'She ne'er approved o Grissell. She thocht her an ill match fir her brither, who wisnae interested in the family's standing. She couldnae unnerstaun Grissell's nature. She wis happy wi her bairns. Naething else mattered tae her. Whit did she care fir the interest o the Hoose of Lammersheugh? Lady Girnington wis aye tellin her how the weans should be brocht up. After the laird's death it wis whae she should marry; then matches fir Euphame an Rosina. Grissell hated few things in the warld, but she hated her. But tae use witchcraft? Never the day, sir.'

'Who was Lady Girnington suggesting that she marry?'

'The colonel hissel. Lady Girnington and Clachdean are thick thegither. I dinnae ken why. She was aye pushin the match. I ken that Grissell shuddered at the very thocht o him touchin her.'

'Who is the woman who made the accusations?'

'Margaret Rammage wis a servant at Aikenshiels. She is now burned tae dust.'

'Is she from Lammersheugh?'

'She lived in Headshaw, beyond Clachdean. Margaret deponed before the session that she'd seen Grissell in a green silk gown at a meeting wi other witches in the wids during the summer. She telt aboot dancin wi the Deil and how a paintin wis made o Lady Girnington, roastit wi brandy and pins stuck in it.'

The wind gusted down the chimney. The dog's ears pricked.

'How could I hae forgotten!' Janet suddenly straightened herself in the chair. 'The news of Euphame has distracted me. I promised Grissell I wid tell ye things I should hae telt ye at the beginnin when ye came in. All yer questions trauchled ma auld mind.'

'Please tell me now, Janet. Take your time.'

The old woman closed her eyes, conjuring from memory

the words she had been told. As she spoke she imitated the cadences of her mistress's speech, so it was as if Grissell herself was speaking in the dark cottage.

'"I could not write these words for fear my letter would fall into the wrong hands. Listen to Janet Cornfoot my old servant."' She opened her eyes and spoke in her own voice briefly: 'that wis what she said, Mr MacKenzie,' before continuing to imitate Grissell. '"Listen well to what I say in my latterwill and testament. Listen well. It will direct you to my commonplace book where everything is explained. It must not pass into the wrong hands. Janet will give you the key to the closet in which it rests."'

The old woman opened her hand to reveal a metal key about an inch long. She handed it to MacKenzie before continuing: '"Read my words carefully. See where my eyes come to rest."' She hesitated for a moment then repeated: '"Read my words carefully. See where my eyes come to rest."' Janet raised her head, indicating the end of Grissell's message. 'Now I hae said ma piece.'

MacKenzie put the key in his pocket. 'I am baffled, Janet. Do you know where the book is?'

'I do not, sir. I didnae ken she kept one.'

There was a noise outside. The dog barked. A scraping sound could be heard at the door. Janet looked fearfully at MacKenzie. 'There was somebody here yestreen, tryin tae scare me.'

He withdrew a small dirk from his jacket. Turning from the old woman, he walked slowly towards the door. He could hear something behind it – a muffled knocking. The dog, held back by its mistress, continued to growl as he crossed the room.

When he reached the door, he stopped. A gentle tapping could be heard. Raising his knife, he pulled the handle. Someone was attaching a dark shape to the lintel. It looked like a carcass about the size of a dog. A masked figure sped into the night.

MacKenzie pushed through the body of the animal, sharp bristles prickling against the side of his face, and followed into the blackness of the woods. After stumbling on for about fifty yards, he tripped on a root and fell to the ground. Fortunately he dropped the dirk a safe distance away. Bewildered, he lay in the pitch black, trying to determine the direction in which the person had fled. But he could not tell. After catching his breath, he decided to return to the cottage. He pulled himself to his feet, picked up his dirk, and headed back through the trees.

After a short distance the light from the window came back into view. He slowly retraced his steps, his senses pricked by fear.

As he entered the garden he remembered the animal hanging from the lintel. When he reached the door he saw that the creature was a badger, fresh blood still dripping from a neck wound. He put his finger to the deep gash, then cut the cord and tossed the body into the earth beside the door.

'I did not catch him, Janet!' he shouted as he entered.

There was no answer. The old woman was slumped in her chair.

He knew at once that she was not asleep. Walking towards her, his eyes darted round the dark interior. He lifted her head back carefully, but when he released his grip it sagged forward. He felt for a pulse on her neck. There was none. He had been out of the cottage for only a few minutes. There seemed to be no indication of strangulation. Removing her bonnet, he pulled up her long grey hair, checking the back of her neck. There was no wound, no suggestion of a struggle. He wondered if the shock of finding the badger had been too much for her. The cottage was just as he had left it. Except that Janet was dead and there was no sign of the dog.

Then he noticed something lying on the stone floor beside the chair. It had not been there when he had sat by the fire. He picked up a striking blue feather about nine inches long.

CHAPTER 16

Sackcloth

EUPHAME STOOD IN the centre of the small, candle-lit room inside the steeple of Lammersheugh Kirk. Above her head was the parish bell which had summoned her to worship throughout her life. Two men, whom she recognised as servants of the colonel, sat on stools by the door.

She heard footsteps. Someone was slowly ascending the spiral staircase which led from the body of the church into the steeple. The door opened and a woman dressed in black entered, a gaunt figure with a sour expression on her face, bearing a bundle of ochre sackcloth in her hands. She walked across the room and dropped it by Euphame's feet.

'Put this on,' she said coldly.

'May I keep on my gown, Miss Rankine?' Euphame asked timidly. The thought of sackcloth against her skin was appalling. As she reflected on her mother's fate, despair rose within her, a feeling of utter hopelessness. She believed she had never knowingly sinned. Three years ago her parents were alive and she was happy. Now they were dead and she was accused of the vilest of crimes.

There was hatred in the eyes of Marion Rankine, hatred and exaltation. She had been looked down on by Euphame and her sister, and by her whore of a mother. But the whore was dead. She was burning in Hell. Euphame was reduced to this. She, Marion Rankine, although a sinner, was promised everlasting salvation by Christ Jesus. 'You must put it on, Euphame. An accused witch must wear sackcloth.'

'I am no witch, Miss Rankine. You must believe me!'

'I know your mother was a witch. You too have been delated by Margaret Rammage. Put it on or I will have the men strip you.' She pointed at the sackcloth.

Euphame was shaking so much she was unable to bend down. Marion Rankine picked up the sackcloth, placed it in her trembling hands and shoved Euphame towards the far wall. 'You must!' she ordered.

Euphame began to undress. She felt the gaze of the men upon her. Rankine stared at her velvet gown and petticoats.

'And the undergarments!'

Pulling the coarse sackcloth over her head, Euphame placed her arms through the holes. It dropped down and she felt the coarse fabric against her skin. Her thin body exposed in such a way. She wondered what her father would have done to this woman, to these men who regarded her lecherously, if he were alive. But he was dead. He could do nothing for his eldest daughter.

'That is better, Euphame. You suit its drab colour. Now you are ready for him.' Marion Rankine smiled venomously before departing.

CHAPTER 17
A Stranger on the Road

27 October 1687

SCOUGALL HAD BROACHED the subject of marriage with his mother over breakfast that morning. As he expected, she was delighted to hear about his intentions and she began to describe a series of candidates without hesitation, listing the advantages and disadvantages of each. Janet Bain was a bonnie lass with a reasonable tocher, but her parents were grim folk. Alice MacLean would be a good catch. She was young. Some might call her fat, but she would deliver fine bairns. There was also the minister's daughter, Ann Grave, who was well educated. She was pious and refined for Musselburgh. Such a match would bring great honour on the Scougall family. And there was Elizabeth Carmichael, the merchant's daughter. At the mention of the name his mind filled with an image of MacKenzie's daughter. She beamed like a sun above the small planets of the Musselburgh lasses. But that Elizabeth was out of his reach. He knew it in his heart. He must think rationally. His mother's recommendations would all make fine bedfellows. He would come to love them, as they him, through the passage of time.

As his horse plodded down the road to Haddington, he tried to raise his spirits. The letter from MacKenzie had pleased him much. He could not resist being praised. Mac-

Kenzie requested his company in Lammersheugh. He was to do everything he could to reach the office of Gideon Purse, a lawyer in Haddington, by two o'clock that afternoon when Grissell Hay's testament and latterwill was to be read. His skills with the pen were required urgently and his knowledge of shorthand might prove of great use. MacKenzie was sorry to interrupt his visit home, but events in Lammersheugh had taken a turn and he required help.

Scougall banished the subject of marriage from his thoughts. Something very serious was occurring, possibly connected with the accusations of witchcraft made against Lady Lammersheugh. He had not told his mother where he was bound, but contrived to give the impression that he was returning to Edinburgh. MacKenzie had asked him not to draw attention to his destination. It felt like lying, and that went against the grain of his being.

The image of the burning body on the Castle Hill came back to him and he wondered if Lady Lammersheugh was a witch. A mixture of fear and excitement made him rouse his horse. Applying his spurs to the beast, he attempted to increase its speed. The lethargic creature trotted for a few yards before slowing again to a walk. The ways of horses were a complete mystery to him.

Scougall had not noticed a man standing at the side of the road beside a horse. As he came up to him, the fellow lifted his hat.

'Your horse has seen better days, sir!' he said.

Scougall tugged the reins, stopping beside him. 'I am not an accomplished horseman, sir. The beast does not respond well to me.'

'Where are you bound?' the stranger asked casually.

'Haddington,' Scougall said without thinking.

'Then let me join you on the road. I am making for an estate nearby.'

The man mounted his horse and they continued together down the rough track.

'It is indeed a fine day!' the man smiled. 'If you do not mind me asking, what kind of business do you have in Haddington?'

Scougall was about to say that he was bound for the office of Mr Purse to hear the testament of Lady Lammersheugh, when he remembered MacKenzie's admonition to keep the business secret. His face coloured, but his companion was looking ahead. 'A little legal business, sir. I am a notary public.'

'What is your name?'

'Davie Scougall. And yours?'

'I am John Kincaid.'

'And what is your profession, Mr Kincaid?'

The man looked Scougall full in the face. 'I am a pricker, Mr Scougall. A pricker of witches.'

Scougall had imagined that he was a merchant of some kind, or a well-to-do artisan, or even a writer like himself, having noticed the bags attached to the back of his saddle. The revelation that he was a pricker was a shock. The uneasiness returned; memories of the burning in Edinburgh flashed through his mind. Kincaid appeared an ordinary fellow. But here was a man who sought out the Devil's Mark, a man who had dealings with witches!

'You look alarmed, Mr Scougall. Please do not be. It's a profession like any other. My father was a pricker; I follow his trade. I was born to do this job. I have spent my life travelling the parishes of Scotland, of service wherever I am required. I provide evidence for the courts. You might say that I am an expert witness. I saw my first witch pricked when I was twelve. I make a living as all men must. I serve my Maker in the way I can.'

Kincaid spoke in an automatic tone, as if he had described

his job in the same words many times before. Scougall felt his pulse racing. He wondered if the appearance of Kincaid was connected with the accusations against Lady Lammersheugh. It occurred to him that he should stop playing the foolish clerk. MacKenzie would not let such an opportunity slip.

Gathering his composure, he worked up the courage to ask a question. 'Where are you bound, sir?'

'I am heading for Lammersheugh where a woman is held on suspicion of being a witch. With God's help I will seek out the Devil's Mark.'

Scougall was excited by the subject matter. 'How many witches have you known, Mr Kincaid?' he blurted out.

Kincaid smiled. 'If you mean how many I have pricked, Mr Scougall, I believe it be more than five hundred.'

'How do you find the Devil's Mark?'

'The Mark is insensible. I use a pin about this size.' Kincaid held his thumb and forefinger about two inches apart. 'It is slipped beneath the skin. If no blood appears and the accused feels nothing – it is the mark of Satan. It may be found on any part of the body, but it is most commonly located here.' He indicated the inside of his thighs. 'Or at the base of the spine. But I have found marks on every part of man and woman.'

'Do they ever resist you?'

'Sometimes they do. Then they must be held down or tied down, especially if they are men. They often curse me, screaming that I will pay for my good work. Others succumb without opposition. Many whimper like animals.'

'Who is the woman you attend in Lammersheugh?' Scougall probed.

'I do not know her name, sir. Word reached me in Tranent that my services were required. I must follow the money, as they say. There is always work for me in the Lothians.'

Kincaid drew up his horse. 'I take the road here.' He indicated a track heading southwards towards the hills.

'Haddington is but a mile distant. I bid you good day, Mr Scougall.'

Scougall watched Kincaid proceed down the track. His thoughts turned to MacKenzie and he reflected that there was real danger in the parish of Lammersheugh.

CHAPTER 18
The Latterwill of Lady Lammersheugh

THE WALLS OF the stuffy chamber were lined with bookshelves crammed with large ledgers and an assortment of legal texts. Gideon Purse sniffed loudly and cleared his throat. From behind thick spectacles, his eyes darted round the room, making sure that everyone was listening. His audience sat in an arc of wooden chairs and stools in front of his large desk. MacKenzie was beside a small sash window which looked down on the High Street of Haddington.

There was a knock on the door.

'Come in,' said Purse, annoyed by the arrival of a latecomer.

Scougall made his apologies, crossed the room and sat on a stool beside MacKenzie.

'My horse proved difficult to handle,' he whispered.

'It was good of you to come so quickly, Davie,' MacKenzie replied in a low voice. He waited until Scougall had settled himself. 'Note down as much you can in shorthand. It may prove invaluable.'

Scougall withdrew a small leather notebook and a pencil from his bag. A slither of excitement passed through him at the prospect of utilising the skills he had learned from Shelton's *Tachygraphy*. MacKenzie had scoffed when he had told him what he was studying as if it was just a passing whim. But here he was making good use of it.

'Lady Girnington, gentlemen. I believe we are all present. Thank you for coming this morning,' the lawyer sniffed again, 'to hear the latterwill and testament of Grissell Hay Lady Lammersheugh, relict of Alexander Hay of Lammersheugh, who died on the twenty-second day of October, the year of God 1687. I will read the document in its entirety as requested by my client. If you have any questions please wait until I have finished.

'"The following is the testament dative and inventory of debts and sums of money pertaining to umquile Grissell Hay, Lady Lammersheugh, relict of the deceased Alexander Hay of Lammersheugh, faithfully written by Gideon Purse, writer in Haddington, conform to this letter dated at Lammersheugh and subscribed on 6 October 1687.

'"The inventory of goods is as follows: money lying in cash in Lammersheugh House £500; household plenishings in Lammersheugh House £2,000; books in the library of Lammersheugh House £500; other sundry goods £50. Debts resting to the defunct by the Laird of Woodlawheid conform to his bond £666 13s 9d, by the tenants of Lammersheugh in unpaid rent £300. Summa of inventory and debts owed to the defunct £4,016 13s 9d."'

He cleared his throat again. '"Debts owed by the defunct. To servants for their fees and bounties: John Murdoch for one year's fee £50; Elizabeth Murdoch for one year's fee £50; Bessie Hodge and Agnes Smith maidservants for one year's fee £25 each. To Archibald Muschet conform to his two bonds of £5,000 and £3,000, in total £8,000. To Lady Girnington conform to her three bonds of £2,000, £10,000 and £5,000, in total £17,000. To John Murray merchant in Haddington conform to his bond of £1,000. To Andrew Hunter merchant in Edinburgh conform to his bond of £5,000. To John MacKenzie, advocate in Edinburgh, for legal expenses £500. The defunct's funeral charges £20. Summa of debts owing by the deceased £31,670. Therefore, the debts exceed the goods by £27,653 6s 3d."'

The lawyer moved one sheet of paper across his desk and picked up another. 'I will now read the latterwill,' he said, sniffing loudly again.

"'I, Grissell Hay, Lady Lammersheugh, being of sound mind, leave to my sister-in-law Lillias Hay, Lady Girnington,"' he raised his head to meet the eyes of a large woman in a billowing blue velvet dress sitting directly in front of him, "'The Dutch clock that sits on my mantelpiece in my chamber."'

Scougall gawked at the huge figure, reflecting that she was repulsively fat. MacKenzie's elbow gently reminded him that he was to note everything down. Lady Girnington maintained an air of indifference.

"'I leave to Adam Cockburn of Woodlawheid the engravings in the library at Lammersheugh which my late husband collected on his journey to Europe as a young man."' MacKenzie noted a finely dressed man nod to Purse.

"'I leave to Mr Cant, minister of Lammersheugh, for his troubles in instructing my daughter Rosina Hay, the Bible published in Paris in 1555, to be found in the library at Lammersheugh."'

The minister nodded to the lawyer, and then looked at Lady Girnington. He noticed MacKenzie watching him.

"'I leave to Archibald Muschet, merchant in Lammersheugh, the sum of £100 for his loyal service to the House of Lammersheugh."' A soberly dressed merchant shook his head in an aggrieved manner.

"'I leave to Theophilus Rankine the sum of £100 to be administered by him on behalf of the poor and sick of the parish."' A gaunt figure with sunken cheeks, also dressed in black, nodded to Purse.

'"I leave to my loyal servant John Murdoch, who has served the House of Lammersheugh for forty years, the sum of £200 and an annual rent of £50 from the lands of Lammersheugh in his retirement. I leave to his wife Elizabeth Murdoch, also a servant of the House of Lammersheugh, the sum of £50."' MacKenzie recognised Murdoch from his visit to the house. His head remained bowed, eyes fixed on the floor.

'"To my beloved Janet Cornfoot who has served me through all the days of my life and who has been a beam of light unto me, I leave the sum of £200."'

'She cares more for her servants than her kin,' Lady Girnington scoffed. Her refined accent had little suggestion of a Scottish brogue.

'I am not quite finished, my lady. "To my husband's legal agent in Edinburgh, Mr John MacKenzie, advocate, Clerk of the Court of Session, I leave the small picture which hangs in the library at Lammersheugh. And to his daughter Elizabeth MacKenzie..."' The mention of the name took Scougall by surprise. He felt his face redden. He hoped that no one, especially MacKenzie, would notice. '"...to his daughter Elizabeth,"' the lawyer repeated, '"I leave an exquisite emerald to be found in the box in my chamber."'

MacKenzie's elbow nudged Scougall again. 'Record every word, Davie,' he whispered.

'The sums of money will be distributed later today. The legacies will be surrendered in Lammersheugh House at midday tomorrow.'

Scougall was perplexed, but continued writing until he had recorded every word. He looked down with satisfaction at the tightly packed symbols in his notebook.

Lady Girnington indicated to the man beside her that he was to help her to her feet. When he rose Scougall noticed he was as tall as MacKenzie, but considerably heavier in build. He placed a large hat with a long black feather on his head, before helping her from the chair. 'Great dishonour is done me by that woman, Mr Purse. Collect my clock for me. Good day, gentlemen.'

The others rose to their feet as Lady Girnington left with the large man. Murdoch, MacKenzie and the fashionably attired laird remained seated. Scougall found himself rising involuntarily, but he was held down by MacKenzie's hand.

'She did not show much sympathy for her sister-in-law, Davie. Come, I have much to tell you.' MacKenzie appeared to have lost the good humour which he had shown in Musselburgh.

They had to wait while Lady Girnington descended the stairs. As they emerged from the front door onto the High Street of Haddington, the laird was waiting for them. He wore a large hat with a feather protruding from a black ribbon, a long periwig and a silk suit.

'I am Adam Cockburn of Woodlawheid, a close friend of the family.'

'I am pleased to make your acquaintance, sir. I am John MacKenzie. This is my assistant, Davie Scougall.'

'You were Alexander's man of business in Edinburgh. He spoke fondly of you,' Cockburn said in a friendly but serious manner.

'I am here to settle the affairs of the estate. Recent events complicate the picture.'

'The parish is afflicted by madness, Mr MacKenzie.'

'You speak of Euphame.'

'Indeed. You could not meet a more delightful young woman. She has been greatly wronged. As was her mother.'

'I believe your son found Lady Lammersheugh's body, Mr Cockburn?'

The laird hesitated. 'Yes. At the Devil's Pool.'

'What of Janet Cornfoot? I found her body last night.'

'She was infirm. A seizure of some kind is suspected. The

sheriff-deputy will no doubt take a statement from you at some stage. Justice moves slowly in these parts.'

'Who is the sheriff-deputy?'

'Colonel Dewar of Clachdean – he left with Lady Girnington. He does not carry out his duties with the celerity we might wish.'

MacKenzie did not seem disposed to divulge the details of what had happened in the cottage: 'I wonder if you could do us a service, Mr Cockburn. I want to see the place where Lady Lammersheugh's body was found. There are a number of aspects of this affair with which, from a legal point of view, I am not happy.'

'I can take you there this afternoon on my way back to Lammersheugh. Let us meet in the Bell at two o'clock, if that is convenient.' The laird removed his hat, bowed and departed down the street.

MacKenzie waited until he was out of earshot before turning to Scougall. 'Let us find somewhere we can talk.'

They wandered down the busy High Street, stopping by a low wall at the end of a row of houses with a view of undulating rigs leading to the Lammermuir Hills. MacKenzie described what had occurred since he left Musselburgh. Scougall was disturbed to hear about the death of Janet and the arrest of Euphame.

'How was she killed, sir?'

'I am not sure, Davie. I could find no signs of violence. She may have died of natural causes, but the timing is highly suspicious. I found this on the floor beside her chair. I am sure it was not there when I left the cottage to pursue the intruder.' He removed the feather from his pocket and handed it to Scougall. 'It could have been blown to where I found it by a draught when the door was opened, of course.'

'Why would a killer carry a feather with them?' Scougall was thinking aloud.

'Why do you think, Davie?'

'It may have fallen from a hat.'

'That is quite possible. A feather is a common accessory to a cap or hat.' He took it from Scougall and examined it closely. 'We must take notice of the head-gear of all we meet. Now, tell me everyone who had a feather in their hat in Purse's office.'

As Scougall had been concentrating on recording the lawyer's words, he had paid little attention to the dress of those in the room. 'I can only recall the hat of Mr Cockburn.'

'Good, Davie. I noticed that Colonel Dewar also had a feather in his hat, as did Lady Girnington. It may be nothing, but it is all we have at the moment. I do not believe that Janet died of natural causes. She told me that someone had tried to scare her the previous night. The appearance of an Edinburgh advocate at her cottage may have sealed her fate.' MacKenzie looked south across the brown rigs which gave way to muirland before rising to the hills. White clouds were drifting across their rounded tops. 'The affair is darker than I had expected. We have two deaths and a young woman accused of the gravest of crimes. Euphame Hay is in great danger. It may already be too late to save her. She does not look as if she has a strong constitution.'

The accusation against Euphame troubled Scougall. Mothers and daughters had been known to sell themselves to Satan together. If Lady Lammersheugh was a witch it seemed to him likely that Euphame was one also.

'Do you think that the same person killed Lady Lammersheugh and Janet?' he asked, trying to lay aside his train of thought.

MacKenzie ignored the question. 'We have much to do. First we must visit the Devil's Pool, then speak to all those involved. I fear we have little time. Euphame has already been shattered by the death of her mother. She may not survive long in prison. We need to get her kin to stand caution for her.'

Scougall summoned up the courage to say what was on his mind. 'What if Euphame is a witch, sir?'

'There are no witches, Davie!' MacKenzie replied gruffly.

CHAPTER 19

The Pricking of Euphame Hay

'I THANK YOU for your quick response, Mr Kincaid.' There was a slight echo from Cant's voice from the church bell which hung above them. He was standing with Rankine and Muschet in the steeple of Lammersheugh Kirk.

Euphame Hay was sitting on the floor with her back against the wall. She recognised the new arrival. She knew what his leather bag contained. John Kincaid was the son of John Kincaid, pricker of witches. He had terrified the children of the parish with his repulsive father when she was young.

She vomited onto the floorboards and found she was unable to move her arms or legs. In horror she watched a dark stain seep through the sackcloth as she lost control of her bowels. She prayed to God, not the harsh God of these men, but the one she had glimpsed in the New Testament. Was such a God dispelled from this blighted land? She looked at Cant. He had been welcomed to Lammersheugh House as the spiritual guide of her sister. Now he was overseeing her torture. She felt a terrible breathlessness. The tightness across her chest was unbearable. She tried to scream, but could not.

She had been kept awake the whole night, a servant appearing every ten minutes to rouse her with a stick if her eyes were shut. She had no blanket or cushion on which to rest her head. She was forced to sit against the cold stone wall, drawing her knees into her stomach, pulling the stinking sackcloth round her.

Even when they did not use harsh words, she knew they sought to break her, make her confess to being a witch, to planning evil deeds and fornicating with the Devil. She could never confess to that – whatever they did to her. She had not lain with any man. Now she never would. She would never be a mother. Never hold a bairn in her arms. That thought was the saddest of all. They had broken her life, destroyed it. If she lived, what man would want her? She recalled his handsome face. He would not have her as his wife now. No man in Scotland would. The image of a burning stake appeared in her mind, the fire taking her soul, roasting her to nothing. They had said that she might sleep if she confessed she was a witch; if she confessed to lying with Satan; if she confessed that her mother had introduced her to him; if she confessed that they planned to kill Lady Girnington using witchcraft, creating a wax doll in her image.

'Hold her down.' Kincaid's calm words struck like a hammer. His tone was workmanlike compared with the nervous banter of the others. Two servants lifted her by the armpits. She was a lithesome thing. That was how her father had described her. They carried her to the centre of the room where she looked up into the bell, trying to read the inscription. But the words made no sense. She felt her nerves were full of bees, stinging everywhere inside. She retched; the bile dripped down her chin onto the floor, staining the boards bright yellow. She recalled yellow flowers in the garden at Lammersheugh – the beauty of summer, the view of the hills from her chamber. How could she account for such good things against this?

Kincaid withdrew a leather bundle and unrolled it in front of her on the floor. He selected a metal pin of about two inches in length and tested its sharpness against the skin of his thumb.

Raising her head, Euphame watched him approach. But her fear had subsided. Hatred gave her strength. She discovered that she could move her arms again.

She closed her eyes and thought of the garden again. Her father laughing as he picked her up, throwing her into the air. She fell back towards him, secure in the knowledge she would be caught in his strong arms. She loved him. She must hold on to that. He was a good man. He did not hunt witches.

'Hold her down!'

Kincaid's breath was on her cheek.

CHAPTER 20
The Devil's Footprints

THE DEVIL'S POOL, an expanse of black water, moved slowly towards a channel where it became a vigorous burn that ran northwards towards Haddington and the Firth of Forth.

'This is the Devil's Pool, gentlemen,' Cockburn said, leading the way round the edge of the water towards the boulder on the north side.

'Why is it so called?' Scougall ventured.

'It is said that witches meet the Devil here, Mr Scougall. But such stories are no more than superstition.'

'That is where my son says he sat.' The laird pointed to the boulder. 'Let us take a closer look.'

They continued uphill to a spot where they could cross the burn by hopping over a few small stones. It was an easy ascent of a couple of feet onto the large rock. On the two sides facing the pool, the boulder was only a couple of feet above the water, but the drop on the other sides was about five feet. Its top was flat, about nine feet square, large enough for them to stand on together. MacKenzie's slightly bulging eyes observed the scene carefully. He turned to complete the view – the birchwoods to the west, the pool, the channel, the muir, then up to Lammer Law, perhaps five hundred feet above them. It was a lonely spot. He could understand why the boy came here. Childhood memories came back to him, happy times fishing with his foster brothers, before the country fell into civil war.

Scougall looked down at the smooth surface of the rock. There was a long crack which he followed until it deepened into a crevice about a couple of inches deep. He crouched down and began to poke into it with a stick.

'Sir, Mr Cockburn, look.' MacKenzie got down on his knees beside him and peered into the crack. A few decaying apple cores were visible. A black beetle scurried into the shadows. But there was something else, something which sparkled as it caught the light.

Scougall carefully fished it out. He held up a small pearl necklace.

'I believe this belonged to Lady Lammersheugh,' said MacKenzie. 'Janet told me it was missing. But how did it find its way in there?'

Cockburn's voice broke as he spoke. 'A fine woman is dead.' As he paused the trees released a few more leaves to the earth in a chilly gust of wind. 'My son sat here eating an apple. He noticed something on the far side, in the shadows over there, beneath that tall tree.' The laird pointed to a silver birch overhanging the western side of the pool. 'He ran round to take a closer look and discovered the body. Then he saw a figure in the woods. He was terrified and ran home.'

'Let us look at the other side,' suggested MacKenzie.

They retraced their steps down the eastern fringe of the pool. MacKenzie noticed footprints on the ground by the water. He kneeled down to examine them, letting the others continue, but was back on his feet in a few seconds.

They followed the burn downstream below the channel where they could cross the rocks, and then came back up the other bank to the edge of the woods. The birches had shed most of their leaves. Beside the large tree there was a jump down of a couple of feet to a small area of sand. MacKenzie pointed to more footprints.

'Who came back to retrieve the body?'

'I believe the colonel's men, John Dunbar, George Pringle and Patrick Abernethy,' the laird responded. 'I was told they left the cart where our horses are. They pulled her out of the water, placed her on a board, then carried her back.'

MacKenzie kneeled down. 'We have the footprints of three men and a boy.' Turning to the laird, he observed him carefully. 'Where did your son see the figure?'

'He was standing here, looking into the woods. It was growing dark. Someone appeared in the trees about thirty yards away.' He pointed into the birches.

'Who was it?' Scougall asked solemnly.

'Who do you think, Mr Scougall?' There was a hint of bitter humour in the laird's voice.

'I do not know.'

'Perhaps it was the Devil.' The laird hesitated, watching the reaction on Scougall's face. The word shot into him like a bullet. 'The black fellow, Mr Scougall. Geordie is adamant that he saw the Devil.'

Scougall saw again the witch's face staring at him on her journey up the High Street; the fevered night with Sinclair's book; his mother's words at the dinner table – 'Satan walks in Scotland.'

'Who do you think your son saw, Mr Cockburn?' MacKenzie interjected.

'He saw a man like you or me, Mr MacKenzie. At the root of evil are men. Perhaps the Devil was acting through a man.'

'Which man might that have been?'

'I do not know.' The laird reflected for a while. 'But I did see Murdoch and his wife out late on the road the night before the body was found. It was very cold, but I noticed he was wearing only a shirt.'

'What were they doing?'

'I do not know. It was after midnight. They seemed to be making their way back to Lammersheugh.'

'What were you doing out so late yourself?'

'I often walk round the gardens at night when I need to think.'

'And what were you thinking about on that evening?' MacKenzie asked in an affable manner.

'My usual concerns, Mr MacKenzie. The wellbeing of my son and wife.'

'Let us explore the wood,' said MacKenzie. He climbed onto the bank and walked in the direction Cockburn had indicated. The laird followed and then Scougall, reluctantly, listening to the strange wailing sounds made by the wind in the birches.

MacKenzie proceeded for about fifty yards. As the trees were not tightly packed, it was easy to move through them into the centre of the wood. 'Please stand perfectly still, gentlemen,' he said, then he began to speak in Gaelic. The words possessed a haunting quality: *Seileach allt, calltainn chreag, feàrna bhog, beithe lag, uinnseann an deiseir*. I must apologise, Mr Cockburn. Gaelic is my native tongue. Let me translate for you – Willow of the brook, hazel of the rock, alder of the bog, birch of the hollow, ash of the sunny slope.' MacKenzie smiled. 'The proverbs of my people come to me in Gaelic before I think about them. They have much to teach us, representing the collective wisdom of the Gael. They often direct my thoughts down new pathways. They are a useful tool.' He observed the laird carefully before smiling.

'Sadly I do not speak your language, sir. I have never been to the Highlands,' he replied.

Scougall recalled his own visit to Glenshieldaig Castle in the West Highlands the previous year; the cateran's dagger on his neck, the attempt on their lives by Glenbeg. His sense of unease grew.

'It is too beautiful a spot for the Devil,' said MacKenzie, sensing Scougall's fear.

Scougall mustered a half-hearted grin.

'We must search the wood in case the Devil left anything behind.' A peremptory tone entered MacKenzie's voice which Scougall recognised as an indication of purpose, but it surprised the laird, whose expression suggested he was not used to being told what to do. 'The wood is not large,' MacKenzie continued, 'head in that direction, Davie. Mr Cockburn, please go that way. I will search this way. Shout if you see anything. But take your time – *Buinnigear buaidh le foighidinn* – Patience wins victory. We may be lucky and come upon the Devil's footprints!'

Despite the grim series of events, he was feeling well. The blackness was vanquished. Lightness engrossed his spinning mind. This was a dark puzzle, but a puzzle nonetheless. And he would solve it.

Scougall set his eyes on the floor of the wood and he plodded like a sullen child, examining each clump of grass and heather. Every so often he stopped to look up into the thin branches. They reminded him of skeletal fingers. He saw no beauty in this spot as suggested by MacKenzie. After about twenty yards, he turned to watch the figures of the other two receding into the distance. The presence of evil was palpable. He wished keenly for human companionship. Another look over his shoulder added to his gloom. Cockburn and MacKenzie were far off on the other side of the wood, almost unrecognisable as human, black streaks against the silver bark of the trees.

He was nearing the end of the wood. Before him was the pool, the Devil's Pool, black water, a dark mirror of the sky. He was wondering how deep it was in the middle when he caught sight of an object lying in the heather near the edge of the trees. Kneeling down, he saw that it was a finely carved pistol, the length of his hand with an exquisite ivory handle.

'Sir... sir... Mr Cockburn... over here... I have found something,' he shouted.

He looked down at the small gun. It was strange to see such a valuable weapon lying there. But the discovery cheered him. After all, why would the Devil need a pistol?

CHAPTER 21

The Dreams of Euphame Hay

SHE WATCHED HIM walk away, the sound of his boots on the wooden floorboards echoing within her head. She prayed that the pain was over. She heard him talk to the others. She did not understand what they were saying. A look of agitation was on the face of Cant. She had watched him from her pew in church each Sabbath. In the kirk his eloquence shone. It was different here. He looked exhausted. The pricking was something he had not witnessed before. Muschet also looked drawn. However, Rankine's expression was as self-satisfied as ever.

Euphame's body ached everywhere. They had removed the sackcloth. They were the first men to see her naked. It should have been her husband.

As the two men held her down, Kincaid had applied the pin to every inch of her body. She had tried to resist, but she was too weak. Sometimes the metal seemed to slip into her almost without pain, like a knife dropped into butter. In other places, it was agonising.

For a while she felt light, as if she was looking down on her torture from above. She was glad that her father was dead; that he did not live to see his daughter suffer like this. The thought gave her some strength. She would accept the pain in remembrance of him. She would meet him again when she died. The thought of death did not scare her.

She began to drift into unconsciousness. Her thoughts became confused. She was a girl back in Janet Cornfoot's cottage watching her prepare a meal. Her mother arrived in a beautiful green gown. Euphame was startled by her youthful beauty. It was as she must have looked when she was first married.

'Euphame, Euphame, wake up! Wake up!'

She had no idea how long she had slept, one minute, two – an hour. She did not know if it was day or night. She did not know what day it was.

The minister's voice. 'You may not sleep yet, Euphame...'

The colonel's men were behind her, pulling her up so that she was forced to sit against the wall. Her three accusers, Cant, Muschet and Rankine, stood once more before her, black intent in their eyes as they looked down on her.

'The Devil's Mark has been found on you, witch!' Theophilus Rankine was the first to speak. 'Kincaid has found marks on your thigh and the small of your back. The pin was inserted a full inch. There was no blood. You felt no pain. Witch!'

She wanted to spit in his face. But she was powerless. She knew what they sought. They wanted to break her, to wear her down by waking her again and again until she told them that she was a witch and her mother and Janet and others were witches. Then they would let her sleep. She looked at their faces, but said nothing. Her eyelids drooped. Her head fell forward. All of a sudden she felt a jolt on her face. It was not a hand. It was water, ice-cold. She came back to consciousness. They had miscalculated. She was awake again. She knew that if she was alert she would never give in. But in that place between sleep and wakefulness, in that halfway house she had less control. In that place she was not sure if she was in life or in a dream.

'Euphame.' The minister was not full of condemnation like the session clerk, but he was insistent. 'Euphame, the pricker has found the Devil's Mark upon you. We know you are in covenant with Satan. We know you have met him in the Blinkbonny Woods and at the Weird Heugh. We know that you have conspired with your mother and other witches to harm Lady Girnington. You must seek God's forgiveness. You must repent. If you confess, you may rest tonight.'

She summoned up the energy to speak, but her voice was weak and hoarse. 'I am no witch, Mr Cant. I am Euphame Hay, daughter of Alexander Hay of Lammersheugh, grand-daughter of John Hay of Lammersheugh, great-grand-daughter of Robert Hay of Lammersheugh.' But her words were unintelligible.

She was lost somewhere. It was the feeling you got as a child when you ran too far into the woods and, for a few minutes, you could not find your mother or father. Then with a jolt she was back in the steeple. She was not sure if she had slept. Now there were only two of them in the room. The minister had retired to bed.

Rankine kneeled down beside her so that she looked straight into his reptilian face.

'Confess you are a witch! Whore of Satan! Fornicator with the Devil! Polluter of the parish – witch!'

'I am no witch.'

Rankine understood what she said. There was pain again on her face. This time it was a hand, a slap, a burning feeling on her cheek. Again she was roused. Again she claimed victory. God must be watching. These men would surely burn in Hell for what they did.

'No, Mr Rankine! We are not to touch her. We do not have the authority. We must follow procedure.' Muschet's anxiety was evident.

She let her head rest against the wall. Visions of happy

times before her father died came to her. Just as she was falling asleep the cottage of Janet Cornfoot appeared again, full of the old woman's laughter, a place where she felt at home. On the spit in the hearth she watched meat roasting, a creature of some kind. She could not tell at first what it was, but there was a sweet smell. She gazed on long glistening muscles and white sizzling tendons.

But when she realised what it was, she screamed as she had never screamed before. She was watching her own body roasting before her.

CHAPTER 22
A Reception at Girnington House

'ONE FINAL QUESTION, Mr Cockburn,' MacKenzie said as he dismounted at the gates. 'Where were you the afternoon Lady Lammersheugh died?'

'Do you assume the role of sheriff-deputy, Mr MacKenzie?' Cockburn was clearly nettled.

'It is only my inquisitive nature getting the better of me. As the family's lawyer, I need to find out what has happened to Lady Lammersheugh. It may help Euphame.'

Cockburn's tone softened. 'I am sorry. Clachdean shows little application in his position. I had a meeting with Purse in Haddington.' He took off his hat and bowed. 'Until we meet again, gentlemen.' Rousing his horse, he set off at a trot in the direction of Lammersheugh.

MacKenzie and Scougall entered a drive leading to Girnington House. MacKenzie observed the impressive structure as they approached, noting the Dutch gables tied across the front by a balustrade and fine portico. 'What do you make of this afternoon's discoveries, Davie?'

'I am relieved to be away from the pool, sir,' began Scougall. 'I felt the presence of evil there. I have never experienced it so powerfully before.'

'But what do you think about the necklace and the gun?'

'Lady Lammersheugh may have taken her own life. I have

heard of accused witches who have done so,' he proposed.

'Yes. She may have been overwhelmed by the accusations against her.' MacKenzie stopped walking and turned to Scougall. 'However, she would have expected protection from her kin if the case went to trial. She may have ended her life to escape the pain of grief. On the other hand, we have evidence that she was a devoted mother. The letter suggests that she believed that her life was in danger. Let us assume for now that she did not take her life. Clachdean, the colonel as he appears to be known in the parish, thinks it was an accident; a woman who could not swim fell into a deep pool. This is also possible, of course, but unlikely. He does not know about the letter. In addition, he may want little attention drawn to her death to minimise his workload. The presence of the necklace may indicate that Lady Lammersheugh was on the rock before she died, or that someone found it and placed it there for safe keeping, George Cockburn, for example. However, it was very careless to lose such a fine weapon in the woods. I must confess I am confused, Davie.' They continued walking towards the house.

'The presence of the gun may be unrelated, sir.'

'Entirely possible. What do you make of the initials?' MacKenzie withdrew the pistol from his cloak and handed it to Scougall. 'AH has been carved at the bottom of the handle.'

Scougall examined the weapon, turning it round to observe the base. 'Do you know anyone with these initials, sir?'

'None of those I have met thus far – Lillias Hay, Adam Cockburn, Robert Dewar, Archibald Muschet, Theophilus Rankine, John Murdoch.'

'It could have been purchased from someone else,' suggested Scougall.

MacKenzie walked on for a few paces, deep in thought. 'There were other footprints at the pool, Davie. I noticed some on the eastern side as we walked north. You may have seen me kneeling to tie my laces. And we have a shoe size!'

MacKenzie removed a piece of string from his pocket, holding it up to show Scougall. Bending over, he placed it beside his foot and then his companion's. The string was longer than Scougall's by an inch, and half an inch longer than his own. 'It does not seem to belong to a woman unless Lady Lammersheugh had very large feet! Nor was it one of those who retrieved the body for I compared the length with them. We know that a man with large feet visited the pool alone over the last few days. But we cannot tell if this was before or after she drowned. We are fortunate that the weather has been clement over the last week, and rain did not wash them away.'

'I had not noticed them, sir.' Scougall was impressed by MacKenzie's forethought to measure the prints.

'Fear can heighten the senses, but it can also blunt them. Do not waste time thinking about Sinclair's tales. Grissell's death has nothing to do with the Devil, Davie. The answer is to be found among the inhabitants of Lammersheugh. As you know I am a student of human nature. Combining the pieces of evidence we find with a close scrutiny of the characters in the parish will help explain her death and, hopefully, save Euphame.'

Scougall was relieved by MacKenzie's assurance that human agency was at the root of events. 'It is possible that someone pushed Lady Lammersheugh into the water, found out that she could not swim and then threw the weapon away,' he suggested.

'Janet Cornfoot found a slight bruising on her temple which could have been caused by a fall into water,' replied MacKenzie. 'Drowning is the most likely cause of death. But much depends on the boy's testimony.'

They had reached the front door of the house. MacKenzie

indicated with a nod that Scougall was to knock. After a long wait a smartly dressed servant answered, gave them a cold stare and enquired as to their business.

'I am John MacKenzie, an advocate in Edinburgh. This is my assistant, Davie Scougall,' MacKenzie said politely. 'We seek an audience with her ladyship on legal matters relating to the estate of Lammersheugh. Announce our arrival and arrange for our horses to be cared for.'

The servant bowed his head, but left them waiting outside. MacKenzie turned to take in the view of the gardens to the front of the house. He bent over to examine a shrub, smiling appreciatively. 'Ah, Cytisus – *Cytisus sessiliflorus* was introduced from Italy in the early part of the century. And here is Trumpet Honeysuckle, *Lonicers sempervirens*, a native of America. Lady Girnington has employed an adventurous gardener.'

'Her ladyship will see you.' The servant had re-appeared.

They were escorted through the hall into a large room on the right. Lady Girnington was seated by the fire. She was wearing a dark silk gown. A luxurious blonde wig enclosed a vigorously powdered face.

MacKenzie reflected that Lillias Hay, Alexander Hay's elder sister, had put on a great deal of weight in the twenty years since they had last met. She was arrogant then. He doubted if age had mellowed her. A great beauty in her youth, she had made a stir in London in the days of Cromwell. But there had been a scandal. He could not remember the details.

Mesmerised by the billowing dress, Scougall was reminded of a queen on her throne.

Lady Girnington did not rise to greet them. 'That will be all, Leitch,' she snapped. 'Mr MacKenzie, it is a pleasure. I expect you are well,' she continued in barely more mellow tones. 'And who are you?' The question was directed at

Scougall, causing his face to turn red.

'My assistant Davie Scougall, a writer in Edinburgh,' MacKenzie interceded. 'He hails from Musselburgh.'

'An inhabitant of Musselburgh. I see...' Holding back none of her condescension, she turned to MacKenzie: 'To what do I owe the pleasure of your company? I do not remember seeking legal advice.' Lady Girnington shifted herself slightly. 'Sit,' she ordered.

Scougall dropped into a finely upholstered French chair. MacKenzie took his time to make himself comfortable on another. 'Thank you, my lady. I am very sorry we visit Girnington under such circumstances,' he began in a slightly obsequious manner, 'I believe we met many years ago. I am not sure if you remember.'

'I do not, sir. Lawyers make little impression on me,' she replied.

'I believe it was over twenty years ago. The laird was still alive.'

'I am happier as a widow than I ever was as a wife,' she smirked.

MacKenzie returned the smile. 'It was with great sorrow that I learned of the death of your sister-in-law. She was a charming woman who will be greatly missed by her children.'

'You are right, Mr MacKenzie. However, their future is secure in my hands. Grissell was a soft creature who gave no thought to the future of Lammersheugh. Debts were built up, but little was done to improve the estate. Under my stewardship there will be change. You must remember that I was a child of the house. It is a place which means much to me. I have fond memories of it.'

MacKenzie had long experience of the arrogant wives of aristocrats and lairds. 'Your ladyship, I seek to clarify some points of law relating to my deceased client. I am particularly interested in financial encumbrances upon the lands of Lammersheugh. As one of the guardians of Euphame and Rosina, I thought that you might be able to shed some light on them.'

'I do not concern myself with such matters, Mr MacKenzie. I fear your journey has been wasted. Purse will help you with the financial details.'

MacKenzie sat forward, a serious look coming over his face. 'I must remind you that Euphame languishes in sackcloth in the steeple.'

'I am doing all that I can to secure my niece's release,' Lady Girnington replied. 'But when the parish zealots get hold of a witch it is difficult to restrain them. Their appetite for persecution grows. The kirk session must have its day. However, I am sure Euphame will not be convicted. The case would be laughed out of court!'

'I fear we must make haste if we are to save her from the humiliation of a trial in Edinburgh. She may not survive incarceration in the Tolbooth.'

'It will not come to that, Mr MacKenzie. I have influence over Cant and the other little men of the parish. Persuasion will rein them in. After a night in the steeple she will be released. I am sure of it. I will stand caution for her.'

'I presume you have already been in contact with the minister.'

'Be assured that I am doing all I can to secure her release.'

MacKenzie took a deep breath. 'I believe you are owed substantial sums from the estate of Lammersheugh?'

'You attended the reading of Grissell's will – it is public knowledge. Debts are, however, not purely financial in nature. I have no intention of going to law to get money back from my own family.'

'What of your relations with Lady Lammersheugh?'

'You ask too many questions, Mr MacKenzie. I am not to

be cross-examined in my own home. Relations were as one might expect. I am as shocked as anyone by the terrible course events have taken since the death of my brother.'

'Can you think of any reason why anyone might want to kill her?'

Lady Girnington hesitated before answering. 'Mr MacKenzie, I am not in court. I do not need to answer your questions. All I will say is that I know of no reason why anyone might want rid of her. However, I do know that she was sorely afflicted by melancholy following Alexander's death. This can drive some to seek unwise remedies.'

'What do you mean, my lady?'

'I mean that her servant, Janet Cornfoot, had a reputation for charming.'

'You are surely not suggesting that Grissell was involved in such things?'

'I am not suggesting anything. I think it is time for you to take your leave, Mr MacKenzie. If you have any further questions concerning the debts, address them to Purse.'

But MacKenzie was persistent. 'What about Euphame's marriage?'

Lady Girnington could not resist replying. 'Euphame's value would appear to have fallen. We may find someone once she is released. The Laird of Clachdean is unmarried. He may be willing to accept her – on certain terms.'

'Is he not too old for her?'

'The caresses of an old man have been forced on many a maid. I doubt if she will have many suitors. Most men are reluctant to marry a woman accused of witchcraft, although I know a few who have taken one into their bed.' She gave a humourless laugh.

'Where were you on the twenty-second of October?'

'Are you suggesting that I could have killed my sister-in-law?' She laughed in derision. 'Look at me, gentlemen. I am a fat old woman. It is difficult for me to stand unattended. I am helped into the gardens. I am carried to my coach. I am afflicted by grossness of the body, as my mother was.'

MacKenzie rose, indicating that Scougall was to do likewise. 'I have only one more question, madam. A clock is hardly a generous gift to a beloved sister?'

'The silly game of a deranged woman!' Lady Girnington shook her head.

'We have taken up enough of her ladyship's time, Davie.'

They were shown out by Leitch, who observed them with unveiled suspicion. At the front door MacKenzie turned to him. 'Was Margaret Rammage a servant on the Girnington estate?'

'Yes, sir. She bided in Headshaw. A poor misguided creature. God rest her soul.'

At the gates they allowed a horseman entrance. The bulky frame of Clachdean was perched on top of the beast. He nodded sullenly to them as he passed.

CHAPTER 23
A Meeting with the Colonel

THE MINISTER WAS nervous as he entered the room. The colonel always made him uneasy. It was partly his gruff manner; as a soldier who had survived bloody battles, he cared little for men of the cloth. But it was also that he made no secret of his life of sin, boasted of his conquests, even to him, a minister of the Reformed Church of Scotland. Did the brute have no care of his immortal soul? On their last meeting he had told him all the details of a liaison with Jane Nisbet, the Laird of Skirt's servant. Cant did not have the strength of will to upbraid him on the evils of fornication. In the church before his congregation he felt confident, but in the presence of the colonel he was diminished, a fearful boy before a man. Another troubling matter was that Clachdean never attended church on the Sabbath, deliberately ignoring the Kirk's admonitions. He would not have the word of God flouted in his parish.

'I did not see you in church last Sunday, Colonel Dewar,' he said as he occupied the chair in front of the desk. Clachdean was at the window, looking out at the hills, seemingly deep in thought. He turned abruptly and gave Cant a scathing look.

'You will not see me in your church, Mr Cant. I worship God where I want, not where I am told.'

'Would it not set a good example to your servants?'

'My servants need no such example. They will not serve me more loyally for imbibing a little scripture. Too much religion makes men troublesome.'

Cant moved the conversation onto another subject. 'I was deeply shocked by Lady Lammersheugh's death. It was a terrible accident...'

'A terrible accident, indeed,' Clachdean repeated. 'I am told she could not swim. The pool is deep in parts. She must have slipped on the rock. She was a very fine looking woman. You have lost your witch, Mr Cant.'

'She did not confess, sir. She was named in Rammage's confession...'

'But there is now another in the grasp of the session,' the colonel sneered.

'It is an awful shock to me. I am spiritual adviser to her sister. Euphame appeared such a pure girl, but she is infected with sin. The pricker has found the Devil's Mark on her.'

'All women are polluted by sin. They are good for only one thing, are they not, Mr Cant? Only yesterday I fucked a very fine wench in Haddington for a few pennies.'

Cant did not reply. He realised that he hated the colonel.

'You have overreached yourself, Mr Cant. Euphame is an innocent girl, accused by a dolt.'

'The case troubles me much, sir.'

'Her ladyship expects her niece to be released.'

'I must follow procedure, Colonel Dewar. I cannot overrule the session. The authorities in Edinburgh have already been informed.' Cant was adamant.

'Her ladyship will not be pleased.' said Clachdean menacingly.

Cant was sweating. He wanted to get away from the colonel as soon as he could.

'We are in great danger, sir, grave danger. The Devil has found succour in Lammersheugh. Cockburn's boy saw him in the woods by the pool. Many are accused throughout Lothian and across Scotland. As minister of this parish I must do all that is in my power to root out such evil. And now Janet Cornfoot is dead. It is surely the Devil's work, also.'

'Janet was an old woman. She died of natural causes. I have inspected her body. She was afflicted by some kind of fit. Unfortunately, the lawyer MacKenzie was with her. I believe he may be trouble, Mr Cant. He is an Episcopalian degenerate! We must watch him. There is much at stake beyond the parish of Lammersheugh. For all our sakes it would be best if you carried out the wishes of Lady Girnington. If not, I may have to take further action. You may go now.'

Cant looked up at the huge face lowering over him. The colonel's scarred hand rested on the handle of his sword. He wondered whom he feared most – Clachdean, or the Devil.

CHAPTER 24
The Wake of Janet Cornfoot

28 October 1687

THERE WAS A commotion outside Janet Cornfoot's cottage when Scougall and MacKenzie appeared through the woods. A small crowd of mourners were in the garden; an old woman was wailing loudly. She fell silent as they entered through the small gate.

'We come to pay our respects,' said MacKenzie.

John Murdoch came forward with a worried expression, beckoning them to follow him round the side of the building. He waited until they were out of earshot. 'God help us! God help us!'

'What is it, man?' asked MacKenzie.

'Bluid! Bluid! We were aw roond the coffin, when Jean Paterson suddenly screams – "Bluid! Bluid!" I looked within. Fresh bluid wis drippin frae Janet's mooth. Then Jean starts shouting "The killer is here! The killer is here!" It is said a corpse bleeds in the presence o the one who killed it. We aw began tae look roond the room, eyeing each ither.'

'There will be a rational explanation, Murdoch,' Mac-Kenzie reassured him.

'I dinnae ken what it can be, sir. I saw the blood masel, clear as day.'

MacKenzie marched round to the front of the cottage and

made his way through the throng. The door was ajar. He pushed it open and entered, Scougall behind him, fearful of what they might find. Murdoch followed, but remained just outside the door.

There was no one inside the cottage. The coffin lay on top of the wooden table in the centre of the room. MacKenzie and Scougall looked down on Janet Cornfoot. There was a dark red trail emerging from her slightly open mouth. The wood of the coffin was stained beneath her head. Scougall edged back, glancing round the room as he recalled the description of the badger hanging at the doorway.

MacKenzie removed a small pair of tweezers from his pocket. Holding Janet's nose with thumb and forefinger, he pulled down the jaw, jabbing into her mouth with the instrument. Scougall took another pace back, fearing that something might burst out. MacKenzie carefully removed what looked like a leather pouch about the size of an apple. It reminded Scougall of an old golf ball.

'There, we have it!' MacKenzie was delighted with the discovery. 'There is no witchcraft here. This is the work of man, or woman! Look, Murdoch. A bladder of blood was placed in the mouth. A piece of metal was secured inside; the hole sealed with wax. When it was pulled, the bag was ruptured, releasing the blood.' MacKenzie showed Scougall the tiny slash in the bladder. 'The timing was perfect. Could it have been someone in the room? Think, Murdoch!'

'I saw naebody touch the body, sir.' The old servant looked bewildered.

'What do you think, Davie?'

'Perhaps a thread was yanked from somewhere.' Scougall was relieved that the explanation involved no supernatural agency.

They searched the room, but found nothing. MacKenzie noticed that the window was slightly open. 'A cord might have been pulled from there by someone outside.' He looked through the open door where the crowd was dispersing. 'The folk of the parish believe that Janet's killer is amongst them. They will not trust any of their neighbours. Keep this in your pocket, Davie. We must examine it closely later.'

Scougall gingerly pocketed the shrivelled object.

'Does it tell us anything about how Janet died?' he asked.

'It tells us that she did not die of natural causes, despite what the sheriff-deputy believes. But we knew that already.'

'I must return to the house, sir,' said Murdoch from the doorway.

'Before you go, I have a couple of questions for you,' said MacKenzie, moving towards the servant.

Murdoch looked down at the floor. 'Aye, sir.'

'You and your wife were seen the night before Lady Lammersheugh died. What were you doing out so late?'

Murdoch rubbed a large hand on his trousers as if trying to remove a stain. 'We were returning frae ma sister, sir. She bides in Craw, five miles frae Lammersheugh.'

'I understand you were wearing only a semmet on a cold evening.'

'I had taken aff ma coat. It's a lang walk hame. I wis sweating.'

'Was there any other reason you were out so late?'

'No, sir.'

'I hope you are telling the truth, Murdoch.'

MacKenzie waited, but the servant said nothing.

'Janet spoke of strange sounds in the village during the night, faint screechings,' said MacKenzie.

'I have heard them, sir. The spirits o the deid. The Devil walks in Lammersheugh.'

MacKenzie's frowned. 'Please do not say anything about what has happened here to Rosina.'

Murdoch nodded.

'Do you trust him?' Scougall asked MacKenzie after Murdoch had departed.

'I do not trust anyone in a witch-hunt, Davie! But he has been a loyal servant of the House of Lammersheugh, as has his wife. We must not let his manner prejudice us against him. They could have acted together to engineer this morning's conjuring trick. But what would they gain from stirring up such trouble in the parish?'

'They were beneficiaries of the will,' observed Scougall.

'The sum they received was not great. According to Euphame, Murdoch was in the house on the day of Grissell's death. However, it is possible he was paid to cause trouble at the wake.' MacKenzie took a piece of string from his pocket and threw it to Scougall. 'I want to take another look at the body. While I am busy here, search the gardens. Look for footprints under the window.'

CHAPTER 25

The Library of Lammersheugh

MACKENZIE LET HIS eyes wander round the bookshelves. Like him, Alexander Hay had been a devoted bibliophile. He noticed a selection of works by the poet William Drummond of Hawthornden: *Flowers of Sion*, *Forth Feasting* and *Teares on the Death of Moeliades*. And there was a copy of Spenser's *Faerie Queen*. There was *Ekskubalauron* by Sir Thomas Urquhart, a neighbour in Ross-shire. A very fine writer, but quite mad. His translations of Rabelais, which the author had shown him in manuscript, were of the highest quality, though his other works were tiresome.

'Here is the picture, Mr MacKenzie. It is not the best likeness of my mother,' said Rosina.

Scougall and MacKenzie looked at a small portrait which hung above a darkly-stained desk on the only wall not lined by books. Grissell's head and shoulders were painted against a black background.

Scougall was struck by her dark eyes, voluptuous lips and long brown hair. He felt himself being drawn into the painting, and a slight light-headedness. Her beautiful eyes were captivating. He found that he was not able to look away. It flashed through his mind that she was a witch, that he was bewitched.

Then he experienced the beginnings of sexual arousal.

God forgive him! He turned his eyes away.

Rosina was looking sadly at her mother, to whom she bore a striking resemblance. There was something wild about her, a slight look of an Egyptian.

He closed his eyes and tried to focus on the last instrument he had completed in his office before leaving Edinburgh. His excitement dissipated.

Rosina removed the portrait from the wall. 'There you are, Mr MacKenzie. Let us find your daughter's jewel.'

They descended a spiral staircase to the first floor and entered a large room lined with wooden panels. The ceiling was a swirl of coloured flowers, the walls crowded with Italian landscapes and family likenesses.

'This is my mother's chamber.'

Scougall looked at a huge canvas above the fireplace.

'My mother and father with my sister and me, in happier times, Mr Scougall,' said Rosina.

Scougall watched MacKenzie's eyes devour each detail. Following the advocate's example, he tried to place everything in his memory.

The Laird of Lammersheugh was a tall man with a short beard and piercing blue eyes. He wore a blue velvet suit and a large hat with a long black feather. Lady Lammersheugh stood a full foot shorter, dressed in a stunning green velvet gown. She gazed down on the children. The thin girl of about five or six must be Euphame, the younger one Rosina. The family was grouped under a large oak tree; two wolfhounds lay on the grass beside them. He looked out of the window. The same tree still stood there. Scougall moved forward to read the artist's name and the date: *Thomas Warrender, 1675.*

Rosina opened a wooden casket on the dressing-table.

'Here it is.'

She handed MacKenzie a small jewel.

He held the emerald up to his eye.

'It is very fine. My daughter is honoured by your mother's generosity.' He placed it in a handkerchief which he slipped into his pocket. 'How is your sister, Rosina?'

'She suffers so much. You must do something to help her.'

'I believe that Lady Girnington stands caution for her.'

'How long will it take? She has been sorely abused.'

'It should only be a little time.'

MacKenzie was observing her closely. Her demeanour did not suggest that she had just lost a mother, or on top of that had a sister accused of witchcraft. There was something very determined about her. 'I have been told that you and Mr Cant are well known to each other,' he commented.

'He comes to the house once a week to instruct me on religious matters. I give him little thought otherwise.'

'What does he think of you?'

'I do not know, Mr MacKenzie.' There was a hint of annoyance in her voice. 'Ministers are beneath me, whatever you may be insinuating.'

'Some have said you would be a beneficiary of your mother and sister's demise.'

Rosina's eyes burned with anger. 'I do not care to be spoken to in such a manner. Murdoch will show you out.'

She turned on her heel and left the room.

MacKenzie returned to the portrait. He tried to remember Purse's words. 'Find the details of Lady Lammersheugh's latterwill in your notes, Davie.'

Scougall flicked through the pages of his notebook and began to read slowly from his shorthand. '"I, Grissell Hay, Lady Lammersheugh…"'

'Move to the section about my bequest,' MacKenzie snapped impatiently.

Scougall turned the page:

'"To Mr John MacKenzie, advocate, Clerk of the Court of

Session, I leave the small picture which hangs in the library at Lammersheugh. And to his daughter Elizabeth MacKenzie I leave an exquisite emerald to be found in the box in my chamber…"'

MacKenzie knew these words must be significant. But he could make nothing of them.

CHAPTER 26

The Steeple

A WINDING STAIRCASE led into the steeple of Lammersheugh Kirk. At first Scougall could not make out Euphame in the shadows of the windowless room. Only a couple of candles burned beside the guards who sat in a corner. A shape like a sack of grain was revealed at the far wall as his eyes adjusted. She was lying forward as if asleep, knees pulled up to her chin.

One of the guards rose, took a long wooden pole which lay against the wall, and walked over to her. He prodded her with it. She raised her head, opening startled eyes.

MacKenzie and Scougall looked down on the exhausted face of Euphame Hay. Scougall covered his mouth with his hand; the smell of excrement was overpowering.

'It is John MacKenzie, Euphame. Your mother's lawyer,' he said softly.

Euphame's bloodshot eyes appeared to recognise him. But her words were so hoarse as to be incomprehensible.

As MacKenzie kneeled beside her, she recoiled.

'It is all right, my dear. We are here to help you. I came to visit you at the house before you were imprisoned.'

A gurgling sound came from her mouth as she tried to speak. She wanted to tell them about her torture. How the daughter of Alexander Hay of Lammersheugh was being abused by the men of the parish. She wanted to ask if her sister was accused; if the servants of the house were safe. But her throat could only emit the sounds of a suffering animal.

'Do not try to speak, Euphame. Keep your strength. We are doing all we can to secure your release. I have employed Rosehaugh on your behalf. Lady Girnington is appealing to the session. She will stand caution for you.' MacKenzie bent forward and whispered in her ear: 'For your sister's sake, for everything you hold dear, for the memory of your mother and father, do not confess. Do not confess.' He whispered the last words as forcefully as he could without being overheard by the guards. There was a slight nod of her head followed by another unintelligible reply.

Scougall was horrified by Euphame's appearance. He was also beset by conflicting emotions. He did not know if she was a witch or not. The minister and elders had the interests of all the parishioners at heart. The kingdom was in danger. If she was a witch, MacKenzie was assisting a creature beholden to the Devil. However, it was possible that she was innocent. Some were accused wrongly. If so, she had suffered terribly. Those who brought the charges against her had sinned.

They descended the steep staircase and entered the body of the kirk. Scougall looked round the simple interior. It was a fine building. He noticed writing on the walls. Moving closer, he read in swirling black script: 'Thou shalt not kill.' The Ten Commandments were scrolled on the whitewash. His eyes moved along – 'Thou shalt not bear false witness against thy neighbour.'

'Let us pay a visit to Mr Muschet,' MacKenzie interrupted.

Proceeding down the High Street, they came to a three-storey house and entered a shop on the ground floor. It was crammed full of merchandise: fruit and vegetables, clothing, ironwear, wooden tools. MacKenzie addressed the woman behind the counter.

'We seek Archibald Muschet.'

'My brother is not here. Who might I say is calling?'

MacKenzie introduced them. 'Do you know when he will be back?

'There is a meeting of the session. They have much business to attend to. The number of witches grows!'

'Have there been more arrests?'

'A confessing witch has named others.'

'A confessing witch!' MacKenzie looked grave. 'Do you mean Euphame Hay?'

'She does not confess yet. But she will. They all do eventually. The pricker has found the Devil's Mark on her. She is a witch, like her mother.'

MacKenzie inhaled deeply. Time was running out. He let his eyes wander round the shop. 'We will return later,' was all he said. By the door there was a display of hats, some of which had long blue feathers attached to them. 'Look, Davie. These are identical to the one I found on the floor of the cottage,' he murmured.

'We must find out who has purchased them,' replied Scougall.

MacKenzie took one down and tried it on. Turning to Muschet's sister, he asked the price.

'Five pounds, sir.'

'That is very high.'

'They are manufactured in London.'

'Have you sold many?'

'I have not sold one. My brother might have.'

At that moment a young woman dressed in a dirty linen skirt with an old bonnet on her head deposited her messages on the counter.

'We will not serve you here,' Muschet's sister snapped.

'You have no credit, Helen Rammage.'

'I hae siller, Mrs Thomson.'

The shopkeeper examined the coins in her hand and took two of them. Gathering the goods in her apron, the young woman left the shop.

MacKenzie was struck by the blue stains on the hands of Muschet's sister.

CHAPTER 27
A Visit to the Manse

'YOU DO ME a great honour, Rosina.' Cant beckoned her into his chamber. He was greatly surprised by her arrival; surprised, and exhilarated.

'I will not waste time on pleasantries, Mr Cant.' She tried to curtail her natural haughtiness. 'You must do something to secure Euphame's release. My sister is in a pitiful state. Surely you cannot believe that she is a witch.'

'We have the confession of Margaret Rammage. She has been pricked by Kincaid. She did not bleed from her inner thigh and the small of her back. There were similar accusations against your mother.'

'Rammage was a common peasant! How can her words stand against those of my sister, who is a laird's daughter?'

'The session must investigate all cases of witchcraft.'

'I believe my aunt has appealed to you on Euphame's behalf. I advise you not to stand in her way.'

'I have heard nothing from her ladyship. But I must let the law follow its course.'

'Are you sure, Mr Cant? I was told by MacKenzie that she has demanded her release and will stand caution. My sister is sorely abused!'

'Rosina.' Just saying the word gave him pleasure. 'We cannot always account for the actions of others. All are tempted by sin. Your mother and sister have covenanted themselves with Satan. They have chosen evil. You must accept this. Prayer will help. Ask God to give you strength. He will guide you through these difficult times. He will assure you of his bounty.'

'Is there nothing that can be done, Mr Cant?' Her voice softened.

'Thou shalt not suffer a witch to live,' replied the minister. But the words were not said with the venom with which they had been declaimed in the kirk.

Rosina closed her eyes. 'I feel faint. Perhaps I might take off my cloak until I am recovered enough to return home.'

Cant stood up to help. Underneath the long black cloak she was not dressed in mourning, as he had expected, but in a green velvet gown. He recalled the description of Grissell in Margaret Rammage's confession. Green was a colour like any other. It was a coincidence, nothing more. He had hardly slept over the last few days. The pricking of Euphame had taken much out of him. God was asking much of him. He reminded himself that Rosina was feeling faint.

'Would you care for some water?' he asked.

'No, thank you.'

She lowered her head. Tears were on her cheeks.

'Please, Rosina. God will give you strength.'

The sight of the dress had aroused him. He wanted to touch her, to feel her. He needed to hold another human being. He had never done so as an adult. He could feel his penis hard as stone. The blood was pumping in his head. He knelt down beside Rosina and took her hands in a comforting gesture. But he did not want to comfort her. He wanted to possess her. His mind was inflamed by visions of them lying together. Dare he raise his hand onto her arm, touch the soft white skin? Dare he kiss her hands? Dare he confess that he worshipped her? He took his hand from hers and raised it up her lower arm in a slow caress. She did not move it away. She did not move!

The feelings inside his groin intensified to a pitch and then released. He groaned slightly. As he did so, she turned to him. The tears were gone. There was a smile on her face. But when she spoke, it was with none of the gentleness that she had shown before. Her voice was suffused with the disdain of her class for his. 'I am sure there is something we can do for her, Mr Cant.'

At that moment his mind seemed to explode. Blurting out 'Excuse me,' he staggered from the room. He closed the door behind him and stood with his back against it, shaking, his mind pulsing with images from the confessions of witches. Satan was close, so close. He had been tempted. He was shown to be weak. Then, another dreadful thought swept through him. He wondered if they had accused the right sister.

CHAPTER 28

A Few Hours in Haddington

PURSE INDICATED THAT they should sit. Scougall recalled the reading of Lady Lammersheugh's latterwill the day before – the hushed sense of expectation followed by bemusement. He had been agitated after his late arrival. He now had time to examine the office more closely. It was the workplace of a country writer. Once he had dreamed of working as such a lawyer in Musselburgh. But he did not want to settle there now. He had seen too much of the world. His small office on the High Street of Edinburgh was a stone's throw from St Giles' Kirk. He could watch national events unfold from his window. Provincial life no longer had any appeal.

'Mr MacKenzie, Mr Scougall, I was expecting you.'

Without his wig, Purse looked younger than he had seemed the day before. Scougall guessed he was in his mid-forties.

'There is work to be done, gentlemen. The trustees will administer the Lammersheugh estate until the girls come of age or are married. I believe that will not be long.'

'Why do you say that, Mr Purse?' probed MacKenzie.

'Euphame.' He stopped briefly before continuing. 'I am forgetting myself. I have heard that Rosina is to be married to the Laird of Clachdean. That is what I have been told by her ladyship.'

'And when Euphame is released?'

'You know as well as I that she will be difficult to settle on a husband after such accusations.'

'So, in one way or another, Lady Girnington will have authority over Lammersheugh?'

'Until the girls come of age, or marry.'

'How are relations between the Laird of Clachdean and Lady Girnington?' asked MacKenzie.

Purse hesitated. 'You put me in a difficult position. I act for both parties. I will tell you only what is known on the High Street of Haddington. Financial obligations exist between them. The laird has led a dissolute life and is heavily in debt. I believe he owes large sums to her ladyship.'

'So she may control Lammersheugh and Clachdean?' added Scougall.

The lawyer smiled. 'You are very perceptive, Mr Scougall.'

'Let me see, Mr Purse,' continued MacKenzie, 'how much would you say the rents of the three estates add up to?'

'I do not know, sir.'

'Well, let me guess. Girnington provides perhaps £10,000 a year, pounds Scots of course, Lammersheugh £10,000 and Clachdean £5,000. How much does that make in total, Davie?'

Scougall, who was noting down the figures, quickly added them up. '£25,000, sir.'

'A very healthy sum, Mr Purse.'

'I do not believe it would be so much. Clachdean is not a productive estate. It has not been well managed.'

MacKenzie's voice lost its playfulness. 'I am perturbed. Euphame and Rosina are vulnerable young girls. A terrible accusation hangs over one. If something was to happen to Rosina, the Lammersheugh estate could pass to Lady Girnington by escheat.'

Scougall looked up from his notebook. 'What drives her

on so? She has surely reached an age when she should be thinking of retirement.'

Purse turned to Scougall. 'Men and women seek to accumulate. Her ladyship may feel that she has not been given the recognition she deserves. She was a great beauty in her youth before grossness afflicted her, a rival of the Duchess of Lauderdale in London in the days of Cromwell.'

'Revenge, sir?' proposed Scougall.

'A kind of revenge...' added Purse.

'But she is an old woman who may not live long. Who will benefit from it all if she dies?'

'The terms of her ladyship's will are secret.' Purse's eyes moved from Scougall to MacKenzie. He coughed loudly.

'Who are the curators of the Lammersheugh estate?' asked MacKenzie.

'Her ladyship, the colonel, Woodlawheid, Muschet, Rankine and myself. We must meet soon to discuss how it is to be administered.'

MacKenzie rose slightly from his chair, as if on the point of leaving, then dropped down again and posed another question. 'Mr Purse, may I enquire where were you on the twenty-second day of October, the day on which Lady Lammersheugh died?'

'I was in my office all day. I met with her ladyship and the colonel in the morning,' Purse replied, unruffled.

'What was the nature of the meeting?'

'That is confidential.'

'Did you meet the Laird of Woodlawheid later?'

Purse thought for a moment. 'No. I did not see Cockburn on that day.'

MacKenzie's expression lightened. 'How do you stand on politics, Mr Purse?'

The lawyer was surprised by the change of subject. 'I'm afraid I do not follow you, sir.'

'There is a pamphlet on your desk.'

MacKenzie pointed to a sheet of paper sticking out from a pile of documents. He leaned forward and read out the title – *The Sad Sufferings of an Afflicted Church.*

Purse was taken aback. 'I like to keep abreast of developments. Change was ever in the air. The King is not popular. His policies disgruntle many.'

MacKenzie was enjoying himself. It was always good to disarm an opponent during an interview.

'Do they disgruntle you, Mr Purse?'

'Politics is bad business for a lawyer. We must make money whichever way the wind blows. All I will say is that having a Catholic King is dangerous for this kingdom.'

Scougall nodded in agreement. The thought of such a monarch on the throne of Scotland was abhorrent. The recent conversions to Popery were very worrying, suggesting the rising power of Antichrist. But he was not sure why MacKenzie was asking Purse about this.

'Would you support an attempt to change the monarch by force?'

MacKenzie waited, but a reply was not forthcoming. He changed tack. 'Could you tell us about the condition of Cockburn's wife, Mr Purse?'

Purse looked relieved. 'I believe she suffers from a malady of the mind and fears to leave her chamber. She spends all her time in doors, oppressed by melancholy. It has been very trying for the laird.'

'It has been very trying for the laird?' MacKenzie repeated.

'It has been difficult for such an ambitious man. He was parliamentary representative for the shire, considered by many as one who might do great things for King and country. But his wife's decline sapped the spirit from him. He retired to his estate and took no further part in public affairs. He has become increasingly morose. He is barely civil to me now; even grunting a good day is hard for him.'

There was a knock at the door. The clerk's head appeared. 'Mr Kincaid is here to see you, sir.'

'I have a client, gentlemen. You will have to excuse me.'

CHAPTER 29
Redemption of a Debt

MUSCHET ROSE FROM the front pew at the sound of Cockburn's boots on the stone floor.

'The twenty-eighth of October in the Kirk of Lammer-sheugh, Mr Muschet. I am here to repay what I can,' Cockburn said in a serious tone.

'What you can,' echoed Muschet, an unpleasant smile spreading across his face. 'I had expected payment in full, Mr Cockburn. I believe the harvest was a good one for you.'

'The harvest was reasonable. But my other ventures have returned little. My share in the *Hope* has provided nothing. She is not yet returned from the Indies. I would be obliged to you, sir, if you might extend credit to me of half the amount for another year...'

'A year you say, Mr Cockburn... let me see...' The merchant was enjoying himself. Moneylending was his element. 'I assume you have half the principal and annual rent in ready cash with you?'

Cockburn withdrew a small money bag. 'It is all here, in silver.'

Muschet took it, weighing it in his hands. He poured the contents onto the table by the lectern and began to examine the coins for soundness. He had a keen eye and years of experience. There was 1,100 merks, half the principal and the annual rent on the full amount. 'I will lend you another 1,000 merks at a rate of twelve years' purchase for my trouble.' He put some coins to the side and returned the rest to the bag.

'Very well, sir,' Cockburn replied, without betraying any hint of emotion. The bag was thrown back to him.

'I will have Purse draw up a bond. We will sign in his office.'

'What news of Euphame, Mr Muschet?' Cockburn asked.

The question punctured the merchant's calm. He was forced to bring back to mind the pricking of the previous night. At first, he had been intoxicated. But her nakedness reminded him of a lanky boy, all bones as opposed to the voluptuousness her mother had possessed. It had become a grim affair. What was particularly disturbing was Rankine, the way the session clerk had observed the process as if being taught a new skill. Cant had not been able to watch at all and had stood by the door in prayer.

Muschet gathered himself. 'The Devil's Mark was found by the pricker, Mr Cockburn. She is a witch. There is no doubt. She must stand trial in Edinburgh for her crimes.'

The laird closed his eyes. He was sweating. It was claustrophobic inside the kirk. The thought of Euphame being pricked made him feel sick.

'She is an innocent young girl, Mr Muschet.'

'Do you question the evidence provided by the pricker, sir?'

'I do question it. She is tortured because of the testimony of a deluded woman.'

'I heard the confession of Margaret Rammage. She spoke with such earnestness. There is a terrible evil unleashed in our parish. Euphame was misled by her mother. She seemed a fine woman, but was in covenant with Satan.'

The laird took a deep breath. To have to tolerate this man was excessively irksome. 'Her mother was an honest woman. She was greatly wronged.'

'And how is your wife, sir?' asked Muschet, ignoring the comment.

'No better.'

'I am sorry. I am deeply saddened by the state of our landed men who must borrow from poor merchants like me. The houses of Lammersheugh and Woodlawheid both face difficulties. I hope they will find better days with God's grace.'

Cockburn wanted to throw the sanctimonious upstart to the ground and run him through with his sword. How the world was changed, turned upside down, indeed! Vile little men of trade risen high were now pulling the strings. The old families were reduced to begging from them. The more Muschet lent, the greater the hold he had over the lairds.

But there were more important matters to attend to than bothering about this insect. Cockburn reflected that at least he had got what he wanted.

'I bid you well, Mr Muschet,' he snapped. Without waiting for a reply, he made his way down the aisle.

CHAPTER 30
A Wax Painting

SHE LOOKED DOWN on the little figure she was carving. It was almost finished. She brought the spatula round for a final time. The wax doll was complete. God help her, she hoped that it wid wirk this time. They had risked sae much the previous week. But it had wirked years afore when they were young. She had feared that she might lose him then, also.

Memories of that time came to her. She had woken him at midnicht. She remembered helping him frae his sickbed. He had coughed aw the way tae the burn. He stood in the sooth-runnin water in only his semmet an turned thrice widdershins. Then she had dooket him in the freezing water an they had dropped the figure in the stream. It floated awa in the moonlicht. She said her chairm, the ane taught her by her mither lang ago.

She had felt powerful, something strang within her, a force acting thro her. She looked up at the moon an a pulse o joy shot thro her. She had touched him on the foreheed. They baith stood in the water fir a minute longer. She felt his shiverin body beside her. She was young an she wanted him inside her there an then, she wis so aroused by his nakedness. But he wis ill an had nae appetite fir sic things.

She helped him frae the water an dried him wi the cloth beside the burn. They plodded back thegither tae the cottage in the moonlicht, hoping that they widnae be seen. His teeth were chatterin as she pit him tae bed. That nicht she feared that he wid dee. A fever raged thro him. He cawed oot tae her in his dreams. She begged the Lord tae save him. She feared that the magic widnae wirk. But it did, as her mither had telt her it wid.

Sure enough, as dawn broke on that cauld winter day, he was brocht back tae her, the fever disappearing as the sun rose, his cough easing. He wis able tae sit up in bed, his muckle haunds roond the wee bowl o soup. Within a week he wis fully restored tae health an back at wirk.

He had rarely been ill since, certainly naething as serious, not till last week when the hacking cough came on. Her mither wis lang deid. But she kenned whit she must dae. An the wirds were etched in her mind. She dare nae speak them oot till they were at the burn again.

She feared that they had been seen returning tae the village the first time. But it wis a risk they had tae take.

Times were haird. The ministers had witches on their minds. But she wis nae witch. She wis just using the skills she had been taught as a girl. She believed in Jesus Christ an the Bible. She went tae the kirk every Sabbath. She prayed wi the congregation an looked up at the young handsome minister. She wis a guid woman. She wirked haird aw her life. But she didnae want tae be alane now. She loved him tae much, the auld fool.

They had been thegither sae lang. An now there wis the death o her mistress.

At least they wid be comfortable enough. Lady Lammersheugh had provided fir them. But the ithers were putting pressure on him, wanting him tae help. He wisnae fool enough to dae that, fool enough tae be hung as a traitor.

She thought o puir Janet, taken as weel, her auld friend. She had complained o pains in her chest an she had tane a remedy to her the day afore she wis found deid by the tall lawyer.

She didnae trust him, wi his dark threatenin een. She had tauld him tae say naething tae them.

CHAPTER 31

A Glass in the Bell

MACKENZIE AND SCOUGALL sat in a corner of the inn, the remains of their meal in front of them on the table. MacKenzie had spoken little since the interview with Purse.

'I do not care for Lady Girnington, sir,' said Scougall, breaking the silence.

'There are not many who do, Davie. She is arrogant and bitter. She hated Lady Lammersheugh's beauty and despised the hold she had over her brother. It is difficult to disguise such feelings. But why would she risk killing Grissell or having her killed? We must lay our personal feelings about her to one side. Now please excuse me while I go to pass water.'

Scougall sat back, reflecting on Lady Girnington's character. He hated the landed gentry when they were puffed up with self-importance. That woman had all the qualities which he did not seek in a wife. His mind drifted to Elizabeth MacKenzie. He was lost in thought for a few minutes, sipping wine from his glass. When he raised his head, he noticed the man at the next table, a dishevelled looking fellow in late middle age dressed in ill-fitting clothes. Scougall turned away as the man caught his eye. When he looked back his gaze was still on him. He lifted his glass to his lips and took another sip.

'Did I hear you talking about Lady Lammersheugh?' the stranger asked. And before Scougall could reply he went on: 'I have heard she was delated as a witch.'

'I think that is true,' replied Scougall hesitantly.

'Some scoff that there are no witches.' The man became agitated: 'You must beware the misguided utterances of Atheists and Sadducists!'

'I did not know Lady Lammersheugh – did you?'

'No, I did not. But these are dark days.' The voice became an intense whisper. 'Our King is a servant of Antichrist. A Papist King in reformed Scotland! Heresy spreads throughout the realm, Godliness is banished from our shores. Men talk of no God. They mock the world of spirits!'

'Are you a minister?' asked Scougall.

'I am not, although my brother is a man of God, an exile in Holland. He could not prostrate himself under such an Erastian church. I was once a professor at the College of Glasgow. I was expelled for my beliefs. I follow the suffering remnant of the true Presbyterian church with all my heart and soul. Now I live by my wits. My name, sir, is George Sinclair.'

Scougall was stunned. 'The author of *Satan's Invisible World*?'

'I am, sir. You have read my work?'

'I have a copy here.' Scougall rummaged in his bag and removed the book. 'I found it most enlightening, a very...' He could not think of the right word, '... enjoyable read.'

'And you are, sir?'

'David Scougall, a writer in Edinburgh.'

'And your companion?'

'John MacKenzie, Clerk of the Session.'

'I have heard of him. He is an Episcopalian.' Sinclair shook his head. 'What do you think of my book, Davie Scougall? Did my arguments convince you?'

'You did... at least I think they did...'

'As I pointed out, atheism is the reason folk disbelieve in witches and spirits. Why is there so much atheism in the world?' Sinclair threw his head back in full-throated declamation. 'There are many reasons, but two main ones. Firstly, there is a monstrous rabble of men who follow the Hobbesian and Spinozian principles, slighting religion and undervaluing the Scripture. They think that all that is contained in the universe comes under the notion of things material and consequently there is no God, no Devil, no spirit, no witch. The Englishman Hobbes is well known for his atheistical writings...'

Scougall lost the thread of the argument as it moved at pace through the works of a number of thinkers. A feeling of unease rose within him. 'There is a second reason,' continued Sinclair, 'namely the absurd principles of Cartesian philosophy. They do not assert there is no God, but rather seem to prove as much. It is self-evident that their principles are absurd and dangerous. I shall mention a few of them which are maintained publicly abroad, especially in Holland...'

Sinclair babbled on, gesticulating vehemently and not allowing Scougall the opportunity to say a word. Looking around for MacKenzie, he spotted him on the other side of the room, in conversation with the innkeeper.

'Stretch your hands to help, strengthen, encourage and comfort a poor wasted, wronged, wounded, reproached, despised and bleeding remnant, setting ourselves against all the injuries and affronts done to our blessed Lord Jesus Christ, against the man of sin, the kingdom of Antichrist, James, Duke of York, though a professed Papist and excommunicated person, now King of Scotland, England and Ireland.'

The words poured in a torrent from Sinclair's toothless mouth.

'But God will save us, sir. God will save the poor bleeding remnant that is the true Presbyterian Church of Scotland!' At that, he appeared to relax. 'Now you must excuse me, Mr Scougall. It has been a pleasure to meet a reader who has gained so much from my books. It encourages me in my work. Our day will come again, Mr Scougall. The brethren will return. Scotland will embrace the true Church. The Covenant will be restored. The malignants will be driven from this land, the rule of bishops cast asunder! Good night to you, sir.'

Scougall watched him limp towards the door. There had been something in his eyes which made him feel very differently about the book which he had hitherto held in such high regard. When reading it, he had skipped the philosophical arguments in the opening pages, seeking the tales of witches and ghosts. The author in the flesh reminded him of some of his contemporaries in Musselburgh who burned with a similar fervour for Presbytery.

When MacKenzie returned to the table, Scougall could not contain himself. 'I have just met George Sinclair!'

'Who, Davie?'

'The author of *Satan's Invisible World*.' He held up the book.

'That is an interesting coincidence,' was all that MacKenzie said.

'He talked of his works, of the danger of atheism.'

MacKenzie appeared to ignore what Scougall had just said. 'Let us take some night air so we can discuss what we have learned today.'

As they rose to leave, the door crashed open and a group of men entered in boisterous spirits. MacKenzie bowed his head to the Laird of Clachdean. 'Colonel Dewar, we meet again.'

Clachdean was dressed in an old velvet suit. A dirty

periwig descended beneath his hat and a box sword swung at his side. He towered over Scougall.

The colonel addressed his cronies: 'Lawyers from Edinburgh, gentlemen,' before turning to MacKenzie: 'What business do you have in these parts?'

'I act for the family of Lammersheugh.'

'The family of Lammersheugh,' one of the colonel's companions mockingly repeated.

'The family of Lammersheugh have much need of your services, sir,' replied Clachdean.

'A coven of witches! I hear they rut with the Devil…!' another shouted.

MacKenzie kept his eyes on Clachdean. 'I believe you are a beneficiary of Lady Lammersheugh's death?'

'What are you insinuating?'

'I have heard you are to marry Rosina Hay.'

'You are mistaken, sir. I would not touch the progeny of witches… Your meddling is not welcome, MacKenzie. I suggest you complete your business and return to Edinburgh.'

'We will be gone as soon as I have brought the legal affairs of the family to order and secured Euphame's release.'

'I fear the latter may be beyond your skills,' sneered the colonel.

MacKenzie appeared unperturbed. 'What happened to Janet Cornfoot?'

'She died of natural causes. She was long in years and in bad health. There was no indication of violence upon her.'

'But you have not spoken to me. I was with her the night she died. Someone attached the carcass of a badger to the lintel. A few days before that, a cat was garrotted and tied to the same place. Someone was seeking to scare her. '

'As sheriff-deputy, I decide to whom I speak.'

'What of the death of Lady Lammersheugh?'

'Lady Lammersheugh fell into the Lammer Burn. She could not swim.'

'Have you considered suicide? She was under suspicion of witchcraft.'

'Do not interfere in our affairs, gentlemen. The witch-hunt will burn itself out, as it always does.'

Clachdean turned his back on them and rejoined his party.

CHAPTER 32
A Last Drink

THE WOMAN STAGGERED as she left the tavern. She kenned she had drunk tae much. But she had wanted a wee celebration. They had aw been through sae much recently. She deserved a drink as much as onybody, she had siller in her pocket. She had enough tae see her thro the winter. Her bairns wid hae food on the table. She pulled the ragged shawl round her shoulders against the cold. It wid be a lang walk hame.

She left the High Street and plodded along the Lammersheugh road with her lantern.

She wisnae feart. She kenned the way like the back o her haund. She had walked it a hundred times at nicht.

After half a mile she squatted down on the verge to urinate. As she was crouching in the long grass, she heard the sound of a horse approaching from the town.

It wis perhaps a late drinker returning frae a nicht o revelry. She might hae a few wirds, perhaps share a dram, or something mair. They could lie thegither in the field ayont the dyke. She felt that she wanted a man. She carried a small bottle of rum in her basket. It wis fir her mither. A few nips wid dae nae hairm.

She pulled up her garments.

The sound of the hooves echoed closer. She sauntered on, then stopped and turned. A horseman emerged from the darkness about a hundred yards away, the silhouette of his hat visible against the sky.

If it wis a gentleman she might make some mair siller. She wisnae a bad lookin lass. She had these. Men always wanted them.

She opened her shawl and squeezed her breasts together.

The horseman slowed as he approached. He must have noticed her. Then she remembered she was carrying a lantern. How stupid she was. She raised it to see if she could identify who it was.

'Wid ye care fir a wee drink, sir?' She took the bottle from the basket, holding it up.

As she did so, an object swung through the air.

CHAPTER 33
A Conversation with Archibald Muschet

29 October 1687

EUPHAME'S FRAGILE FRAME, supported on either side by a guard, emerged from the kirk. There were gasps from the crowd as she moved forward, a miserable skeletal figure in stained sackcloth, more like a pauper than a laird's daughter.

'Puir creature...' a woman standing beside Scougall murmured; her husband shook his head: 'The House of Lammersheugh, fallen tae sic a state.'

Beside the coach waiting by the gates of the churchyard, Euphame fell into Rosina's arms, a hint of affectionate recognition on her dirt-stained face. Tears ran down the cheeks of the younger girl.

MacKenzie moved through the throng. Taking Euphame by the hand, he whispered: 'I must continue my search here. We are close to establishing your innocence.'

She looked up at him with an imploring expression.

'Be strong Euphame, be strong. You still have friends,' he managed to add before he was pushed back.

She was lifted into the coach by the guards, who took up position at either side of her. The coach took off down the main street.

'May I have a few words?' asked MacKenzie, intercepting

Muschet who was on the point of leaving.

The merchant looked aggrieved at the delay. 'I fear your attempts on Euphame's behalf are ill-considered, Mr MacKenzie. There is unassailable evidence of her witchcraft – the delation of Margaret Rammage, the pricking by Kincaid. She did not bleed. She is a witch. She will confess soon. Now, you must excuse me. I have business to attend to.'

'I am a man who prefers facts, Mr Muschet. I examined the papers at Lammersheugh House this morning. There are a series of bonds made out to you for substantial sums of money. How much are you owed?'

The thought that he might see the return of some cash lifted the merchant's mood. 'Five thousand pounds Scots, I believe.'

'A tidy sum.'

'The family were not good payers!'

'But you went on lending to them.'

'I did them service when others would not. They offered security – fertile lands.'

'Did you make any further demands upon the family?'

'I do not understand what you mean, Mr MacKenzie.'

'Did you make an offer to Lady Lammersheugh?'

'What kind of offer are you referring to?'

'An offer of marriage?'

Muschet glared. 'I did not, sir. Marriage to such a woman was not an appealing prospect!'

'Then you deny that any such offer was made?'

'I do...'

'Do you have designs on the daughters of the family?'

'Designs, on a witch! My only object is to have my money back, Mr MacKenzie, by legal means. If they cannot pay I will proceed through the courts. I will take what is due to me.' He raised his right hand in a fist. MacKenzie noticed there were blue stains on his fingers.

'I see. You have cleared up a misunderstanding. What do you think happened to Lady Lammersheugh?'

'I believe she took her life rather than confess her sins and beg forgiveness.'

'She did not slip, as Clachdean thinks?'

'I do not believe so.'

MacKenzie smiled. 'I noticed some fine hats with blue feathers in your shop priced at five pounds. How many have you sold?'

'I have sold three.'

'Who bought them?'

'A merchant does not usually reveal such information. But I will tell you. I sold them to Clachdean, Woodlawheid and Purse.'

MacKenzie turned to make sure that Scougall was noting everything down. 'Who was the woman I saw in your shop yesterday morning?' he continued.

'Which woman are you referring to?'

'The peasant whom your sister had words with.'

'Helen Rammage.'

MacKenzie's eyes burned into Muschet's. 'Is she related to Margaret Rammage?'

'She is her sister.'

'She had money to spend in your shop, Mr Muschet.'

'Indeed. That was a surprise. She lives in a hovel in Headlaw.'

'Where might she have come upon such funds?'

'I do not question customers about where they get their money. My only concern is that they are able to pay. I will not give credit to the likes of her. I have long experience of the family.' As Muschet turned to leave, he added: 'I warn you, gentlemen. The family of Lammersheugh have embraced evil since the death of the laird. There are other creditors who cry out for payment. Families rise and fall. It is the way of things. You will know that well, being a Highlander, Mr MacKenzie. Clans grow like plants, then fade to nothing. I bid you good day, gentlemen.'

MacKenzie was not quite ready to take his leave. 'Where were you on the day Lady Lammersheugh died?'

'That day the session had a meeting that lasted hours. I was in the church with Mr Cant and Mr Rankine.'

He strode off down the main street in the direction of Lammersheugh House.

CHAPTER 34
The Hovel of a Witch

THE BUILDING WAS one of four squat stone structures with thatched roofs comprising the village of Headlaw. An old man smoking a pipe directed them to an open door. A line of dirty faces looked up as they entered. Five children were sitting on the floor, eating from wooden bowls with their hands. An old woman occupied the only chair in the cramped darkness of the cottage. She stopped stirring her pot and turned with a terrified expression.

'Are you Helen Rammage?' MacKenzie asked in a friendly manner.

'No, sir. I am Margaret Rammage. Helen is my dochter.'

Scougall was shocked to hear the name. Was this the witch, brought back to life before them?

'You are the mother of Helen and Margaret Rammage?' MacKenzie's question settled him. He must learn not to leap to conclusions.

'I am, sir. God forgie me. My ain dochter brunt as a witch. God forgie us aw.'

'I am John MacKenzie, a lawyer from Edinburgh. This is Davie Scougall, my writer. We are looking after the affairs of Lammersheugh. If I may, I would like to ask you some questions.'

The old woman looked bewildered. 'Margaret burnt as a

witch. Lady Lammersheugh accused o witchcraft. Now Euphame Hay tane tae the steeple. God gie me strength. We are puir servants. I hae naethin. And now Helen's nae back frae Haddington last nicht.'

'What do you mean?'

'She did not come hame yestreen. She may be lyin in a ditch sleeping aff the drink, leavin her bairns wi me, puir relict that I am.'

MacKenzie put his hand in his pocket. He took out a few coins and gave them to her.

The old woman's face lit up. 'Thank ye, sir. Ye are maist generous.'

'Does your daughter often visit Haddington?'

'Only when she has a few bawbies. She likes a drink, like her faither. Whit else dae we hae?'

'Please tell us when she returns home, Mrs Rammage. We stay with Porteous in Lammersheugh. It is very important that we speak to her.'

The woman nodded. 'She is aye happy to talk wi a gentleman, as I am, sir. Aye happy.'

'You are a servant of Aikenshiels?'

'I was, sir. Just like Margaret and Helen.'

'Can you tell us what happened to Margaret?'

The woman indicated with a movement of her hand that the children should leave the cottage. They silently walked out in a line.

'I ken not when it began, sir. Margaret served Aikenshiels since she was a girl. She was canny wi her mistress. They were aye thick thegither in aw things. But I didnae ken they had sauld themsels tae him. He is aye tempting ye, ken. He has come tae me mony times in the nicht when the bairns are asleep, asking me tae lie wi him. He's asked me tae gae tae the wids wi him. I hae been tempted. But I aye said no. Margaret couldnae say no. She was ill-treated by her man. He left her wi child, then she had anither by a sailor. The session were aye tryin tae reform her, makin her sit in the stool in the kirk. She hated them for that.' The old woman was becoming more and more animated. 'She was a wild thing. She loved tae run wi them. Fornicating in the fields, fucking ony man she liked the smile o, leaving me wi her bastards. Excuse ma wirds, sir. She wis often oot aw nicht. I didnae ken whaur she wis. But in she wid come in the mornin. I now ken whit she wis aboot. The hail parish kens which she wis aboot. An now her bairns an mither must live wi the disgrace. I wid leave the parish if I could. But who will hae an auld relict an six bairns?'

Scougall felt disgusted by the lives of these Godless peasants.

'Do you know why Margaret might have added the names of Lady Lammersheugh and Euphame to her delation?'

'It is aye the way o witch-hunts, sir. A few are named, then a few mair come tae mind, an then mair, until aw the women in the parish are accused an a few men as weel!'

'Does Lady Girnington ever come here?'

'No, sir. Why wid she pay court tae the likes o us? I hae ne'er spake tae her and I hae served her tenant as servant fir forty years.'

'What about Clachdean?'

'The colonel has nae business here.'

'Did he ever pay court to your daughters?'

The woman eyed MacKenzie suspiciously.

'Please, Mrs Rammage. Euphame's life is in danger. She is no witch.'

'I believe the colonel wis known tae them, sir.'

'Known to them?'

'He has lain wi baith. The youngest child is his bastard.'

'Who is the mother?'

'He has a witch as mither.'

'Does he support his son?'

'He provides a few pennies. But he is aye wantin value fir whit he gies tae us.'

'What do you mean?'

'Helen is carryin his bastard tae.'

CHAPTER 35
Questions for Mr Cant

'MAY WE HAVE a few words, Mr Cant?' The minister was surprised by the appearance of MacKenzie and Scougall. His mind was full of Rosina. She had promised to visit him again.

He recovered his composure. 'Are you walking to your lodgings, gentlemen?'

'We are,' replied MacKenzie.

'Then I will accompany you. I return to the manse.' He spoke politely to Scougall: 'I do not believe we have been introduced.'

Scougall had been taught from the cradle to revere the ministry, especially those from the Covenanting tradition, and he knew that Cant inclined towards the brethren, although he had accepted the recent Indulgence. As Scougall shook his hand he recalled that he himself had aspired to the profession of minister when a boy. But he was too shy, entirely lacking the self-confidence to speak in public. He felt a rush of admiration for the young man of God, whatever MacKenzie might think of him. He liked his serious demeanour, his Godliness.

'This is Mr Scougall, my assistant.' MacKenzie intervened as Scougall stood speechless.

'It is a pleasure to meet you, Mr Scougall. The law is, I hope, a rewarding profession.'

'Thank you, sir,' was all that he was able to say.

They walked down the High Street in the fading light. An icy cold had descended and a few stars flickered above them.

'Rosina tells me that you have care of her spiritual education,' MacKenzie commented.

'I have long had her under my wing, guiding her studies, answering her questions. She has been through so much recently. I am very worried about her. A mother accused of witchcraft, and a sister...' A vision of Rosina in his study came back to him. He prayed to God to direct him away from sin.

'Is the family not dangerous company for a minister?' Scougall picked up the sneer in MacKenzie's voice and was tempted to say something about rudeness to a minister, but recalled the face of Mr Hope when they visited him in his manse the previous year, and the unpalatable fact that the clergy were not immune from sin. There must be a reason for MacKenzie's abruptness.

Cant was not used to being addressed in such a manner. The reverence paid to him was one of the most enjoyable aspects of his position. He struggled to smother his irritation. 'I seek to lead her to the path of righteousness – like my parish – like the kingdom – there is much at stake in Lammersheugh. I must ensure that Satan does not take the soul of Rosina as well. I will fight with everything I have to preserve her for God.'

'You talked scripture with Rosina, sipped wine at Lammersheugh House while her sister languished in the steeple of your kirk half a mile away. She now rots in the Edinburgh Tolbooth.' There was venom in MacKenzie's voice.

'I have visited Euphame constantly during her confinement in the steeple. I sought to gain her return to God,' Cant insisted.

'And her confession!' interrupted MacKenzie.

'We all seek her confession. She has been accused of witchcraft by delation. The pricker has revealed her guilt. Now she must stand trial.'

'I am very sorry this has happened, Mr Cant. I do not believe that Euphame is guilty of anything. She is the victim of the evil of others.'

'Let me assure you, I have only the best interests of my parish at heart. I must look after all my flock. There will always be some who turn from God. But the parish will be cleansed.'

Cant's confidence was returning. He would master Rosina. He would master himself. But the memory of touching her was painful.

'And taking the life of Euphame Hay is part of the cleansing, is it?' MacKenzie's voice resonated with scorn.

'It must be so, sir.' Cant raised his voice as if conducting a sermon. 'We follow scripture which is the word of God. Thou shalt not suffer a witch to live, Mr MacKenzie.'

'What if you are wrong? What if Euphame is innocent?' MacKenzie leaned towards him.

'I am not wrong. I have God's assurance. He has told me that I am doing good work in rooting out such evil. I am doing His work in hunting the witches that pollute our parish.'

'Then we must differ, Mr Cant.' MacKenzie shifted key again, effacing his true feelings with an urbane smile. 'Was Margaret Rammage one of your flock?'

'Her extirpation rids the parish of great evil. She confessed under no compunction. She was regularly before the session for fornication. She had three bastards to different fathers.'

'But she changed her confession. The first delation did not include the name of Euphame Hay.'

'That is correct. But the list of witches was long. Many

others have been accused. It might not be expected that she would remember all those who attended such meetings.'

'I would have thought that she would have recalled the name of a laird's daughter. Why did she add other names to the list?'

'She told us that she had remembered further details. Mr Rankine took down her confession. I was not able to attend the second interview. However, the minutes in the session book are public records.'

'Perhaps Mr Scougall might peruse their pages?'

'Of course, it can be arranged. I can provide him with access if he comes to the manse. Here are your lodgings, gentlemen.'

'I would prefer that he accompany you immediately to examine the book.'

Cant was annoyed. He had wanted to see Rosina. Now he must entertain this gauche notary public. 'If that is what you wish, Mr MacKenzie.'

'Go with the minister, Davie. Look at all the entries in the session book of the last few weeks. Do not let your eyes miss a trick.' Before Scougall could answer MacKenzie was crossing the road. 'I must have a word with young Geordie Cockburn.'

CHAPTER 36
A Walk Through the Graveyard

SCOUGALL JOINED MACKENZIE at the table and withdrew his notebook. 'I looked at all the entries over the last two months and have copied down the dates on which each session gathered. They met on the twenty-second of October with Cant, Rankine and Muschet in attendance. None of them could have been at the Devil's Pool on the day of Lady Lammersheugh's death.'

'Very good, Davie.'

'I then read the confession of Margaret Rammage.' Scougall now had MacKenzie's full attention. 'I made a close examination of the lists of names in the delation. A group of names were added in the margin at a later date, Euphame Hay's being one of these. However, her name was written in ink of a slightly different shade, suggesting it was an even later addition.'

MacKenzie nodded. 'This suggests manipulation of the session records, possibly by Rankine.' He sat back in his seat and looked out of the window of the inn, highly impressed by Scougall's eye for detail.

'There is Rosina, sir!' Scougall pointed at a woman dressed in a black cloak walking down the High Street.

MacKenzie took hold of his arm. 'Follow her, Davie!'

'But to follow a young lady at night... if I was seen...'

'Take the air! An evening stroll to clear the mind. A walk in the gloaming for religious reflection... Go now!'

The urgency of MacKenzie's words had the desired effect. Scougall was soon on the High Street. The thought of spying on Rosina was less disgraceful if she might be involved in some way. It seemed that she did not fully comprehend the enormity of the accusations against her mother and sister. Or perhaps she did not care. It was possible that she was in league with Cant, or hoped to gain from their demise. The thought was appalling. But Scougall recalled MacKenzie's advice. He must let his mind follow all paths, wherever they led. It was necessary that they should find out as much as they could about her.

Turning right, he spotted Rosina about fifty yards ahead of him on the empty street. The sun had almost set and it was very cold. Bending down, he pretended to tie a lace of his boot. He counted to ten before following.

Despite MacKenzie's injunction to adopt a relaxed air, Scougall kept to the shadows beside the houses, walking with an awkward gait at a fraction of his usual pace. He kept his eyes pinned on Rosina. As she passed the mercat cross and public weighing beam, he could hear the echo of her shoes on the cobbles.

Suddenly a figure emerged from a door on his right and collided with him. There was a muffled scream. Scougall found himself face to face with a thin middle aged woman. 'You scared the life out of me, creeping in the shadows at such an hour! See what you've made me do,' she squawked.

'I'm very sorry, madam. Let me help you.'

Scougall sank to the ground to pick up papers that had fallen from her basket. He handed a pile back to her, noticing the title of one in the half light – *The Wrestlings of a Withered Remnant*. He owned a copy of the pamphlet himself, purchased from Mr Shields for one penny.

'Wheesht, boy! Out of my way.'

She bent over and scooped up the rest of the sheets.

'I am sorry, madam,' he repeated, 'I take the air. A short walk to clear the mind.' He watched Rosina in the distance look over her shoulder.

The thin woman appraised him suspiciously. 'You would do well to keep to the inn tonight. The woods are dangerous for those who don't know them. The Devil has many traps. You must be careful.'

'I will... I do not believe we have met.'

'I am Marion Rankine, sister of Theophilus. Everyone in Lammersheugh knows who you are, Mr Scougall. I bid you good evening.' The woman bowed her head and scuttled back in the direction of the inn.

He could now barely make out Rosina and he quickened his pace. She disappeared into the gathering mirk. After about a hundred yards he came to the gates of the kirkyard. She must have entered here, Scougall thought. The kirk was in complete darkness, so he turned towards the manse, where there was light coming from a window. The minister must be at home. However, he would have to walk through the graveyard to reach it! The thought caused a burst of anxiety. Rosina must have done so, and she was just a woman. But he had never liked such places. Now he was to walk through the graves in a parish infested by witches. He might interrupt a meeting with the Devil. Fingers of fear crept through him as he became acutely aware of his surroundings; the damp smell of the grass; the sounds of the night, an owl hooting somewhere; dark tombstones encrusted with skulls, hourglasses and other symbols of mortality. Noticing the noise his feet were making on the stone path, he moved onto the grass verge.

His courage began to slip and he considered retracing his steps. But how could he tell MacKenzie that he had lost her?

He knew that he would be sorely disappointed in him. And, above all, he wanted to prove himself a worthy assistant. He might yet have acted the timid clerk, the fearful boy from Musselburgh, had he not thought of Elizabeth again. He knew that Seaforth's brother would have been brave enough to find out more. And then another terrible thought struck him. If he was found wandering among the graves, he might be accused of witchcraft himself. His mother's horrified face appeared to him: 'Ma Davie, a warlock!' It almost made him laugh.

He reached the centre of the graveyard. The kirk loomed above him on the right, the manse lay about a hundred yards away, down a slight incline on the left. It would not be beyond his capabilities to reach the window, look inside, or wait to see if Rosina emerged from the door.

At last he came to the side of the manse, an old building on two levels. He reached the window, hoping to have a quick look in, but the curtain was drawn. About five yards from the door there stood a large tombstone. He crept behind it, pulled his cloak under him, and sat on the cold ground. The light from the window eased his anxiety. A man of God would surely have power over Satan. He decided to stay for half an hour and return if nothing happened.

Scougall judged that he had been shivering there for ten minutes when he heard a noise. A light appeared on the pathway leading through the churchyard from the Haddington road. He kept his eyes fixed on the white lozenges as they grew. Three figures came into view. He feared that they might be witches.

As they came closer, he was relieved to find that he was looking at men. He did not recognise the one holding a lantern. Behind him was a huge shambling block with the unmistakeable gait of the colonel. He was followed by a limping figure. Scougall was shocked to realise it was George Sinclair.

The man holding the lantern passed in the gowns of a

preacher and knocked on the door. Scougall caught sight of Cant's worried face as they entered without exchanging greetings. His mind raced back through the words that Sinclair had spoken in Haddington. His exiled brother would return soon. He was perhaps in Lammersheugh tonight. He decided to tell MacKenzie what he had discovered. But as he rose, another light appeared on the path. He waited until Muschet and Rankine had also entered the manse.

CHAPTER 37
Clachdean Castle

30 October 1687

THE NEXT MORNING was cold and grey as MacKenzie and Scougall rode past the kirk, taking the fork to the right for a couple of miles until a small castle appeared on the top of a high bank. Beyond, the rounded hilltops were covered in low cloud.

As they approached Clachdean Castle, it became obvious that it was a rotting pile. The driveway had been neglected, the gardens left to run wild. The castle itself was in a state of decay. The colonel was known to be short of cash, but surely the lands provided enough money to maintain a home in reasonable order, thought MacKenzie.

As they stood at the door, it began to rain. Scougall was disgusted by the dilapidation of the structure. Green stains of slime covered the white harling. Windows were broken, some boarded up.

'It must have been a fine house when it was built about a hundred years ago,' began MacKenzie. 'The gardens have been laid out with care. Now they're a sorry sight. The colonel applies little of his capital to the upkeep of his house. And this is where Rosina is to be installed as wife!'

MacKenzie knocked on the blistered door. Scougall shivered, pulling his cloak tightly around him. He watched crows crossing the sky, an ill omen. A longing welled up inside him to be away from the parish of Lammersheugh and its witch-hunt. A meal in his mother's kitchen on the road back to Edinburgh would cheer him. He longed for a game of golf on the Links. And he had barely given the matter of his marriage any consideration.

The door was opened by an old servant. 'The colonel isnae at hame,' he barked.

'We wish to speak with him. We are lawyers from Edinburgh. May we wait until he returns?' asked MacKenzie.

'He has gone tae Embro.'

'What business has he there?'

'His ain.'

'Might we have a cup of ale before we return to Lammersheugh?'

'We do not entertain at Clachdean. The colonel has nae wish to welcome visitors.'

MacKenzie smiled. 'I see. Perhaps some water for our horses?'

'There's a trough roond the back o the toor,' the servant said sharply and closed the door.

MacKenzie adopted a serious manner as they returned to their horses. 'We must not let this opportunity slip, Davie. As we say in Gaelic, *Buail an t-iarann fhad's a tha e teth* – We must strike while the iron is hot. We need to have a look inside the castle. I suspect that he is the only servant, given the state of the place. We must plan a distraction. I'm relying on you.'

'Me, sir?'

'I will take care of the servant. You must get inside. Climb the stair on the left. I believe the colonel's chambers will be above.'

'How do you know that?'

'The architecture of the building suggests so.'

MacKenzie turned to face the tower. He pointed to the turnpike stair leading up the left wall and the oriel window on the first floor.

'I often try to visualise the interior of a building from without. It is an amusement, but a useful one.'

'How am I to get out, sir?'

'Trust me, Davie. I will keep him occupied as long as I can.'

It went as much against Scougall's nature to enter a house without permission as it had done to follow a young woman at night. 'What am I looking for?' he asked, without concealing his lack of relish for the task.

'I want to know in what state the colonel lives. Make a quick search for any documents or papers. Do not spend time reading them. Determine what they are. If they look important, take them!'

'That would be an infringement of the colonel's rights!'

MacKenzie took hold of his arm. 'An innocent girl rots in the Tolbooth. She may be dead soon. Our actions are justified, Davie. I assure you.'

Scougall bit his lower lip.

'Look at it this way,' continued MacKenzie. 'God is setting you a task infinitely more important than writing an instrument of sasine. It is within our grasp to save Euphame's life. Her future, if she has one, is in our hands. We must act!'

Scougall nodded reluctantly. If a girl's life was in danger, he must follow MacKenzie's instructions. But it still niggled. It was possible that they were acting on behalf of a witch.

They led the horses to the troughs on the other side of the castle, where a group of ruined outhouses formed a courtyard. MacKenzie entered an open door. It was empty. He tried the next outhouse. A pile of firewood filled a corner.

Returning to Scougall, who was standing by the horses, he

issued a rapid stream of orders: 'Stand against the castle wall, Davie. I will call the servant. When he opens the door and comes towards me, slip inside. Do not hesitate! I judge you may have about twenty minutes, if my diversion is successful. Take up position. If he asks me where you are, I will tell him you are retrieving the horses. Quick!'

Scougall walked back towards the castle, taking up position at the left side of the door so he would not be seen by anyone exiting. MacKenzie smacked the hindquarters of both horses and they sped off towards the road. He disappeared into the outhouse.

Time seemed to stand still. Scougall must have been waiting for five minutes. He counted slowly to sixty – still nothing. Another long minute passed. Then a light was visible through the small window of the outhouse. It glowed orange. As MacKenzie emerged from the door, flames shot up behind the window, bright against the grey of the afternoon. The outhouse was on fire. The crime of arson was to be added to that of housebreaking!

MacKenzie began to shout and wave his arms. 'Fire! Fire!'

Scougall pushed himself against the damp wall. The flames had kindled his resolve. MacKenzie would not have resorted to such desperate tactics if it was not absolutely necessary. He must conquer his fear.

The door burst open.

'My pipe fell on some kindling! Where are the buckets?'

The old servant swore violently as he ran towards the outhouse. Scougall slipped inside.

CHAPTER 38
The Edinburgh Tolbooth

ROSEHAUGH WAS FEELING weary. He was finding it difficult to sleep, haunted by a recurring dream. William Carstares, a minister who had been tortured by the Privy Council a few years before, was about to inflict pain on him. He did not know the manner, whether by thumbscrew or boot, or some other device, for he always awoke just before the pain was to begin. But he had seen the fear on the faces of the tortured, the loss of dignity, of control. How the shit spilled on the floor.

He wondered if it was reasonable to inflict agony on one's fellow creature for the security of the kingdom. He had thought it was justified when Scotland was threatened by religious extremists in open rebellion. Now he was not so sure. But a nest of vipers laid in wait. They had failed two years before. He recalled Argyll's head dropping like a lump of meat from the Maiden. So much blood spilled in this country; the Campbell's father executed in the same manner in 1661. The words of Macbeth came to him: 'in blood stepp'd in so far that, should I wade no more, returning were as tedious as go o'er.'

He passed through the small door on the High Street and entered the Tolbooth, an ancient stone conglomeration on the north side of St Giles' Kirk. He stopped in the corridor, putting his hands on his stomach. There was the pain again. He stood for a moment waiting for it to ease, as it usually did. He did not have long left. He must do some good before it was too late. Make some amends for what he had inflicted on others.

He recalled visiting witches in the Tolbooth in the early 1660s. He had written that they were much less common than many supposed, knowing in his heart that there were none. But folk clung to the old views, even his colleagues in the law. He hoped he would never again have to witness anything like the executions of 1661. He was then a young man working on his romance, *Aretina*, alive with the possibilities of the future; and ambitious, so ambitious. He had craved recognition – as an advocate, as a writer, as a politician. The words had flowed from his lips in court like a Highland stream. Men had listened.

Perhaps he could do some good for this young woman.

As he entered the low-ceilinged room, four guards rose to their feet. He was no longer Lord Advocate but he still commanded respect. There was the possibility that he might return to office. 'I am here to see a client – Euphame Hay.'

'Follow me, sir.' Taking a large key from his belt, the guard opened a door at the far end of the room. Rosehaugh followed him down a dank corridor into a cavernous chamber. A hellish scene opened up before him, one which he knew only too well. The room was full of despairing cries, a grim sarcophagus of suffering replete with the reek of human excrement.

They walked through the squalor and entered another corridor. The gaoler opened one of the low wooden doors. Rosehaugh looked at the crumpled figure in the cell.

'She has not confessed yet. She is woken every twenty minutes,' said the guard perfunctorily.

Rosehaugh stood on the festering floor looking down on

Euphame. He did not know her family but he trusted his kinsman MacKenzie, who rarely asked for favours. Her head was slumped forward. He gently lifted it back to reveal her emaciated face. 'No... no,' she groaned.

She must be strong to have lasted so long without confessing. Her trial was set for two weeks' time. They would expect a confession by then. If she survived, she had a good chance of acquittal. He would attack the evidence like a hawk. He had written to Tweeddale in London and to Lady Girnington. The Hay kin would hopefully come to her aid. She was the daughter of a laird, if a minor scion of the name, unlike the peasants who usually burned. The thought brought him some cheer. However, he did not think it likely that she would live to see her trial. She was a bag of bones. She could be dead by tomorrow. Her head slumped forward again. She murmured something from between parched lips, a word he did not recognise. He whispered into her ear: 'I am George MacKenzie of Rosehaugh, kinsman of John MacKenzie. I am your advocate.'

After the door was locked he handed the guard a silver rix dollar. 'Let her sleep tonight, Mr Moscrop. Let her sleep tonight.'

CHAPTER 39

The Cellars of Clachdean

SCOUGALL'S HEART WAS pounding and he was sweating. He raised his hand to cover his nose. There was a stale meaty odour. His eyes took time to adjust to the gloom as no candles were lit. The interior of the castle was as grim as the outside.

Following MacKenzie's directions, he climbed the spiral staircase to the first floor and entered the room at the front. He looked for the oriel window. MacKenzie was right. It was a wood-panelled chamber which must have been impressive in its day. He noticed vermin droppings by his foot; rat rather than mouse. He walked to the window and looked down, catching sight of MacKenzie and the servant carrying buckets into the outhouse. The dingy interior was cold and dark, old curtains and decaying furniture, a few dirty paintings on the walls. He made a quick search but found nothing of interest. There was a door into an adjoining room at the far side.

The smaller chamber possessed an animal reek and there were signs of habitation. Scougall gauged that the bed had been slept in recently. The stinking sheets were swept back. There was the imprint of a head on the filthy pillow. In a corner was a wardrobe. He carefully opened the door. It was empty. His eyes darted round the room, trying to take in as much detail as possible. There seemed to be nothing else.

Dropping down on his knees, he looked under the bed. A sheet of paper lay crumpled on the floor. He stretched his arm across the dirt to pull it out. It was a pamphlet: *The Wrestlings of a Withered Remnant*. He stuffed it into his pocket and made a hasty search of the rest of the room, but found nothing.

He looked in the other chambers on the first floor. There was little in each except for ancient hangings and the odd piece of furniture. He went back to the stairs and climbed to the second floor. Again the four rooms were deserted. It was as if the castle was no longer inhabited, as if it had been cleared. The colonel must spend most of his time elsewhere.

Scougall descended the stairs. MacKenzie would be disappointed. There was no sign of a charter chest.

On the ground floor he took his bearings. He guessed that the only rooms he had not examined were towards the front of the castle. Opening the door on his left, he was surprised to see steps disappearing into the darkness. They must lead to the cellars. He was about to close it when he thought of MacKenzie. He rummaged in his pockets, found the stub of a candle and his tinder box. After a couple of attempts, the wick took flame.

At the bottom of twenty worn steps a vaulted room of arched alcoves opened to view as he raised the candle. It was the castle's wine cellar. But the alcoves were cleared of all bottles of burgundy and claret.

Something moved on the floor. There was a scurrying into the darkness, other movements. The rats would not often be disturbed down here.

After about thirty yards he came to a wall. He placed his hand on the cold stone. There was something different about the alcove on the right. He noticed objects covered by sheets. He pulled one back to reveal a large barrel. There was the smell of gunpowder. Long implements were sticking from another. He moved the candle down and counted the muzzles of twelve muskets. One by one, he dragged off all the sheets. There were ten barrels, enough powder to blow the castle to the four winds, and above two hundred weapons, sufficient for a small army. He wondered why the colonel needed so much firepower. He had been a soldier once. Was he now a trader in arms?

Scougall suddenly realised that the weapons must be for those who opposed the King. Men who wanted to overturn the rule of the Papist tyrant. Another rebellion was being planned. He withdrew the crumpled pamphlet from his pocket. Presbyterianism was to be restored by force. The rebels had failed two years before. This time they might succeed.

He remembered his excitement on hearing the news of the risings in 1685. He had followed the history of Argyll's ill-fated attempt closely. The Cameronians would not join one who was not a Covenanter. Argyll was captured in Renfrewshire and executed, the glorious Monmouth meeting a similar end.

Scougall had sympathised with the aims of the rebels. They wanted to re-establish Presbytery, restore Godly rule to the kingdom and end the despotic reign of James Stuart. To remove a king who was the servant of Antichrist was surely just. But these weapons unsettled him. They would cause death and destruction. He recalled the words of George Sinclair: 'Do not give up hope, Mr Scougall. The time comes.' The meeting at the manse was surely concerned with some kind of plot. 'We will not fail.' Sinclair's brother had returned from exile. Hundreds of others were waiting in Amsterdam and Groningen until the time was ripe. With the help of William of Orange, they might succeed.

It dawned on him that he had discovered something of great importance, something much bigger than the affair of

Euphame and Lady Lammersheugh. The thought was daunting, exciting. He would enjoy telling MacKenzie. He knew he had no time for such zealots. The MacKenzies were a clan that opposed the Campbells. MacKenzie despised those who advocated violent insurrection. He was an Episcopalian who thought ill of Presbytery. For an instant Scougall wondered if he should tell him. There was a chance that the plotters might succeed if he did not. The reign of Antichrist would end. But his desire to please MacKenzie was stronger. This was about a girl's life, not politics.

He replaced the sheets and retraced his steps, judging that about fifteen minutes had passed since he entered the castle. He climbed the stairs with care. At the top he blew out the candle, slowly opened the door, and advanced into the half-light of the hallway.

At the back door he noticed a pair of riding boots. Kneeling down, he took a piece of string from his pocket and measured the length of a boot as MacKenzie had shown him. He was delighted by this other discovery.

Scougall did not see the figure in the shadows at the end of the corridor.

He came out of the back door just as MacKenzie and the servant disappeared into the outhouse. The flames were no longer visible. As he moved gingerly round to the front to find the horses, he remembered that he had not searched all the rooms on the ground floor. But it was too late to go back in.

CHAPTER 40
A Conversation with Theophilus Rankine

A THIN WOMAN with piercing blue eyes answered the door. Scougall recalled with embarrassment that he had bumped into her the night before. She bore the same disgruntled look on her face. MacKenzie conquered his feelings of repugnance. 'I wish to speak with Mr Rankine please. Is he at home?'

The sides of her mouth dropped even further. 'Who is calling upon him, sir?'

'We are lawyers from Edinburgh. I seek your husband's...'

'He is my brother,' she interrupted. Noticing her reptilian neck, Scougall reflected that disgust seemed to be her natural disposition.

'I seek your brother's opinion on a legal matter of some consequence.'

'I will ask him if he will see you.' She closed the door. After a short while she returned, the scowl still on her face. 'This way,' was all she said.

They followed her down a hallway to a chamber at the back of the house containing a few pieces of dark furniture. Rankine stood in the middle of the room rubbing his hands. He was a thin creature like his sister. Scougall felt sure they were earnest Presbyterians. He shared some of their views, particularly on church government, but the puritanical zealotry which derived satisfaction from such bare surroundings had no appeal for him. He thought of the warmth of his mother's house. He was a Presbyterian who liked home comforts.

'Welcome, gentlemen. Perhaps we might share a few words of the Lord before talking.' Rankine nodded towards a large Bible resting on the table. 'I am reading from Genesis Chapter 19.' He closed his eyes and recited: 'The sun was risen upon the earth when Lot entered into Zoar. Then the Lord rained upon Sodom and upon Gomorrah brimstone and fire from the Lord out of heaven. And he overthrew those cities, and all the plain, and all the inhabitants of the cities, and that which grew upon the ground.' He looked up for a moment to meet MacKenzie's eyes.

'But his wife looked back from behind him, and she became a pillar of salt.' Scougall completed the verse.

'Ah! I see you know your Bible, Mr Scougall.' There was a sarcastic note in the session clerk's voice.

'We have no time for theology, Mr Rankine,' said MacKenzie.

'Of course, I forgot that you are an Episcopalian. You care little for the Word of God.'

'I do not care to discuss theology when Euphame Hay's life is in danger.'

'Thou shalt not suffer a witch to live!' said Marion Rankine from a rocking chair at the window on which she had settled. 'God's words are as clear as fresh water. The young whore is a witch. Her mother was a witch!'

MacKenzie had to control an impulse to slap the woman across the face. He wondered how humanity could spawn such bitter creatures. But he smiled, kept his voice even, and turned to her brother.

'I have some questions on a matter of law. I believe you are a creditor of Lammersheugh.'

'Only for a small amount, sir. I have no grievance with the

house. The laird always paid interest. Lady Lammersheugh did the same.'

'What about the Laird of Clachdean?'

'What about him?'

'Were there financial obligations between him and Lammersheugh?'

'I believe not. But he owes considerable sums to Lady Girnington.'

'Is the colonel an honourable man?'

Before Rankine could answer his sister cut in shrilly: 'He is a debauched sinner. The vilest of hypocrites! He whores wherever he rides – in Lammersheugh, Haddington or Edinburgh. His bastards are the spawn of witches! He has brought eternal damnation upon himself.'

Rankine gave her a look. 'The laird is a soldier. He has lived the life of a soldier. He finds it difficult to follow a settled life in the parish.'

MacKenzie turned to Marion Rankine. 'I have heard that he is an honourable man, Miss Rankine. A fine soldier…'

'He is an oaf! He abused me in the street, pulling me into a vennel. I had to fight off his drunken advances!'

'He mistook you for another,' snapped Rankine.

'He is a vile fornicator who should be dragged before the session. I do not understand why he has not been.' She looked accusingly at her brother. 'I believe the minister is as afraid of him as the rest of you.'

'What do you make of Woodlawheid?' Again MacKenzie addressed the question to the sister.

'He is a malignant! A vile Erastian – a companion of witches!'

'What do you mean?' probed MacKenzie, guessing her proclivity for hysterical denunciation might work to his advantage.

'He was always in Lady Lammersheugh's company after

Lammersheugh's death. They were seen often in the hills together. Meanwhile his wife rotted in darkness, afflicted by melancholy. He was polluted by lust.'

'What is wrong with his wife?'

'A malady of the mind, I believe. I have not seen her for years.'

'And what is your opinion of Lady Girnington?'

This time she looked at her brother before answering. Her bile seemed to have abated. She did not say anything.

'Her ladyship is a devout woman. Now, I have work to do gentlemen,' replied Rankine.

There was a knock on the front door. Rankine's sister rose and left the room. When she returned there was an excited look on her face. 'A body has been found in the midden,' she announced.

CHAPTER 41

Clem Bell's Midden

THE REEK HIT them as they approached. A crowd stood around the steaming mound as a man raked through the detritus of Lammersheugh.

'Where is it, Mr Lorimer?' Rankine held a hand over his mouth. The man stopped raking and pointed to a bundle lying on the ground. MacKenzie knelt down and pulled back the blue blanket.

A woman's decapitated head and a long piece of bloody flesh lay side by side. Scougall thought that he was going to vomit. The other object was an arm. Something small rested in the palm of the upturned hand. MacKenzie kneeled down to have a closer look. 'It is a tiny child, Davie!'

Scougall observed the perfect little body. The foetus was about the size of an apple. 'Dear God!' he gasped.

MacKenzie shook his head. 'Who is she?'

'It is the head of Helen Rammage,' said Rankine. 'The sister of the witch. The child has been ripped from her by the Devil!'

There were gasps from the onlookers.

'Who discovered her?' MacKenzie directed his question to the innkeeper, Porteous, who was standing beside them.

'An Egyptian girl found the head this morning on the top of the midden. The child was beside it. Mr Lorimer is searching for the rest of her.'

'It is the Devil's work,' said an onlooker.

'Satan walks in Lammersheugh. We have sinned gravely,' said another fearful voice.

'She must have disobeyed her master.'

MacKenzie examined the head. He judged it belonged to a woman in her twenties. He tilted it sideways to look at the cleaved neck, then spoke to Rankine. 'The sheriff-deputy must be informed. She has been beheaded and quartered.'

'I've heard it said that she was a witch,' said a woman.

'A whore,' barked another. 'Three bastards tae different men.'

'What are we to do, Mr Rankine?'

The session clerk replied calmly. 'I will inform the minister. We must intensify our search. The parish must be cleansed.'

CHAPTER 42

The Sleep of Euphame Hay

SHE WAS NOT sure if she was asleep or awake. She was aware of someone beside her, a man. She could tell from his voice – a refined one. It was not that of the pricker or the others. She did not know who it was. She watched a thin face encased in a long wig. Was he a lawyer or judge? He was talking to her quietly, but she could not understand what he was saying. A thought suddenly filled her with terror. Was this her executioner, the hangman who was to strangle her before she was burned to dust? But he did not speak with the voice of such a man. He was surely wealthy, perhaps a rich kinsman come to rescue her.

The presence faded. A young girl was at her side, dabbing her forehead with a wet cloth and stroking her hair. She felt momentary relief from the soft cool fabric. There was still tenderness in the world. But the girl was soon gone. The men were back. They woke her with violent prods, telling her to confess.

She was in the woods holding the hand of a young man. He was looking down at the ground. She could not see his face. She knew he was the one she was to marry. She would enter his family, establish a house and have his children.

She was in bed waiting, a deep longing within her for him. It was her wedding night. He sat with his back to her. She admired his white shirt across broad shoulders. He threw his wig on the floor and pulled off his long boots. She called on him with sweet words, saying that he was her love and that she wanted to give herself to him.

But when he turned his head, she fell. She fell into the pit. She fell into the pit of despair. It was not the face of her love. It was the countenance of Kincaid. He had stripped her and admired her nakedness, the lecher who had used a pin on every part of her body. He was her husband.

CHAPTER 43
A Picture of Grissell Hay

THE PORTRAIT SAT on the small table against a pile of books. In front of it lay the shrivelled bladder found in the mouth of Janet Cornfoot. From their chairs, MacKenzie and Scougall stared at both items. MacKenzie was thinking of a portrait of his wife Elizabeth in his lodgings in Edinburgh. He saw her sitting for the picture at The Hawthorns. Although it was a fine piece of work, it did not capture the essence of her. Art could never do that. In his mind's eye he saw himself standing behind the painter, watching him work, admiring his wife's beauty. How lucky he had been. By the time the portrait was finished she was pregnant with their daughter. She had wanted it hung in Libberton's Wynd so that he might see her as he worked. A few months later she was dead. He had killed her. The thought opened up like a chasm within him.

'Do you think there is something important about it, sir?' Scougall's question dragged him back to the matter at hand.

'I am not sure, Davie. It seems like any other picture of a laird's wife in her prime. She is dressed in a fine gown, she wears a pearl necklace. On the table beside her is a book which we cannot identify.' He stood up and turned to Scougall. 'But it has been given to us for a reason – everything has been planned by Grissell.'

Scougall turned his attention back to the picture. He was

scared to look into the eyes for too long. He had heard so much about this woman. He wondered what she had been like in the flesh. It was quite possible she was a witch, but he kept this thought to himself.

'I have sent word to Edinburgh about your discovery this afternoon. Dragoons should be in the parish tomorrow.'

'What if your message does not get through to Edinburgh?'

'We must hope that it does. If it does not, I will have to send you.'

Scougall hoped that they were not in danger. 'Do you believe that a rebellion is planned soon, sir?'

'It is possible, Davie.' MacKenzie began to pace around the room, looking as grim as Scougall had ever seen him. At last he continued: 'Helen Rammage has paid the ultimate price, as has her unborn child, the colonel's bastard, if we are to believe her mother. The size of the boot at Clachdean Castle suggests that the colonel may have been at the Devil's Pool on the day of Grissell's death. It is also possible that Cockburn was there. Rankine, Muschet and Cant were in Lammersheugh attending the session. Purse was in Haddington. Lady Girnington could not get to the pool herself. We also have the pistol.'

'What about the bladder?' added Scougall.

'What does it tell us?' MacKenzie picked it up and tossed it to Scougall who caught it with a shudder. He could not think how they might link it to anyone.

'Why was Helen Rammage killed?' he asked, placing it beside the portrait.

'I believe she was paid to be quiet, Davie.'

'Margaret Rammage was paid to alter her delation.'

'Yes. It would provide something for her children. She was perhaps resigned to her fate.'

'It is also possible that Rosina is involved. She is close to

Cant. Or is some other man, like Kincaid?' Scougall looked puzzled.

'Let us sleep on it, Davie. Tomorrow we must meet the elusive George Cockburn.'

CHAPTER 44

An Uncomfortable Night

SCOUGALL RETIRED FOR the night disturbed by what had been found in the midden. The vision of Helen Rammage's head was foremost in his mind; the soul of the child another cause of concern. He was full of doubt. He had believed that Lady Lammersheugh was a witch. However, he conceded that it was possible she was an innocent woman, the victim of the evil of others. His meetings with Lady Girnington and the colonel had not predisposed him to think kindly of them. She was rude and arrogant, he a devotee of debauchery. It was possible that they had conspired to entrap Grissell. But why might they have killed her? To gain the lands of Lammersheugh by escheat? Or was the spurned Muschet involved? He certainly had aspirations above his station in asking Lady Lammersheugh to marry him. Or were Rankine and his sister the murderers, motivated by a burning hatred to rid the parish of sin?

He opened the window which looked down on the main street of Lammersheugh. Everything was calm; stars sparkled in a cloudless sky. The same cold apprehension remained. He felt the presence of the Devil. Satan might be meeting with his disciples somewhere in the parish at that very moment.

Fearing he would not be able to sleep, he sought his notebook, flicking through the pages, reminding himself of words and phrases he had recorded over the last few days. He found the notes from Lady Lammersheugh's will: *I leave to my sister-in-law Lillias Hay, Lady Girnington, the Dutch clock that sits on my mantelpiece in my chamber.* His eyes moved through the shorthand symbols. *To my husband's legal agent in Edinburgh, Mr John MacKenzie, advocate, Clerk of the Court of Session, I leave the small picture which hangs in the library at Lammersheugh and to his daughter Elizabeth MacKenzie an exquisite emerald to be found in the box in my chamber at Lammersheugh House.* Elizabeth's appearance in this affair troubled him. There must be something of significance in the words. He yawned. Perhaps he would sleep after all!

Scougall put on his white nightgown. As he climbed into bed, he caught sight of Sinclair's book on the table. It was asking to be read. He remembered the words of warning from the author.

Rather than looking at the book he pulled the blanket over him. There was a strange unclean odour coming from it. He pushed it away. The book caught his eye again, sitting in the candle-light. But he feared that if he read one of the tales he would not sleep.

Lying down, he tried to find a comfortable position. He closed his eyes and attempted to think about something other than the events in Lammersheugh, letting his mind drift to the golf course at Musselburgh where he had played as a boy. He imagined that he was a bird following the path of the ball from above. He swooped round the first six holes. But still he could not find sleep. He could not get his head round why God might allow the game of golf, but also sanction the existence of witches.

An image of Lady Lammersheugh, face-down in the dark water, kept interrupting his view of the course. He opened his eyes. He was in darkness. The candle had burned out. He moved slightly and was aware of something in the mattress. He lowered his hand to a lump under his buttocks. He was sure that it had not been there the previous night. Pushing down, he felt something hard within the straw. No wonder he could not sleep. The mattress was full of stones! He pushed harder. It was gone. He lent down with more weight. There it was again. There was definitely something in the mattress!

Pulling himself up, he kneeled down, feeling round the shape. He was quickly out of the bed. He must find out what it was. He lit another candle before heaving back the blanket and sheet. He threw the pillow on the floor, pulled up the mattress and pushed it against the wall.

Having located its position he sought his knife. The blade cut through the fabric easily. Something rolled out and landed on the floor before him.

At first he was not sure what it was. He took the candle from the table, holding it above the little object. He looked down on a wax painting, a doll in the shape of a man, perhaps six inches in height, produced crudely in wax. The shock was like a hammer blow to the chest. He felt it pounding against him again and again.

He moved his hand forward. He turned it over. He experienced pure terror. Despite the crude style it was evident that it represented him. Pins were sticking from each side. He dropped it in his panic.

He was out in the corridor in an instant, banging on MacKenzie's door; nausea sweeping through him. There was an agonising delay. Finally he heard sounds of movement within. The door opened. A small pistol poked out.

'It is me, sir. Davie Scougall!'

'What is wrong, Davie?' MacKenzie, also dressed in a nightshirt, followed him back to his room.

'Look, sir!' Scougall stood back, shaking in terror.

MacKenzie raised the candle and peered down on the wax

figurine. Although simply carved, it did bear a striking resemblance to Scougall. The sculptor had even added dark colouring to the cheeks to draw attention to his vigorous facial hair.

'It is me, sir!'

'Calm yourself, Davie. It is a piece of wax sculpted by human hands, placed here to scare you. You must think rationally. It is a warning. We are interfering in the affairs of the parish. You have made an important discovery today. This is not witchcraft, but the agency of man.'

Scougall was unconvinced. Petrified, he closed his eyes and prayed for God's protection.

CHAPTER 45
A Sister's Love

SHE IS IN the woods in the bright light of summer, standing outside Janet's cottage. The garden is alive with insects, bees buzzing from flower to flower. The butterflies are huge, the largest she has ever seen, their colours vibrant. Janet's dog is lying in the sun by the door.

Her mother emerges from the cottage, smiling. She is wearing a luscious green gown. She walks through the garden towards her. As she approaches, her dress merges with the surrounding green of the garden. She disappears.

He is beside her, the man she is to marry. He is tall and handsome, but his eyes are closed. He opens them. In the dark shining eyeballs is a reflection. She does not know if it is Satan or the pricker.

She cannot understand how she is looking through the library window, two storeys up. She realises that she is hovering like an insect twenty feet above the flower beds. She is elated by the feeling of lightness. She looks inside the room. Cant and her sister sit at a table looking down at a large black book. Cant points to a passage with his finger and looks at Rosina. She stands up. She stares out of the window. She does not see her.

Rosina lets her gown fall to the ground. She wears no undergarments. She stands naked in the room, the minister watching her. From outside she screams at her sister to put her gown back on, to leave his company. She does not hear her. Cant approaches, his eyes enraptured. He removes something from a bag. It looks like a small wand. She realises it is a pin, about two inches long. Rosina is expressionless, staring out of the window. The minister is beside her. He raises the pin, placing it on the surface of her breast. She screams at Rosina to run. She does not hear. As he inserts the pin into the soft flesh, he turns. It is not the face of the minister. It is Him. It is the countenance of Satan, black, handsome, all-consuming.

She was awake again, the dream or vision fresh in her mind. She remembered where she was. The desperate cries of the prisoners, the endless stream of obscenities were audible again. She wondered if they had stopped waking her. She was sure that she had slept. Perhaps they had given up. Then the image of Cant came back to her, his black gowns, the Bible, the pin – the Devil. Cant was the Devil. She must warn Rosina, somehow.

CHAPTER 46
Letters from Edinburgh

31 October 1687

SCOUGALL SAT BESIDE MacKenzie in the dining chamber of the inn, pale and drawn after a sleepless night. A dark shadow covered his cheeks and neck. He had not shaved. His mind was fixated on the wax figure.

'Take your porridge!' MacKenzie urged.

This affair was becoming darker by the hour, their antagonists, whoever they were, more brutal. He wondered if they intended to scare them off. Or was something more sinister planned?

The innkeeper approached the table. 'Two letters for you, Mr MacKenzie. One for you, sir.' Scougall was distracted as he received few letters, only an occasional one from his parents or sisters. He took his without saying a word.

MacKenzie recognised the handwriting on one and opened it. 'Ah, it is from Rosehaugh...' He read it quickly. 'The news is not good, Davie. Euphame weakens. He fears that she will not survive long.' He passed the letter to Scougall.

Edinburgh, 30 October 1687

My dearest cousin,
I have received yours of the 26th October. I will of

course act for the accused. It is fortunate that you find me in the north with a couple of months to spare and little to do. My experience should prove of value.

I have visited the poor girl in the Tolbooth. She is a very lamentable sight, having been denied sleep for a number of nights. Much pressure is applied to her to make a confession. She has stood firm as yet.

I hope her kin will intervene soon on her behalf. My greatest fear is that she will not live to see her trial which is set for 15th November. She is as thin as a skeleton and has the look of death upon her. Please send anything you consider pertinent to me at the above address. I will add my own weight to the voices which have been raised on her behalf. You know that I am sceptical about the crime of witchcraft. It goes without saying that I will need as much evidence as you can provide to help her cause. I enclose a copy of the instrument of sasine which you requested.

I remain your most humble servant,
Sir George MacKenzie of Rosehaugh

PS Our common acquaintance Archibald Stirling wishes you well. He asks me to remind you of the great Montrose. When the occasion allows, after your business is complete in Lammersheugh, please send him your thoughts.

MacKenzie looked deeply perturbed. 'We must do something or Euphame will die soon.' He raised his voice, taking hold of Scougall's cuff: 'This is no time for dark reflections. Euphame needs your help. You are no good to her in this condition. *Am fear a thug air fhèin, thug e buaidh air nàmhaid,* as we say in Gaelic. He that conquers himself conquers an enemy, or as the Bible tells us, "He that ruleth his spirit is better than he that taketh a city." Apply a razor to your face. Meet me here in twenty minutes! Make a prayer to your God!'

Scougall was shocked by the outburst, but he departed with the letter.

MacKenzie unfolded the copy of the instrument and read it carefully. It described the purchase of the Clachdean estate by Colonel Robert Dewar in 1681. In addition, a series of bonds were itemised by which the transaction was funded. The colonel had borrowed significantly from Lady Girnington to purchase the lands. MacKenzie examined the witness list:

Dated at Girnington 4 August 1681 before the following witnesses – Lillias Hay, Lady Girnington, Alexander Hay, Laird of Lammersheugh, Colonel Robert Dewar, Gideon Purse, writer in Haddington.

Rosehaugh had scrolled a short note in the margin of the copied document. The original was witnessed by Colonel Robert Hay, but 'Hay' had been scored out and replaced with 'Dewar'. MacKenzie experienced a revelation. He was making progress, at last.

He opened the other letter, written in a hand which he did not recognise. There was no date or signature on the short note:

I have important news. Meet me at Rooklaw Tower tonight at midnight.

MacKenzie looked round the inn, overcome by a feeling that he was being watched. There was no one in the room. Outside on the street, a couple of women were deep in conversation. He wondered what motivation lay behind the note. Was it advice from a friend or an enticement by an enemy? The awful gravity of the situation bore down on him. Inactivity might cost Euphame her life. He imagined his own daughter chained in a cold cell in the Tolbooth. What vileness could condemn men and women to such humiliation? Zealots, using the cloak of Christianity. He hoped, almost prayed, that the light of reason would one day shine on Scotland.

And there it was, the familiar feeling of dread, washing through him from the black ocean of his soul; a knot deep inside. He knew that he could not afford to fall into melancholy at such a time. It was enough that Scougall was showing signs of the condition, brought on by the discovery in the mattress. The tide receded.

They must act. He would have to risk their lives.

His thoughts were interrupted by the appearance of Cockburn with a worried expression on his face.

'I have just heard the news that there has been another arrest.'

MacKenzie groaned, shaking his head: 'Rosina?'

'No. John Murdoch is accused of being a warlock. He is taken to the steeple.'

CHAPTER 47

The Prayers of Theophilus Rankine

RANKINE AND HIS sister were on their knees. With eyes shut, he clasped a Bible to his stomach, speaking in a voice just above a whisper, so that a person at the other side of the room would have had difficulty hearing what he said. His legs were stiff. He had been in the same position for half an hour, experiencing the intoxification of communion with his maker.

'Lead us through this valley of sin. Lord, give us strength to turn away from sin.' His eyes remained closed. A vision of his sister came to him as it often did during prayer. Was God testing him, or was it the Devil? It was forty years before in the Blinkbonny Woods. The image was as fresh as if it had happened yesterday. The green dazzle of spring sunlight through the birch leaves, the touch of her skin, the awful taste of lust. But he had turned away from sin. He had turned away from Satan. This knowledge gave him a tremendous rush of joy. He had been a miserable sinner, beaten down by the grossest of sins. But he had been forgiven. He was chosen. God had told him he was one of his Elect, his immortal soul saved from the beginning of time. And his dear sister, the receptacle of his sin, the conduit of Satan, she too was promised eternal glory. 'Thank you, Christ Jesus. Thank you Lord.' He opened his eyes. Angels descended through the roof into the room in which they were kneeling. He saw himself and Marion carried aloft by gentle arms, away from this vale of tears, away from this world beholden to filthy lust, away from warlocks and witches.

He heard his sister whisper beside him. 'Thank you Lord. In a parish which is stained with sin I will be thy rod to smite those who follow Satan. They have made compact with Him. They have sold their souls. They follow lust in all its forms – dancing, fornicating, singing. Through this they worship him.'

Rankine's mind was enlarged with a vision of a glorious conflagration. In the centre was a coiling mass of fornicating bodies swirling against the black face of Satan. For a moment he gazed in pleasure, experiencing arousal, but recognising it was the Devil's snare, he continued to pray in a low voice.

'I will serve you Lord. I will seek out witches. I will seek them out and destroy them. Margaret Rammage sinned against you. She is burned to dust. Helen Rammage was a filthy fornicator. She is destroyed. Grissell Hay sinned against you. She is food for the worms. Euphame Hay is a witch. She will be burned for thy glory. Rosina Hay is a whore of Satan. She will burn also. We will cleanse the parish. We will make it as a shining light unto you. Nothing will stop us, O Lord. The time comes when we will rise up against him. The reign of Antichrist is over!'

CHAPTER 48
A Letter for Davie Scougall

FORTUNATELY MACKENZIE HAD removed the figure during the night, but Scougall examined the small room inch by inch, even dropping to the floor and checking under the bed.

Only once he had satisfied himself that no intruder had entered did he sit down to look at the letter. The address was written in an unfamiliar hand.

To David Scougall notary public, at the house of
Mr Porteous, Lammersheugh, Haddingtonshire.

He broke the small seal and unfolded the paper. The hand inside was familiar. The letter was from Elizabeth MacKenzie!

30 October 1687
Libberton's Wynd
Edinburgh

Dear Mr Scougall,
    You must excuse the subterfuge, but I could not risk my father recognising my hand and opening this. I asked my friend Helen Oliphant to write the address.
    I know that I can write to you in confidence as a special friend.

Scougall read the sentence again. The words 'special friend' rekindled feelings which he had suppressed. They resurfaced, dulling his fear. The thought of Elizabeth's pretty face calmed him. His tremors began to subside. What would she think if she could see him in such a state? He continued to read:

We have heard the terrible news of the accusations against Lady Lammersheugh and Euphame Hay. I am worried sick as my father has not written anything to me except a brief note after his arrival. I know he is busy but I am very concerned. I beg you to write to me with haste to set my mind at rest. I beseech you, do not tell him that I have written to you. I fear that great evil is unleashed. There are rumours in Edinburgh that the Whigs plan another rising.

I have another piece of news, Mr Scougall. Euphame's trial is set for 15th November. I took the liberty of visiting her in the Tolbooth. I cannot describe what terrible conditions she suffers under. She is crushed by the accusations and the denial of sleep, surely the vilest of tortures. She can barely speak. Her gaolers believe she will not live to see her trial. Something must be done with great haste or I fear she will die.

You are both in great danger, so tread with the utmost care. I know that my father will look out for you. Please have care for him.

Your affectionate friend
Elizabeth MacKenzie

Scougall placed the letter in his leather bag. His hands had stopped shaking. How could he settle for a Musselburgh wife? But she was to be married to another. Whatever happened, he must live up to her expectations. He could not lie here like a coward.

He got down on his knees and, closing his eyes, began to pray. A vision of Christ came to him with his gentle words on the Mount. He felt his fear dissipate further. God had surely intervened through Elizabeth. He knew that he had the strength to proceed. He would do as she asked. He would do anything for her.

CHAPTER 49
An Interview with George Cockburn

'THIRD TIME LUCKY, Davie!' They had taken up position outside the school house, when a group of boys emerged in a gaggle of laughter. 'Are you Adam Cockburn's son?' MacKenzie addressed the tallest of them.

'No, sir. There's Geordie.' He pointed to a dark-haired boy behind him.

'I am Geordie Cockburn.' The boy had large brown eyes like his father.

'It is good we have found you at last, Geordie. You have not been to school for two days?'

'I have not been well, sir.'

'What has been wrong with you?'

'A fever. It is gone today.'

'How old are you, Geordie?' MacKenzie continued in an affable tone.

'I am ten years old, sir.' The boy looked nervously down at his boots.

MacKenzie smiled. 'I am John MacKenzie from Edinburgh. I am an acquaintance of your father. He may have mentioned me. I was Lady Lammersheugh's lawyer. I now act for Euphame. This is Davie Scougall, my assistant.' The boy looked at them as if he had done something wrong in the classroom. 'Do you play golf, Geordie?' MacKenzie asked in a friendly manner. The boy nodded. 'Then Davie will give you a round on the Links at Leith the next time you are in town.'

This seemed to settle him: 'I have never been so far, sir.'

'But you have been as far as the Devil's Pool.' MacKenzie observed the boy's reaction. Geordie continued to look down. 'Your father told me about what you found there.'

Geordie hesitated before answering. 'He said that you might come to speak with me. He told me to tell you everything I know. He says you are an honourable man.'

'That is very kind of your father. Why don't we walk up to the wall over there where we can talk?'

They sauntered up the High Street for fifty yards until they reached a low dyke. MacKenzie indicated that Geordie was to sit on it.

'What do you think happened to Lady Lammersheugh?' he asked.

'She drowned, sir.'

'How did she drown?'

The boy looked away for a moment, before blurting out: 'The Devil did it.'

'But why would the Devil want to kill Lady Lammersheugh?'

'I do not know.'

The boy was shaking. MacKenzie patted him on the shoulder. 'I want you to help me, Geordie. I want you to tell me as much as you can remember about what you saw at the pool. You do not have to tell me all these things. But I think you would do anything to help Euphame. I believe she is a friend of yours. Is that correct?'

The boy nodded.

'She is in trouble, great trouble. She needs your help. Tell us everything you remember about the day you found her mother's body. There is not a single detail that I do not want to hear, Geordie. I am a man who loves detail. I love tiny facts. Each piece of information you provide will make me happier. Start from the beginning of the day when you awoke in the morning. Tell us everything that happened to you, everybody you saw, everything that occurred at the pool, every thought you had, everything. For as we say in Gaelic, which is my first tongue and which I spoke before I knew a word of English, *Is fheàrr an fhìrinn na'n t-òr* – do you have any?'

The boy shook his head.

'Then I will translate for you, "Truth is better than gold." You should learn some one day. A few words of Gaelic might prove useful. Mr Scougall will copy down what you say in his notebook so that we can remember it. Just close your eyes. Go back to that day – the twenty-second of October. I might ask a question or two when you are finished.'

The boy nodded again. Scougall showed him his notebook, revealing a page of tiny script: 'As you can see, I do not waste paper – I use every inch.'

'What is that writing, sir?'

'It is shorthand, Geordie.' Scougall smiled. 'I have been learning it. I can now write as quickly as a man can talk. You see the symbol there.' He placed his forefinger on the page. 'That means "road" and that one beside it represents "pool"…'

'Thank you, Davie,' MacKenzie interrupted. 'We can return to a lesson later.'

Geordie realised from MacKenzie's tone that he was to begin. He folded his arms across his chest and closed his eyes. 'I woke in my chamber. The day was fine. I ate breakfast with my father. He was not happy. He said little to me. He was dressed in his riding gear, so I enquired where he was bound. He told me he was to go to Haddington on business. I called to my mother, who does not leave her chambers. She bid me good day at school. I left the house at eight o'clock and walked down the Haddington road to the village through the woods, past Lammersheugh House.' He hesitated for a moment. 'I remember little else of the morning. I was tawsed by Mr Richardson. I could not remember my Latin. After school I went to the pool. I often went there before it happened. I walked down the High Street to Lammersheugh House.' He stopped, recalling another detail. 'I saw Euphame in the garden. I waved to her and she waved back. I continued up the road, over the brig and onto the path. As I was entering a field I saw a rider approaching. I stood on the dyke to let him pass. It was the Laird of Clachdean. He looked ill-pleased to see me and said nothing as he rode by. I do not like him. He does not speak to children.'

'You are doing very well, Geordie,' said MacKenzie. 'Please keep going.'

'I walked up to the pool and climbed onto the big rock. When I was eating my apple I saw something and I took a stone and threw it across the water. It hit first time, with a thud. So I climbed down and ran round. When I jumped onto the sand I saw a body in the water.'

'Describe exactly what you saw.'

'She was face down. She had long dark hair and a black cloak. I did not look for long.'

'What happened then?'

'I heard a noise in the woods. I turned round.' A look of fear came over the boy's face as he recalled the experience. 'I saw a black man. I knew it was Him. It was Satan. He called me to come to him.'

'How did you know it was Satan?' asked Scougall.

'He called me by my name, as Satan does. He said, "Geordie! Geordie! Come to me boy." I heard him calling my own name. I ran. I did not look back. I knew if I did he would have me for his own.'

MacKenzie gave some thought to what the boy had said.

'Apart from the death of Lady Lammersheugh and this witchcraft business, is there anything else that you can think of which might be of importance, anything that has happened in the parish recently that might interest an old lawyer.' He looked intently at the boy.

'There is something, sir. A few weeks ago, I was out on the hill. I sometimes go up there after dark. I heard a noise on the road and hid behind a dyke. I saw three carts pass. I wondered if I should follow them. I thought they were smugglers, so I waited until the last cart was out of sight and came out from my hiding place in a gorse bush. They went down the Clachdean road. I followed for a bit. But I grew tired and returned home.'

'Did you recognise the carters?'

'I could not see them.'

'Did you see what load they carried?'

'I think I saw barrels.'

'Thank you, Geordie. You were not the only person to see the carts on the road that night. Janet Cornfoot saw them. You have a very good memory. You would make a fine lawyer.'

'I want to be a soldier, sir.' The boy straightened his back after saying this.

'A fine soldier you will make. I have only one last question. What is wrong with your mother?'

'She is ill, sir. She cannot leave her chambers. The light hurts her skin.'

'How long has she had such a condition?'

'A few years, I think. She will not have me enter her rooms any more.'

'Why not?'

'I do not know, sir.'

'She never leaves the house?'

'She does not leave her chamber.'

'I see. Thank you, Geordie. Now off you go. When this is all over you must visit us in Edinburgh. Mr Scougall will teach you shorthand and we will play golf.'

The boy smiled, lowered himself from the dyke and ran off up the road in the direction of Woodlawheid.

MacKenzie turned to Scougall. 'What do you make of that, Davie?'

'The presence of Clachdean may point towards his involvement.'

'But he may just have been riding to Haddington. What about Geordie's mother?'

'She must be very ill.'

'Not from a malady which kills quickly. Adam Cockburn has said little about his wife. We need to pay a visit to Woodlawheid.'

CHAPTER 50
The Confession of Euphame Hay

SHE WAS IN the Blinkbonny Woods in the green of summer. At the end of a long avenue of trees, he appeared, a distant apparition, walking slowly towards her. They greeted each other. He lowered his head to kiss her softly on the cheek. The memory was blissful.

She was inside Janet's cottage, carrying flowers she had picked in the woods, yellow primroses. Janet was busy preparing something at the table. Suddenly it was dark. There was a knock on the door. She answered it. She was overjoyed to see her mother. They embraced and shed many tears. She looked so well in her green velvet dress, full of life, as she had before her troubles.

A tall man entered the cottage behind her. She did not realise who it was at first for his face was hidden by the brim of his hat. Then she saw her father's face, smiling down at her. He took her in his arms, lifting her up as he did when she was a child. She felt overjoyed to be in his arms, protected. Happiness rushed through her.

She was awake. She could not remember where she was. Memories of the Tolbooth and her torture returned. She let out a sigh. She knew that she was going to die. She could not hold out much longer.

She felt refreshed. She must have been asleep. But for how

long? She wondered if they had forgotten to wake her. She had no way of knowing in the windowless dungeon. It could have been hours. She felt a little stronger. She inhaled the reek of abused humanity. It had a sharper smell than she remembered. She had recovered some strength. A slight taste of hope returned. Perhaps the appeal of her kin had been successful.

But realisation fell like a stone on her chest, terror replacing hope, as she remembered why she had been left to rest. She saw in her mind's eye the journey she would make: the long walk to the stake where she would meet the hands of death. She saw a vision of her body in flames, the exaltation of her accusers, the pitiful end to her life. She was innocent, but God was to punish her like this. The declaration that she had made came back to her.

I confess that I am a witch. I have sold myself body and soul unto Satan. My mother took me to the Blinkbonny Woods where we met other witches. I put a hand on the crown of my head and the other on the sole of my foot. I gave everything between unto him. I was told to kiss his manhood like a stallion's. I took his seed within my mouth. He told me I was beholden unto him. He lay with me in the position of a beast. He was cold within me like running water. With my mother I planned the murder of my aunt, Lady Girnington. We prepared a wax painting which we roasted with brandy over a fire. At meetings in the Blinkbonny Woods were also present Janet Cornfoot, Elizabeth Murdoch, John Murdoch and my sister Rosina Hay.

CHAPTER 51
A Conversation at Woodlawheid

THEY CREPT INTO the house like thieves, Scougall terrified that they might be caught. Holding up his candle, he followed MacKenzie from room to room. They entered a large chamber where the windows were covered with thick curtains. Their candle was the only point of light, hinting at an opulently furnished apartment. There appeared to be no one inside.

Two doors led off the far wall. They walked towards them. The one on the right was slightly ajar. MacKenzie opened it and poked his head round. It was a dressing room full of richly coloured gowns. He pushed gently on the handle of the other door. It opened easily to reveal a chamber where a fire was burning. Someone was asleep on a four-poster bed. They inched across the room, trying not to make a sound. But as MacKenzie raised his candle by the bed, there was a shrill scream.

The figure on the bed lurched forward. Scougall gasped in horror as a huge deformed head loomed at him. He recoiled in terror. But when he looked again there was only a small woman in a white nightgown whimpering on the bed.

'We mean you no harm. Are you Helen Cockburn?' asked MacKenzie.

She was cowering with her knees up under her chin. When she raised her head, Scougall realised that he was mistaken about its size. It must have been an illusion caused by the candlelight. But her face was grotesquely deformed on one side. Her right arm lay motionless.

'What is wrong with her, sir?' Scougall addressed his question to MacKenzie.

'She is a leper, Mr Scougall!' Adam Cockburn's voice thundered from the shadows where he stood, sword in hand.

'I am sorry. I needed to know if your wife was alive,' responded MacKenzie.

'You should not have entered my house in this way. You should have sought my permission,' Cockburn spoke angrily, but he returned his sword to its scabbard.

'It is all right, Adam. I am recovered.' Helen Cockburn spoke in a timid voice. 'I have heard much about you, gentlemen,' she continued. 'But you scared me, appearing unannounced in my chamber. I no longer receive visitors.'

'We have broken the laws of hospitality, Mrs Cockburn. As a Highlander, I regret this very much. But we are running out of time. Euphame faces an agonising death. I am too eager, sometimes. I neglect to think about the feelings of others. Please accept my apology.'

'My wife does not speak to anyone,' Cockburn said.

'How long have you been ill?' asked MacKenzie, ignoring the laird.

'The deformity appeared on my face about two years ago.' She moved her left hand to her cheek. 'At the same time my arm began to wither. I could not suffer seeing anyone like this. I could not bear being called leper, so I remain here with my books and embroidery. I am well looked after. It is the way I choose to live.'

'You will not see your own son?' asked MacKenzie.

'I speak with him every day. I will not have him look upon his mother like this. I will not have him contract the disease.'

Scougall could not contain himself any longer. He felt ashamed by the way he had behaved towards her. 'I am deeply sorry, madam. My rudeness is inexcusable.'

'It is all right, Mr Scougall.' There was a smile on one side of her face.

Cockburn walked round the room, lighting candles on the walls, revealing the fine paintings, rich embroideries and ornate furniture. With her husband's help, she got out of bed and, aided by him, walked over to a chair by the fire. 'Come gentleman,' she said softly, 'Sit a while with me. Tell me how your search progresses.'

MacKenzie and Scougall sat opposite her. Cockburn stood, taciturn, at her side. Once she had settled herself, MacKenzie asked her what she thought had happened to Grissell.

'I fear she killed herself to escape her fate. She desired to be reunited with Alexander. I have thought about the release of death many times.'

'But you have not done so?'

'I am too weak. I could not leave my…,' she hesitated as if unsure what she should say, '… son.'

'What family do you belong to Mrs Cockburn?'

'My father was the Laird of Broadwood. I am a Hamilton. Our estates are to the north of Haddington.'

'What is your father's name?'

'It was Andrew Hamilton.'

'Ah, I remember him…'

'He was taken by plague in 1670 – as was my mother.'

'I am sorry.'

'It was a long time ago. The grief diminishes.'

MacKenzie thought about his wife. He was still haunted by her death, although it was twenty years now. His grief came and went like the rain.

'What is your view of Lady Girnington?' he continued.

'When I was a girl I was often a guest at Girnington House when the old laird was alive. He was a strange little man. Lillias always appeared unhappy. I think she felt she had been treated harshly. A glittering future destroyed before it had begun. Marriage to an old man can be difficult for a young woman to thole, especially a beautiful one like Lillias.'

'Do you know what happened to her child?'

'I am not sure, Mr MacKenzie. It may be nothing. When I was a girl I remember a child at Girnington, sometimes.'

'A child belonging to Lady Girnington?'

'No. A cousin of the family, a strange, malevolent boy. I was scared of him and kept away. I only remember seeing him a few times.'

'Can you remember anything about him?'

'I did not see him after I was about ten. There was one unusual thing. He did not have any hair.'

Scougall was baffled by the smile which appeared on MacKenzie's face.

CHAPTER 52
The Devil's Machine

MACKENZIE AND SCOUGALL stood outside the inn in the darkness of the early evening, listening intently. Scougall was sure that he had heard something – a far off screech or a wailing somewhere in the town. A few minutes lapsed but it was not repeated.

'Are you sure, Davie?' asked MacKenzie in a whisper.

But Scougall knew he had heard something. He raised his forefinger to his lips to indicate MacKenzie was to remain quiet. There is was again – a scraping sound, rising to a screech. It was difficult to tell where it was coming from.

'Did you hear that, sir?'

'I did, Davie.' MacKenzie was smiling. 'Now I can test my theory about the stained hands.'

'What do you mean, sir?'

'Come. Let me show you.'

MacKenzie walked down the High Street, stopping outside Muschet's shop. 'Wait here, Davie.' They both stood in silence. After a couple of minutes there was another similar sound, slightly louder. Scougall shuddered.

'What is it, sir?'

'I believe that Mr Muschet is a follower of the art of Chapman and Millar.'

Scougall was perplexed. 'Let us find out,' said MacKenzie.

He tried to open the door but it was locked. He knocked three times.

There was a long silence. Finally, a woman's voice spoke from the other side of the door. 'Who is it at this late hour?'

'It is me, Mr Cant.' MacKenzie imitated the cloying tone of the minister's voice. Scougall was impressed by his skills of impersonation.

The door opened. But Scougall was not prepared for what followed. MacKenzie forced his way past Muschet's sister. 'What is this intrusion!' she screamed. Scougall followed him inside.

MacKenzie rushed through the shop into the back storeroom. He stood at the bottom of a spiral staircase, listening.

'Such indeceny, Mr MacKenzie, Mr Scougall. My brother is not at home. Please remove yourselves!'

MacKenzie paid no attention. He had heard another, louder screech. It was not coming from upstairs. He dropped to his knees, putting his ear to the floor and waited. There was another. 'Look for a trapdoor, Davie!' he shouted.

Scougall searched the shop while MacKenzie pulled back a rug in the storeroom. There was nothing. 'Here, sir.' Scougall had found something behind the counter.

'This is an infringement of our rights!' Muschet's sister continued to protest. She stood on the trapdoor, seemingly prepared for a fight.

'I must ask you to move, madam,' said MacKenzie.

'I will not, sir.'

'Then Mr Scougall will remove you. Davie!'

Scougall was being asked to manhandle the merchant's sister out of the way. He felt ill-prepared for such an act of violence. Laying hands on a woman was an effrontery.

'Davie!' MacKenzie bellowed again. 'Make use of your strong arms, man!'

As Scougall moved forward, greatly to his relief, she turned and sped out of the shop. He pulled up the trapdoor and they descended into the gloom. They went down for about ten steps.

Scougall had expected to find Muschet, but another figure stood beside a strange wooden contraption which seemed to fill the small room. George Sinclair was working at a printing press; a rasping noise coming from it as he turned the screw echoed round the small room.

'Here is your ghost, Davie,' laughed MacKenzie.

'It is a pleasure to meet you again, Mr Scougall.' Sinclair appeared unperturbed by the intrusion.

MacKenzie looked disdainfully at Sinclair. 'A secret press in the heart of Lammersheugh. Is this not a surprising place to find such a device?'

'The censors have driven us underground, Mr MacKenzie.' There was a smile on Sinclair's face.

'And what do you print? A history of the parish?'

MacKenzie took a sheet from the table beside the press. It was the front page of a pamphlet entitled *Rise against James Stuart, tyrannical Servant of Antichrist*. He crumpled it up and threw it at Sinclair. 'Traitors,' MacKenzie muttered.

CHAPTER 53
All Hallow's Eve

THEY SET OFF at eleven o'clock in the darkness, following the path, which they now knew well, through the gardens of Lammersheugh House into the Blinkbonny Woods. They passed Janet Cornfoot's cottage and began to climb the lower slopes of the Lammermuirs. Rather than forking right to the Devil's Pool, they continued southwards into the wilds of the hills.

Scougall's unease had diminished during the day, but it returned when MacKenzie told him where they were bound. He could not see the sense of risking their lives in such a manner, even assuming the note was genuine. Nevertheless, he recognised that they had to do something. Euphame had little time left.

As they reached the top of a knoll, flames became visible at a distance of perhaps a mile, caressing the blackness of hill and sky. Scougall thought he could see figures. MacKenzie snuffed out the lantern. 'Get down, Davie!'

They crouched in the heather behind a gorse bush. Scougall felt his heart racing. He began to sweat despite the bitter cold. Witches were dancing around a fire over there. They were heading straight into the arms of Satan. It was folly!

'We must get closer!' snapped MacKenzie.

They crept along in the darkness. The fire disappeared as

the path descended, but the flames came back into view as they began to ascend again. Scougall was sure that he could see figures moving against them. They were too far away to hear anything but the wind.

As they came closer they could tell that the fire burned within the ruins of an ancient stone castle. 'Rooklaw Tower,' whispered MacKenzie.

Scougall's courage was melting away. Every grain of his being told him that they should go no further. They were approaching evil. Their souls were in danger. But MacKenzie had a mastery over him, an authority which he dared not disobey. He made a short prayer to God to protect them.

The fire disappeared again as the path dropped into a valley. At last they reached a ditch which declined gradually before rising steeply to the broken battlements. The tower suddenly loomed above them, a black mass of stone. They clambered up the bank to reach a wall, moving along until they found a section which was breached.

The only sound was the crackling of the fire, which was burning about fifty feet in front of them in an empty courtyard. There was no sign of anyone. Scougall watched sparks rising like smouldering moths into the blackness. He had convinced himself that he was about to witness a sabbat. His mind was inflamed by images from Sinclair's book – dancing hags, fornicating witches and the black gentleman. But there was only a fire in a ruined castle. He felt sure that he had seen something. Someone had lit it.

He was about to say something when a black figure appeared from a doorway behind the flames.

MacKenzie could practically smell Scougall's fear. 'Do not move, Davie! It is a man! *A man!*' he whispered insistently.

But Scougall was deep in the hellish world of his imagination. 'Satan is here! The Devil is here, sir! He will have us as his own!' he cried.

'Do not be a fool. It is a man. Now, be quiet!'

There were voices behind them. As they turned, two men appeared from the darkness pointing muskets. Scougall darted a look back towards the courtyard. The masked figure was getting closer. The devilish vision became the body of a large man.

'Thank you, Mr Scougall. Our little trap has worked! Her ladyship said that you would not be able to resist.'

He was now only a few feet away. He removed his mask. The grinning face of the colonel was revealed.

'Are you responsible for the death of Lady Lammersheugh?' asked MacKenzie.

'I had nothing to do with her demise. She was a stupid wench who would not take advice,' said Clachdean gruffly.

'Then there has been a mistake, sir,' continued MacKenzie. 'For the safety of Euphame is our concern, not politics.'

Scougall was confused by what MacKenzie had just said.

'It was unfortunate that you visited my castle,' replied the colonel. 'It would have been better for you both if Mr Scougall had not entered my property.'

Scougall felt his face redden, despite the darkness and the danger.

'We sought evidence that might help Euphame, Colonel Dewar. We found nothing. We have no interest in politics.'

'I do not believe you, MacKenzie. Your scribe was seen entering my cellars. This letter was intercepted yesterday.' He held up a piece of paper. 'The stakes are high. The reign of Antichrist is almost over.' Clachdean had a wry smile on his face so that it was not possible to tell if he meant what he said. 'It is a matter of life and death,' he continued. 'A battle for the soul of Scotland. If we fail, we die as traitors. If we are victorious, the world is ours. The despotic reign of James Stuart will end.' The colonel moved closer, handing MacKenzie the letter written to Rosehaugh the day before. He was only a couple of feet in front of them. 'You are a supporter of that regime, Mr MacKenzie, as Clerk of the Court of Session. Your clan has no love of Presbytery!'

Scougall realised that their suspicions were correct. Another rebellion was planned using the arms in Clachdean Castle. What was happening in Lammersheugh had nothing to do with witchcraft. He had admired the men of the Covenant, the field preachers who risked everything for their beliefs. They were noble in exile. But how was a vile creature like Clachdean concerned with them?

He felt the muzzle of a musket in his back, pushing him into the courtyard. They were ordered to stand beside a wall about twenty feet in height. Scougall noticed a fireplace about ten feet above them, marking where the floor had collapsed.

'If you try to escape you will be shot. This is an old ruin, a dangerous place to visit at night. I will make a confession, gentlemen. I have no liking for lawyers.' He spat out the name of the profession as if it was a foul epithet. 'Those who make a living by the pen, while men like me risk their lives. Do you know how many times I have stared death in the face, what carnage I have witnessed on the battlefields of Cassel, Seneffe and Turckheim? You could not imagine the slaughter, the depravity, the rape and torture.'

'And now there are two other lives to account for before your maker – Janet Cornfoot and Helen Rammage,' replied MacKenzie sternly.

'Both met natural deaths,' scoffed Clachdean.

Scougall looked at MacKenzie, who said, 'The feather I found in Janet's cottage came from your hat, Clachdean. I believe you suffocated her with it. You placed the bladder of blood in her corpse to deflect attention form this scheme.'

The colonel raised his eyebrows and smiled devilishly. 'Very perceptive, Mr MacKenzie. But I doubt if you have evidence that would stand up in court,' he mocked.

'The slaughter of Helen Rammage was carried out by your sword,' MacKenzie continued. 'Her head dumped in the midden to keep witches in the minds of the townsfolk rather than guns and powder. If we go missing, the hills will soon be full of troops.'

'We are ready. We will not fail as we did in '85. The old witch, Cornfoot, saw us on the road. She had to be dealt with. Helen Rammage brought attention to herself unnecessarily. Her family had been well paid. A little discretion might have saved her. She was a fine looking lass.' The colonel rubbed his groin with a claw-like hand. 'And now it is your turn, gentlemen.'

MacKenzie suddenly shouted loudly. The words were incomprehensible. Scougall realised they must be Gaelic.

The colonel continued speaking, but his voice was drowned out by musket shots. Ricochets echoed round the courtyard. One of his men sank to the ground, holding his stomach. As he screamed, Scougall watched his guts spilling from his abdomen.

'Run, Davie. Run!' MacKenzie yelled.

Instinctively Scougall dived to the ground. MacKenzie took cover behind a pile of stones. Clachdean turned, trying to determine the direction from which the shots were coming. Raising his musket, he fired into the darkness. His men took cover and began to return fire. Scougall rolled down an incline and came clattering into a low wall. A bullet whizzed above his head.

He looked back at MacKenzie who was on the ground, gesticulating at him to continue. He jumped over the wall into the darkness, making ground for about ten paces before tripping, but he was back on his feet quickly. Musket shots flowered the darkness. He wondered if he was being pursued. The firing continued sporadically. He ran on, crashed into something and fell again. The pain in his leg was awful, but he knew he had to escape. He must survive. He ran on into the night.

After about twenty minutes he reached flatter ground and noticed water to his left. It was the Devil's Pool, its surface reflecting the moonlight. Scougall's heart sank. He sped downhill until he reached the woods. Once in the cover of the trees he ran on for about ten yards, before diving to the ground. He lay still, his heart pounding, his chest on fire. His leg was agony and his head throbbed. Despondency overtook him. MacKenzie might be dead, the victim of a Presbyterian plot, murdered by men he had once seen as heroes for the true religion. But they were just the same as other men, hungry for power and money, willing to use evil to obtain their ends. He thought about the wax doll he had found in his bed. He knew now that it was just a trick to cover the machinations of rebellion. The lives of innocent women were being sacrificed so that one party might take power from another. He felt in his heart that Scotland would be a better country if bishops were banished. The King was a Catholic servant of Antichrist. But the disregard for human life shown by the colonel went against the teachings of Christ.

Gathering his cloak around him, he decided to remain where he was until dawn. He could still hear distant gunfire, but it soon petered out. The sky cleared and the stars were visible. He prayed to God with all his heart to spare MacKenzie and save the life of Euphame Hay. Scougall was now convinced that she was innocent, Lady Lammersheugh too. He kept praying until he fell asleep.

CHAPTER 54
A Warlock in the Steeple

ELIZABETH MURDOCH PULLED her shawl round her shoulders and shuffled out of the gates of Lammersheugh House. She was in a state of panic, having received a message from the minister in the middle of the night that she should attend her husband in the steeple. She was told nothing more by the messenger. She begged God that the auld fool hadnae confessed, that he had said naethin o their trysts in the Lammer Burn, her attempt tae rid him o his cough, the craftin o the wax figure. She hoped that he hadnae confessed tae somethin worse – meetin wi witches and plannin the murder o Lady Girnington. She kenned sic accusations were nonsense. The auld fool wisnae capable o hairmin onything, even wi those huge haunds – a gentle giant he was kenned as, and he wis a guid husband tae her.

She quickened her pace, trying to run, but her legs were shaking with fear. She thought of Euphame in the Tolbooth, bonnie wee Euphame, such a quiet child, such a saft mistress tae them baith. Wis she now deid like her mither, Lady Lammersheugh, her mistress fir mony years? Such a beauty, wi mair o the witch in her, mair alluring an magical but gane, gane, aw gane. Tears were on her cheeks.

They had passed their lives as guid Christian folk. They had gone tae the kirk every Sabbath, worshipped the ain true

God, had naethin tae dae wi Satan, wirked haird aw their lives, brocht up a family. But now this – John accused as a warlock. He wis weak. She feared that maist of aw, his weakness. The clever men o the parish wid trick him. They wid mak him believe that if he confessed, they might baith gae free. But if he confessed he wid burn, the auld fool. Aw she had ever daen wis say a wee chairm, taught by her mither, a wee chairm tae cure her man, naethin bad. But if he telt them, they wid baith burn!

In the auld days the session wis mair lenient. Janet wis questioned lang syne fir chairmin. She'd been warned tae stop and she had sworn she wid. An that wis aw. The auld minister wis a canny man, no like the new ain. He kenned that aw the women o the parish said a rhyme or twa tae help them through life. Whit guid wid it dae burnin aw the folk in the parish? She cried again. But Mr Cant was fu o the new order – a just warld, righteousness, abomination an aw that. The auld session clerk Tam Brewster aye gave ye a wee smile whan he saw ye, but Rankine and his sister were cauld creatures, Muschet tae. The parish wis taen ower by a cruel crew.

She reached the kirk gates. Pausing, she held the iron railing. She was reminded of the cold water in the burn. She did not want to face what was in the steeple. She did not want to see John Murdoch, a confessing warlock.

The kirk was empty. She plodded down the candle-lit aisle. At the door to the steeple, there was a man. Muschet said nothing to her as he moved aside to let her through the door. There was an impenetrable look on his glum face.

She climbed the stone stairs, breathing heavily. She felt the tension rise within her, a desperate sense of foreboding. As she entered the room she saw Cant and Rankine. She could not stop herself blurting out: 'Has the auld fool confessed?'

'He has not, Mrs Murdoch. I am sorry,' Cant said.

For a moment her heart leapt with pride for her man. He

wis strang aifter aw, strang an true. John Murdoch widnae burn. They were guid folk. God had answered her prayers.

'I am sorry, Elizabeth,' the minister repeated sombrely, beckoning her with his hand to enter and behold.

She turned her head to the right, looking into the shadows. Murdoch lay on the floor on his back. He was covered by a white winding sheet.

'He's deid!' she shrieked.

'He fell into a stupor and could not be revived,' said Rankine.

She knelt down beside him, pulling back the sheet and looking on the face of her dead husband. He lay on the floorboards in sackcloth, stinking of his own excrement. Barefoot and bareheaded. His body covered in hundreds of tiny red marks. His heart could not take the strain of the interrogation, the denial of sleep and the pricker's pin. She collapsed over him, screaming for God's help.

CHAPTER 55
A Discovery on the Road

1 November 1687

SCOUGALL AWOKE UNDER a clear blue sky. He could not feel
his feet because of the cold. There was a dawn frost on the
grass. From his hiding place he recognised the track which
they had followed the night before. Everything seemed calm,
a bright winter morning in the hills.

There were noises in the distance. As he peered out, a cart
appeared on the track accompanied by two horsemen. Other
figures walked beside it.

As they came closer he recognised the gait of a man about
a foot taller than the others. He was on his feet and ran to
greet him.

'Thank God you are safe, Davie!' MacKenzie beamed at his
young friend. Scougall was lost for words. Tears formed in his
eyes and he experienced a feeling of joy such as he had not
experienced since arriving in Lammersheugh. Good was
triumphing over evil. He thought of the wonder of the
Resurrection, of life renewed. He recalled his prayer of the
night before. MacKenzie embraced him warmly.

'We can share our stories over breakfast.'

Scougall joined MacKenzie beside the cart. It was only
then that he noticed its load. He counted six heads among the
bodies slumped on top of each other. He recognised the face

of one of Clachdean's men, but he could not see the colonel himself. They did not speak on the way down to Lammersheugh.

Exhausted and filthy, they were soon sitting in the inn devouring breakfast.

'Last night did not turn out as I had hoped. Much blood has been spilled. I did not tell you that I sent word to Mr Cockburn, asking him to bring his men to Rooklaw. I admit that I was not sure whom we would face as our enemy, Mr Cockburn or the colonel. But one way or the other we would find out.' MacKenzie smiled at Cockburn. 'I believe Clachdean's plan was to collapse the wall on us, Davie. After you escaped, the skirmish continued for about thirty minutes. I could do little with my small weapon, so I hid as best I could. The colonel was hit in the melée but escaped into the night. He has the constitution of an ox. Four of his men were killed. Two of Cockburn's died bravely fighting for the King.'

'We have no time to waste, gentleman. We must make for Girnington House as soon as possible,' interrupted Cockburn. 'I will send word to the sheriff that his deputy is gravely injured.'

Scougall was weary, but resigned to seeing the affair concluded. A few minutes later they were on horseback, following the road to Girnington.

About a mile from the mansion, at the side of the road, a body was slumped against a fence post, head bowed, legs apart. There was a black movement around the groin where crows feasted on an open wound. The colonel's belly was a great white sack from which a trail of bloody sausages extruded. His hat was still on his head, his sword lay on the ground. A horse was feeding on the grass nearby. A dark patch of blood could be seen between his legs where the wound had bled copiously.

They dismounted, scattering the birds. 'I expect he was making for Girnington,' said Cockburn pointing up the track.

'He has met a fitting end.' MacKenzie looked distastefully at the huge figure. 'As we say in Gaelic, *Cruinnichidh na fithich far am bi a' chairbh*, Where the carcase is, the ravens will gather. It is just that the crows have fed upon him!'

Scougall felt no pity for Clachdean. He had attempted to kill them. He was willing to use the innocent for political ends.

'Come, gentleman. We must bring her ladyship news that he is dead. I think she will be surprised to see us,' added MacKenzie.

Before they departed, he searched the colonel's body and found a small leather bag attached to his belt. MacKenzie emptied the contents into his hand. Gold coins shone in the morning sunlight. He put them back and threw the bag to Scougall. 'Count these, Davie. Money is behind much of the evil in this parish.'

MacKenzie removed Clachdean's hat. 'This was probably used to suffocate Janet Cornfoot. His sword dismembered Helen Rammage.' He ripped off the wig to reveal the white baldness of his vast head.

CHAPTER 56
The Genealogy of Girnington

MACKENZIE WAS STRUCK by the quiet beauty of the Girnington estate. Amongst such tragedy it was an island of tranquillity. Cockburn knocked loudly on the door.

A couple of minutes passed before Leitch answered. 'Her ladyship is not able to see anyone this morning.'

Cockburn grabbed him by the throat, pushing him back indoors. MacKenzie and Scougall followed. The servant was thrown across the hall.

Lady Girnington was being attended by her maids. 'What do you mean by this interruption?' she squealed at Cockburn's appearance. Her jaw dropped further as MacKenzie and Scougall entered, but she said nothing.

'You are surprised to see us alive, your ladyship.' MacKenzie's voice held no hint of deference.

'I do not wish to receive guests in my current state of dress.'

'Then you have not heard the news of last night?'

'I have heard nothing of last night, Mr MacKenzie. I do not follow the Papist superstitions of All Hallow's Eve. I leave that to others.' She looked at Cockburn.

'Then I am the bearer of sad news, Lady Girnington.'

'What is that news?'

'Your son is dead!'

Scougall and Cockburn turned in surprise and stared at MacKenzie.

'I have no son, sir.' Scougall noted a slight hesitation in her reply.

'Madam, your son, Colonel Robert Dewar, Laird of Clachdean, lies dead by the road. He ambushed us last night at Rooklaw Tower. Fortunately, Mr Cockburn came to our rescue before we joined the dead in the parish of Lammersheugh. Clachdean was wounded in the fight, but escaped. He bled to death during the night.'

'I have no son.'

'The Laird of Clachdean is your illegitimate son.'

'I have no son!' her voice began to betray emotion. 'I have no son! A woman should have a son!' Her voice broke, her head dropping forward, tears on her red cheeks. 'I have no son!'

'The colonel is not the son you may have wished for. But he is your flesh and blood, tied to you by the bonds of kinship.' MacKenzie assumed the formal tone he often adopted in court: 'If I might take a few minutes of your ladyship's time, I will explain myself. A number of pieces of evidence pointed to this conclusion.'

When Lady Girnington looked up there was still defiance in her eyes.

MacKenzie continued. 'There was, first, the physical resemblance between your ladyship and Clachdean. Some might attach little importance to this. I always pay close attention to characteristics shared by family members. Many of the MacKenzies of Ardcoul have a slight squintness of the eye. I observed that you and Clachdean have a similarity of expression. You also tend to grossness of the body. I was struck by the portrait of your brother's family at Lammersheugh. Although Alexander was a close friend, I could not remember his face clearly. When I looked on the painting I was reminded of Clachdean. Not conclusive, of course, but suggestive of a genealogical connection between you.'

'Really, Mr MacKenzie. Such nonsense...' she mocked.

'There were also financial arrangements between you. The instrument of sasine conveying the lands of Clachdean to Dewar indicated that you had underwritten the transaction. Why would you lend money to such a spendthrift? You are a careful manager of your estates. It suggested to me some other more intimate link between you.'

MacKenzie was standing beside her. He suddenly lunged forward. She screamed as her wig came away in his hands to reveal a bald head. 'Baldness also runs in families. Your brother Lammersheugh was bald by the time he was twenty-five. I knew this as his friend. There is not a hair on Clachdean's head.'

She grabbed the wig and put it back on. 'All right, enough of your games. The colonel is my son. I will explain. I was a young girl in London. Although you may not believe it,' she turned to Scougall, 'I was a beauty adored by all men who saw me, a rival of Lady Lauderdale. I hoped to marry an English Earl, not a Scottish one. The sons of the English nobility courted me.' Her eyes sparkled as she spoke of her past glories. 'But I was ravished by a poet who wooed me with words of love. I was much taken with poetry then, fool that I was. I was left with child at fifteen. My father, to avoid a scandal, removed me from London, forced me to return to the bleak fields of Scotland. I gave birth to a boy, but I was not allowed to keep him. He was passed to others to be brought up, distant relatives of a lower standing. I was only allowed to see him a few times over the years. I married, but I was not blessed with children. I wed an old man who was impotent. I sought out younger men. They also failed me! A legitimate son was denied me. Can you imagine that Mr

Scougall? A girl who thought she would wed an English nobleman, reduced to such a fate.'

Scougall wondered why she was addressing him. His face turned red.

Lady Girnington sighed deeply. 'Clachdean is not to blame. He was sorely abused by the man who brought him up as father, beaten viciously from a young age, shown little love by his foster mother. He left to become a soldier when he was twelve. I never saw him again for twenty years. Then I learned that he had bid for the lands of Clachdean. I sought to make amends. I helped him to fund the purchase and put his name forward when the position of sheriff-deputy became vacant.' She looked down at her hands. 'He was treated badly by the House of Lammersheugh. I must have his body attended to. Despite everything, I still have the feelings of a mother.'

'In good time, my ladyship,' said MacKenzie.

'I have made my confession. You have caught out an old lady. There is no crime in mothering a bastard!'

'I believe not, but we are not only concerned with Clachdean. The life of a young woman hangs in the balance.'

'How am I connected with the fate of Euphame?'

'You are very much involved. If I may describe to you what I believe has happened in the parish of Lammersheugh.'

Lady Girnington took a deep breath. 'It seems I have no choice. But the sheriff will not be pleased when he finds I have been treated in this manner.'

MacKenzie began to walk round the room, gesticulating as if addressing a jury. 'For long I was perplexed by the events here. A young widow found drowned, her daughter accused of witchcraft. I was confused, until I realised there were two plots in the parish. The plots were connected, but not intimately so, although they involved many of the same characters.

'Firstly, there was a plan to be rid of Lady Lammersheugh so that the lands of Lammersheugh might be controlled through escheat, or by marriage of a daughter to Clachdean. This was initially carried out by legal, then I believe, by criminal means.'

MacKenzie hesitated for a moment. Lady Girnington shook her head.

He continued: 'The smear of witchcraft is impossible to wash away. The threat was enough to terrify Grissell; the delation of a confessing witch irresistible evidence. Grissell took her life to escape the humiliation. I believe Margaret Rammage was offered money to include Grissell in her delation. She no doubt felt that her poor family would benefit after she herself was executed. Euphame's name was added later, probably after more money was offered. Helen Rammage, ill-advisedly, became ostentatious in spending it. She paid with her life, just as her sister had done.'

'Grissell was a fool! She might have married the colonel and avoided such unnecessary...' snapped Lady Girnington.

'Why did you do it? The Lammersheugh estate would be in your hands. The Clachdean estate was already under your control. You would be a force to be reckoned with in the shire. The life of Grissell and her daughters meant nothing to you. But there was another reason. You were beautiful like Lady Lammersheugh once. She was blessed with two fine daughters. You had Clachdean. You hated her.'

'Ridiculous supposition!'

'And there was another plot. No doubt such reprehensible plans are being hatched across the kingdom. Indeed, a nest of vipers inhabits Lammersheugh, waiting for their moment to settle old scores. You had many to settle, Lady Girnington! The list of plotters is long. It includes Rankine, Muschet,

Purse, Cant, Sinclair and his brother. But I believe the strings were being pulled from Girnington House. Your greater influence from the control of Lammersheugh would elevate your standing under a new regime. Perhaps you would be rewarded with a marriage to an old Scottish earl! It would go someway to compensate you for your disgrace as a young woman.'

Lady Girnington shook her head. 'This is not the kirk session, Mr MacKenzie. You will not force me into a confession with your fine words.'

'I did not expect you to make any confession. The High Court will try you, assess the evidence and make their decision.'

'You have no evidence,' she said defiantly.

MacKenzie indicated to Scougall and Cockburn that it was time to leave. 'I bid you good day, madam.'

'I hope your daughter enjoys her exquisite jewel,' she said bitterly.

MacKenzie stopped. 'Why of course, Davie!'

CHAPTER 57
Back in the Library

MACKENZIE LOOKED AT the wall where the portrait of Lady Lammersheugh had hung. He saw himself at The Hawthorns reading her letter and then in Janet Cornfoot's cottage. He spoke aloud: 'See where my eyes come to rest. Read my words carefully. See where my eyes come to rest.' He moved backwards until his legs were against the top of the desk, his head at a level where the painting had been. He looked across the room to the bookcase full of leather bound volumes on the other wall. He noticed a copy of Burton's *Anatomy of Melancholy*, a work in which he had spent many delicious hours.

'Find Lady Lammersheugh's will in your notes, Davie.'

Scougall withdrew his notebook, flicked through the pages and began to read slowly from the shorthand. '"I Grissell Hay, Lady Lammersheugh..."'

'Move to the section on my bequest,' he said impatiently.

'"...to Mr John MacKenzie, advocate, Clerk of the Court of Session, I leave the small picture which hangs in the library at Lammersheugh. And to his daughter Elizabeth MacKenzie I leave an exquisite emerald, to be found in the box in my chamber..."'

MacKenzie repeated aloud: 'an exquisite emerald... an exquisite jewel.'

'That's it, Davie! *Ekskubalauron* by Sir Thomas Urquhart,

published in London in 1652. The subtitle of the work is
'The Discovery of a most exquisite Jewel.' He walked across
the room and took the book from a shelf.

Rosina appeared at the door as he opened the volume. He
quickly removed a small piece of paper which he slipped into
his pocket and gave Scougall a sharp look, indicating that
they should move the conversation away from literature.

'Wine is on its way, gentlemen. You will have to excuse
me. I must see to the return of John Murdoch's body.'

'Is he dead?' Scougall was perturbed.

'He died last night under the pricker's examination. His
old heart was not strong enough.'

'The list of the dead grows too long,' said MacKenzie
solemnly.

Rosina bowed her head slightly and left.

MacKenzie walked to the window. He took the paper
from his pocket. 'Look – a map, Davie!'

'What does it show?' asked Scougall.

It was simply drawn, but its message was clear. A dotted
line followed the path from Lammersheugh House to Janet
Cornfoot's cottage. MacKenzie opened his other hand to
reveal a small silver key.

CHAPTER 58
A Discovery in the Cottage

SCOUGALL TRIED TO apply MacKenzie's method of observation as they made their search, concentrating on each object in turn, shutting out all other thoughts. He observed the fireplace, the chair, the table, the kitchen implements – a black kettle, a small cauldron, a few spoons. He got down on his knees to examine the cold flagstones. MacKenzie was also on the floor. Scougall got to his feet again and opened the closet. It was empty.

'We must think, Davie. We have been directed here for a reason. Everything has been planned by Grissell.'

'What if the book has already been found?'

MacKenzie ignored him. 'What did Grissell leave Janet?'

Scougall tried to remember Purse's words. But he could not. Withdrawing his notebook he read: 'To my beloved Janet Cornfoot who has served me through all the days of my life and who has been a beam of light unto me, I leave the sum of £200.'

They raised the candles together, the wooden beams of the cottage appearing above them. Scougall climbed uneasily onto the table in the centre of the room. His head was just above the main beam. He brought his candle along the upper side, but could see nothing out of the ordinary.

He moved over to the edge of the table to examine where

the beam joined the wall. A small raised section of wood jutted out slightly at the far end. 'There is something here, sir.'

He had to come back down so that they could push the table against the wall. At the side of the beam he noticed a thin hole about half an inch long.

'Pass me the key, sir.'

He shifted his weight as he took it, almost unbalancing himself as he moved backwards. It was a perfect fit. A small flap, about six inches long and two broad, dropped forward as he turned it gently. Placing his hand inside the thick beam, he removed a book which he handed down to MacKenzie.

'Make sure that is all!'

Scougall moved his fingers around the secret chamber. There was something at the back. He pulled out a bundle of letters, held together by a piece of scarlet ribbon.

'Is that everything, Davie?'

He felt round each corner carefully. 'Yes!'

'Close the flap and lock it.'

Scougall did as he was told, then climbed down.

'What are they, sir?'

MacKenzie opened the volume and read the words on the first page:

'The Testament of Grissell Hay of Lammersheugh.'

'We have already heard her testament,' said Scougall looking confused.

MacKenzie flicked through the pages. 'It is the commonplace book in Grissell's hand. The evidence we require is in here.'

CHAPTER 59
The Testament of Grissell Hay

I, LADY LAMMERSHEUGH, solemnly swear that what follows is a true account of events befalling me since the death of my beloved husband, Alexander Hay of Lammersheugh, who died on the 12th day of December 1685.

I put these words down on paper not for pleasure, nor for the remembrance of days past, but as a true testament of the evil done me by Lillias Hay, Lady Girnington, my sister-in-law, and Colonel Robert Dewar, the Laird of Clachdean, who have conspired violently against me and my children.

The loss of my husband was a terrible affliction for us. He was a young man in his prime, snatched away. But God will have His purpose. He was only buried a few hours when there was the first hint of discord between myself and my sister-in-law. Lady Girnington spoke to me in the kirkyard of Lammersheugh on the very day that he was lowered into the earth. As we returned from the graveside, she proposed a transaction which disturbed me so much that I was forced to retire to my chamber. Without the slightest consideration for my recent widowhood, she informed me that a match with Robert Dewar of Clachdean would be of great benefit to the houses of Lammersheugh, Girnington and Clachdean, joining them together in an estate of power within the sheriffdom.

Colonel Dewar is a man whom my husband and I have always held in the lowest regard. His life of debauchery was never secret; his whoring in Edinburgh and London, his licence with servants and other women in the parish is well known. His bastards, whom he does little to support, are spread far and wide. The thought of marriage to this man, to whom I would be forced to give my body, was too much for me to bear.

At my next meeting with Lady Girnington I expressed reluctance to follow her advice. She was angry with me and called me a fool. She said that a match with Clachdean was a sound one. I would do no better as my best years were behind me. The marriage would benefit my daughters, raising the House of Lammersheugh and providing the girls with better husbands. I replied that I would not marry him, that I was content to remain a relict. I would look after my bairns and remember the sweet memories of the time with my dear husband. I hoped that such a frank declaration would mark the end of the matter. A number of weeks passed. I was left to my mourning, my heart breaking anew each day as I awoke with the dawn, my grief as bitter as bile.

About a month after the burial, the Laird of Clachdean called on me. He had put on his best suit, dusted down his wig. He was civil enough. For my part I was civil to him – though I could not bear the sight of the brute. The thought of him as my bedfellow was repulsive as I watched him across the table as we dined together. He spoke to the girls, smiled at them, asking them little questions, each one piercing me. I saw his game readily enough.

When the girls left to walk in the gardens, I could tell he was about to say something of importance, for his hands grew agitated. He stammered that he would like to marry me. He would, of course, wait a reasonable time. The match would be a fine one for me, the girls, and the House of Lammersheugh. He added that it would also please Lady Girnington. I think he realised at once that he should not have said this. I did everything I could to cover the feelings that rose within me as I looked upon him – gross and lecherous, his vast stomach like a great stone hanging over the table. I said that I was still in mourning, that I could not yet decide upon the matter, that in a few months I would be in a better way to look to the future. I sought to buy time. My answer appeared to satisfy him, for my words were not said harshly. I kept my true feelings concealed and he left in reasonable humour. But his kiss on my hand sent needles through me.

Thereafter I gave the matter of marriage little consideration. I was busy with the estate which I had paid no attention to before. I met my tenants and their families. I made plans for the future, attending to repairs of the house and the education of the girls. Perhaps six months went by, maybe more. Specks of light appeared in the grey despair that had enveloped me since Alexander's death. I gained hard-won pleasure from my work on the estate and I saw my children grow into fine young women. And in my dreams Alex came to me each night. I lived for our trysts when he took me in his arms again. We walked over the hills together as we used to do, up onto Lammer Law to look down on the world beneath us.

Summer turned to autumn. A letter which I enclose dated 10 September 1686 arrived written in a formal tone by Lady Girnington, reiterating her suggestion. It is

short and to the point. It chilled me to the bone for I
foresaw that she would not let the matter rest. She was
set on a course. I knew then that she hated me. I had
always suspected that she did. She must have known
that I had only feelings of disgust for Clachdean. I
sensed she was gaining pleasure from my pain.

I did not do anything for a few days. Then I summoned up the courage to reply. I wrote a short letter,
eschewing the turmoil of emotion that welled up inside
me, pleading my case, arguing that he was not a suitable
match for me. A copy of the letter dated 17 September
1686 is also enclosed.

Again there was a period of silence. I waited anxious-
ly each day for a reply, but none came. I hoped that the
matter was over, that Clachdean had tired of the thought
of me and was seeking a match with another poor
woman.

But there was to be a further twist to my misfortune. I
received a visit from Mr Muschet, merchant in Lammersheugh. I thought it concerned a financial matter as my
husband was indebted to him for substantial sums. But
before we had exchanged pleasantries, or I had time to
offer him a glass of wine, he blurted out a proposal of
marriage. He hinted that the debts which he held over the
house would be redeemed if I agreed. He said that if I
refused, action in the courts was certain. I knew well I
could little afford this. However, I had to be politic and
pleaded mourning as before. Muschet did not fill me with
the disgust that I felt for the colonel. I felt nothing for
him. I considered a match to a merchant beneath me and
dishonourable to the House of Lammersheugh.

On 17th November 1686 I was in Haddington
purchasing provisions. Lady Girnington's coach appeared in the High Street. Her footman descended and

asked me if I would speak with her ladyship. I was
caught off guard and could think of no excuses, so I was
obliged to step into her coach.

'I will carry you home, my dear,' she said. I agreed,
feeling that to object would be impolite. I told my
servant to return to Lammersheugh with my coach and I
found myself alone with her. I had seen little of her since
my husband died. I noticed that she tended more and
more to grossness of the body. She was so large that I
wondered how she was lifted into the coach. I was very
nervous. But she seemed biddable enough, talking of the
King's policies, which she wholeheartedly opposed,
expanding upon the imminent danger of the rule of
Antichrist. She kept saying how Scotland required
reformation. I know little of politics. My father was
much taken up with such affairs, fighting for King
Charles in the Civil Wars which led to our family's ruin.
I smiled and said nothing.

Then she raised the subject of the recent witch trials
in Fife. It was a topic to which I had given little thought.
She told me that she feared for the parish. She had
warned her servants to be vigilant lest Satan tempt them.
She asked me how my servant Janet was. She did this in
such a way as to hint that she might be suspected of
witchcraft. Janet is known in the parish for her remedies. I believe she was questioned by the session in the
1660s. I ignored these insinuations. I said Janet was well
in her retirement, enjoying her little cottage and looking
after the girls.

I felt Lady Girnington was biding her time. Sure
enough, as we approached Lammersheugh she told me
in a calm voice that she had received my reply. She was
very disappointed that I would not consider Clachdean.
She considered him a fine match. He was perhaps a bit

rough round the edges, but like all husbands he would be improved by a little management. She spun other lies about him which she had already told me. I said that I could not under any circumstances marry such a man.

As I prepared my skirts to step out of the coach she took hold of my cuff, digging her nails into my wrist, saying angrily to me: 'We must find another way to persuade you then, my dear.' I looked straight into her eyes. Behind the make-up, which was lavishly applied, I could see a smouldering hatred. I knew that she aimed to destroy me for no other reason than that her brother had loved me and that she had no children of her own. I said nothing, but took leave. I walked into the house without saying farewell, passed straight to my chamber and stood for a long time looking down on the gardens.

I concluded that I had to make plans. I could not let events overwhelm me. But I did not realise to what lengths they would go to destroy me.

Again there was silence for a time, perhaps a couple of months. I prayed to God with all my heart that I had heard the last of the matter. But I knew that it would not be. Sure enough, another letter arrived from the colonel, dated 12th February 1687, which I enclose. It reiterates his proposal of marriage, stating that it would be the last time an offer would be made on such generous terms.

I did not reply. I knew that they would not give up, but I could not have guessed how low they would stoop. I had imagined that Lady Girnington might call in a debt owed by my husband in order to encourage me to look more favourably on the colonel in the way that Muschet had done.

A month passed. I received a letter from Muschet informing me that because he had not received a formal reply to his offer, he was initiating proceedings for recovery of debt. He was sorry that he was forced to take such action, but he needed money for trading enterprises. This distracted me for a short while as I made enquiries about raising funds to pay him.

Then one grey afternoon when the girls were out riding, Murdoch told me the colonel called upon me. When he was shown into the chamber, I could see that he no longer wore the mask of decency. I smelled drink on him as soon as he came close. He asked me if I had received his letter. I said that I had, but that I had already given him my answer. A written reply was not necessary. Did I not think that he warranted a response as a gentleman, he said. Growing angry, he cursed me in words which I cannot commit to paper. I was appalled by the outburst. I called Murdoch to escort him out of the house. But my old servant did not come. I shouted louder. Still no one came. I screamed for help. Still there was no one.

I walked towards the door so that I might shout down the corridor. Perhaps someone in the kitchen would hear me. But the colonel grabbed me and threw me violently to the ground.

It is with the greatest difficulty that I write what followed. My hand shakes at the pen as revulsion rises within me. The colonel held me down, touching me lecherously. I began to scream. He thrust a hand over my mouth. I fought as hard as I could. But he would not cease. He was like an ox on top of me. I could do nothing to push him away.

I can hardly write what happened. But I must do so. I must put down on paper the crime as testimony of the evil done me. I was ravished in my own home by Colonel Robert Dewar, Laird of Clachdean. When he was done with me he wiped his slavering lips and his man-

hood with a filthy handkerchief. He smiled, saying
something like: 'The session will sanction our match
now that I have bedded you,' as he pulled up his breeches. He left without saying anything else.

I smoothed down by dress and saw to my hair. I
called for Murdoch again and again. At last he came,
saying that the colonel had told him of a dreadful
accident on the road. He had searched all the way down
to Semple's Dyke. But there was none. He asked me if I
was well. I said I wanted my evening meal brought to
my chamber. I retired thither, feeling disgust for what
had been done to me, wondering how a creature created
in the image of God could act in such a way. I believe
that Satan visited me in the shape of Clachdean. I shed
tears for my fate and that of my daughters.

I will freely admit that rage for revenge coursed
through my veins. My mind was in turmoil. I did not
know what I should do. Should I tell someone? It was as
if my life had been destroyed again. There was nothing I
could do to escape my fate.

Later in the evening Janet came to me. I did not tell
her yet what had happened, but I told her of the offer of
marriage by Clachdean and Lady Girnington's encour-
agement. As I shed tears of despair, my old servant
brought me comfort, holding me until I fell asleep.
When I awoke in the morning and recalled my rape, I
knew that I must collect evidence. I offer this statement
and letters as proof of the guilt of Lillias Hay Lady
Girnington and Colonel Robert Dewar, Laird of Clachdean.

Again events took a course which I had not anticipated. Another letter from Lady Girnington arrived,
dated 24th May 1687. It had been drafted carefully. I
believe it must be read in the same way. The hints are

clear. I was to be accused of witchcraft if I did not follow their wishes. If she heard nothing from me in a week she would act on allegations against me made by Margaret Rammage, a confessing witch from Aikenshiels who was a servant of her tenant.

The effect of this letter can easily be imagined. I sank into a pit of despair. Even in the darkest days of my grief was I not so afflicted. I lay in my chamber for two days unable to move from bed. Finally, I mustered up courage. Alexander came to me in a dream, telling me what I should do. I realised that I could not delay. I arranged a meeting with Purse in Haddington to make changes to my latterwill and testament. He is close to Lady Girnington. I do not trust him. I penned this statement and bound the letters together. I hid them in Janet's cottage. I had to ensure that they did not fall into the hands of my enemies. I could not even tell Janet of their existence, lest she was questioned and their whereabouts extorted by torture. Lady Girnigton's power extends far throughout the sheriffdom. I had only a week to make preparations so that evidence survived, whatever happened.

May God be my judge.

Signed, Grissell Hay, Lady Lammersheugh
Dated, Lammersheugh 12th September 1687

CHAPTER 60
A Final Thread

4 November 1687

EUPHAME HAY WAS helped out of the coach by her sister. She was a shattered vision of the young woman MacKenzie had met after the funeral. Her skin was a thin yellow sheet across her face, her body emaciated. But she was alive. They had to be thankful for that. He had thought that she would die in the Tolbooth. But here she was, walking painfully towards them.

MacKenzie took her hand as she spoke in a weak voice: 'I thank you for all you have done for my family, John. You have risked your life to save us. I will never forget it.' Tears formed in her eyes. MacKenzie had to swallow to contain his emotion. 'My mother's faith in you was proved right.' Then turning to Scougall she added, 'Rosina has told me of your bravery also, Mr Scougall. I thank you with all my heart.'

Scougall's face reddened. Unable to think of anything to say, he nodded nervously.

MacKenzie intervened to save him further embarrassment. 'We are delighted to see you back home, Euphame. You have been through so much, literally to the gates of hell and back. None of us can imagine what you have suffered. The evil done to you and your mother is beyond comprehension. I hope that one day our nation will free itself from such barbarity.'

A painful smile returned to her face: 'I hope you are right.'

'Now you must rest,' said Rosina, taking her sister's arm and leading her towards the door of the house.

Euphame moved slowly, greeting Elizabeth Murdoch who was also in tears. She stopped beside George Cockburn: 'Thank you for your notes, Geordie. They brought me some comfort when I had lost hope. One of the guards passed them to me in the steeple. He did not wake me as he should. I clung to these shards of goodness as they were all I had.'

The sisters entered the house, followed by the servants.

'Settle our account with Porteous, Davie. We leave for Edinburgh,' said MacKenzie.

Scougall strode off confidently, overjoyed by the prospect of their return. Geordie ran away to play in the gardens, leaving MacKenzie and Cockburn alone.

'I must also thank you, John. The girls will be safe now. I will see to that.'

'Davie and I will always be indebted to you, Adam. I must apologise again for the way in which we entered your house. But desperate times call for such actions. Let us walk for a while in the gardens. There is something I must ask you.'

MacKenzie's eye was taken by the herbaceous border as they wandered down the lawn. He had given horticulture little thought since his arrival in Lammersheugh. 'The Tulip Tree,' he spoke appreciatively. 'I have a specimen at The Hawthorns. You must visit us there... all of you. Your wife would benefit from a little Highland hospitality.'

Cockburn smiled. 'I thank you.'

MacKenzie walked on a few paces before continuing in a leisurely tone, 'There is a thread which hangs loose. It is unsettling my mind.'

'What do you mean, John?'

'The thread is hanging from your jacket, Adam,' MacKenzie smiled.

'Me, sir!'

MacKenzie looked at the laird intently, but spoke in a friendly manner. 'I am going to pose a question which you do not have to answer.' He waited for a moment before continuing: 'Were you at the Devil's Pool on the afternoon Grissell died?'

Cockburn did not speak.

'There is evidence, of course. The pistol that Davie found was yours. The initials AH are your father-in-law's – Andrew Hamilton of Broadwood. I believe Geordie saw his own father calling in anguish from the trees. Am I right?'

Cockburn continued to gaze up towards the hills. It was a fine cloudless November morning. At last he turned to MacKenzie. 'You are right, John. I was there on that terrible afternoon.' He took a deep breath. 'I will tell you what happened. But I must ask that it should remain between us as friends.'

'As a friend you speak in the strictest confidence.'

The two men continued to walk along the border. 'I have not been entirely truthful with you,' continued the laird. 'Please forgive me. I must begin with myself. My marriage is a loveless one. It was a match dictated by others. My wife has been ill for a long time. The deformities appeared gradually. I have grown fond of her, but I do not love her. I never have.' He hesitated, looking up again at the hills. 'I have always had feelings for Grissell – what man would not? I kept them to myself. She and Alexander were childhood sweethearts. I was a friend on their periphery. But following his death we saw more of each other. I now understand she sought someone who might help her out of the dreadful circumstances which she found herself in. I am ashamed that I had my own selfish motives. I witnessed the pain of her mourning. At first I remained at a distance. I tried to comfort her as best I could.

'But I could not control my emotions. I began to think of nothing else but her. When I woke in the morning she was always there in my thoughts. She was the only thing that I lived for. My desire was inflamed. I confess I have committed adultery a thousand times in my mind. I was haunted by her.'

'She finally gave in to my pathetic pleadings. Of course that was not enough for me. How could it be, for a man who had been denied love for so long? I relished each kiss she planted on my lips on that evening. I was bewitched, a man possessed. In love, if you will. I was in love for the first time in my life. I could do nothing to quell the feelings. I did not want to do anything. It was ecstacy.'

The laird closed his eyes, recalling Grissell's embrace.

'I see now that this was the last thing she needed. She was concerned with her own life and her daughters. But love is a wave which overwhelms us. There is nothing that I could do to stop it.'

MacKenzie nodded sympathetically.

'I met her on the twenty-second of October at the Devil's Pool. I confessed my love for her again. I told her that I would do anything for her, give up everything, travel to the ends of the earth for her. But she rejected me. She said it was too dangerous. She had set other plans in motion. She was going away to another land. I asked her where she was bound. She would not say. We argued. I attacked her with cruel words. I was relentless with all the selfishness of a man in love. We both shed tears. Then finally in her desperation she blurted out that she was with child. At first my heart rejoiced at such news. But she held that she must leave Lammersheugh. I pleaded with her, holding her so tightly that her necklace broke and fell onto the rock where we stood. We argued bitterly again. She screamed that she wanted to be alone. I departed for the village. But on my way down I realised that I still held the bonnet that I had taken from her head in my distraction. I retraced my steps to return it.

'As I approached, I saw she was on the rock, looking down into the pool. The next moment she was gone! She had launched herself into the water. I knew she could not swim. She had sought escape from the evil of this world in the other land she had spoken of, for herself and her unborn child.

'I ran as fast as I could. The climb seemed to last for ever. When I reached the pool, I could not see her. I launched myself into the ice-cold water. It was a number of minutes before I found her submerged in the middle. I dragged her to the side. I tried to revive her. I spoke to her, attempting to coax her back from death with words of love. But it was to no avail. She was gone to the other land that she had spoken of. Now, perhaps, she is at peace with Alexander.

'I knew not what I should do. I was paralysed with indecision. I realised that if she was found at the water's edge there would be questions. So I pulled her back into the pool and let her drift, giving her soft cheek one last kiss. She floated slowly with the current across the water and under the trees.

'I cursed my existence. I stared down at the pistol in my hand, the one given to me by my father-in-law on the day of my marriage and I came close to blowing my brains out. I stood for a long time pondering the simple beauty of its craftsmanship, feeling that an end to my troubles was in my hands.'

MacKenzie touched the laird gently on the arm.

'But my reverie was broken by the sound of someone approaching. I ran for cover in the woods, crouching behind some bushes. You can imagine my shock when I saw my own son appear. I crawled deeper into the trees, watching him on the rock. I saw him notice Grissell's body and throw a stone. He then ran round. I knew not what I should do. Grief and guilt overwhelmed me. I called out for him to come to me. The words that escaped from my mouth did not sound like a human voice. My throat was so twisted by despair. He ran away fearing I was the Devil.

'In my distracted state I cast the weapon into the woods, then wandered the hills for hours, intending to drown myself in a loch. But as the tumult of emotion began to subside, I knew that I could not abandon my son and wife. I returned home.' Cockburn's eyes remained focused on the hills. There were tears on his cheeks.

'You have my confession, John. The pain lives on. I miss her as she missed Alexander.'

MacKenzie nodded grimly. 'I am glad I know the truth, Adam. You should tell Geordie what happened. He is convinced that he saw the Devil. It is not healthy for a boy to carry such a memory.'

'I will try to explain, when the time is right.'

The two men walked back towards the house.

'I hope you will honour me with some business one day!' MacKenzie said, changing the subject. 'You have a fine son. Look after him well. Rid yourself of guilt about your wife. Some things are beyond our ken. We must simply do our best. We are all driven by desires which we cannot control. But I lapse into philosophy. It must wait for another day. Come to Edinburgh. Dine with good Scots lawyers. Let us share a few pints of wine and discuss metaphysics!'

'I will, John. I bid you farewell.' A brief smile returned to Cockburn's face as he walked off in the direction of the Blinkbonny Woods. MacKenzie turned to look at the house. Scougall was waiting for him at the front door. The young man had been through much. He was governed by his upbringing and clung to superstitions. But he had conquered his fear. He would proceed carefully with him over the next couple of days. He had proved himself to be a worthy companion.

A Visit from Euphame Hay

12 February 1688

'THERE IS SOMEONE to see you, sir.' MacKenzie was at his desk in his chambers working on an account of Montrose's arrival at Inverness.

'Show them in please, Meg.'

When he looked up again, Euphame Hay stood before him. She was a transformed figure; she had put on weight and a healthy colour was restored to her face. She was a young woman again.

'Euphame, my dear. You look so well.' MacKenzie was surprised to see her. Taking her hand, they embraced. 'I did not expect to see you in Edinburgh so soon.'

'Thank you, John. It brings me cheer to see you again.'

'Please be seated.'

She sat by the fire, MacKenzie taking the chair opposite her.

'I have made good progress. The horror begins to fade, somewhat.'

MacKenzie nodded his head, smiling at the young woman. 'Would you care for some refreshments?'

'No, thank you. I will not keep you long.'

'Do you call on a legal matter?'

'I do, in a way.' She looked down at her hands then burst

out, 'My sister and I have decided to leave Scotland. A coach waits for us on the High Street. We cannot remain at Lammersheugh. We are haunted by memories. We have decided to travel to London, Paris, Italy, wherever the wind takes us.'

'I think that is a fine idea,' said MacKenzie. 'My days of travel were among the happiest of my life.'

'I would like you to look after the affairs of the estate in our absence,' she said sadly. 'I cannot thole Purse having anything more to do with us. Someone must see to the collection of rents and send us money.'

'I will be only too happy to act for you, Euphame. I might assign the task to Davie Scougall, if you are content with that arrangement. I would oversee his work, of course. It would be useful experience for him, a change from the dull instruments he writes, a new challenge.'

MacKenzie smiled as he foresaw Scougall's initial reluctance. But he knew he would perform the task with diligence.

'I believe Mr Scougall will be a most exact accountant,' said Euphame.

'Do you have any further requests, my dear?'

'Only...' Euphame looked troubled as if searching for the right words to begin what she wanted to say.

At last she spoke without meeting his eyes. 'I must leave this country – it is full of evil men – the kirk – the ministers – the pricker. It is a nightmare from which I cannot escape.' She pulled her hands across her chest as she recalled her imprisonment. 'He comes back to me each night, you know – Kincaid,' she continued. 'If I ever have children, how am I to explain to them what happened to their mother and grandmother? The young man whom I hoped to marry is betrothed to another. He does not speak a word to me. My childhood was a time of love. My father was doting. I had dear Janet, the gardens, the house and our dogs. My mother adored us. How am I to account for all that beside so much evil?'

'I share your concerns,' replied MacKenzie. 'Scotland is a blighted land. A fever takes hold of the hearts of the people fed by the zealotry of self-righteous ministers. But I believe it will burn itself out as all distempers do. Unforeseen forces were unleashed by our change of religion in 1560. The reformers desired to mould our lives towards a greater good. But they ushered in much evil. In the Highlands the ministers still have little sway. Our chiefs maintain power rather than the church, although they too begin to fade.' MacKenzie took a deep breath and exhaled as he shook his head. 'At times I fear for our country. I wonder if I should take my daughter to London or America. But there are grounds for hope. New currents in philosophy take hold. The spirit of commerce grows. Making money may interest the young more than witch-hunting or debates about church government. We may soon base our society on sound rational principles.'

Euphame's earlier buoyancy was gone. Her face darkened. 'Such evil – such hatred in the name of God. I do not know if we will return to Scotland, John. We have lived through too much pain.'

'I hear that Lady Girnington is condemned to hang. There was insufficient evidence to bring the others to trial,' said MacKenzie. But he regretted moving the conversation in this direction.

'It gives me little cheer to learn of more death,' Euphame said.

The conversation ceased as they both watched the fire. MacKenzie's eyes moved to the portrait of his dead wife. He felt her eyes accusing him.

'There is something I must tell you.' Euphame continued to stare at the flames. 'I must tell you one last thing before I leave. I tell this to you and to no other – not even my sister. I do not know why I need to speak of it, but someone must know the truth so the chapter may be closed. I need to confess, but I have no confessor.'

'You may confess to me, Euphame.' MacKenzie's eyes moved from the portrait of his wife to the picture of Lady Lammersheugh which now hung in his chamber.

'I have held back some of what happened.' She stared deep into the fire. MacKenzie noticed that she was shaking. The Tron Kirk bell began to chime. She waited until it struck twelve times before continuing. 'In early September I became very worried about my mother. She seemed to be wilting before our eyes. On one occasion she spent two days in her chamber without speaking to anyone. We were unable to rouse her from her melancholy. Thereafter I kept a close watch on her. I could tell she was suffering under great strain. Then one night I was looking down on the gardens as I often did before I retired to bed, remembering the days when my father was alive, when I saw a figure in the moonlight. It was her. I watched her disappear into the woods, so I quickly pulled a cloak over my nightgown. I know the path like the lines on my hand. I soon caught up with her. I watched her enter Janet's cottage. I waited for a few minutes. It was usual to treat the cottage as my own, so I entered without knocking.

'The sight within struck me like a slap on the face. Janet held a cat in her arms and with a long knife was slitting its throat. Blood was dripping into a bowl in front of her on the floor. The last cries of the creature are seared on my memory as deeply as the pricker's footsteps.

'On the spit over the fire was another cat, recently slaughtered and skinned. The cottage was full of the sweet smell of roasting flesh. I stood transfixed at what I was witnessing. My mother came to me. She told me to sit on the chair. I became hysterical, screaming that what they were doing was wrong. She took me in her arms, trying to calm me. She explained that a recipe made by Janet using the blood would allow her to look into the future. I told them that it was witchcraft. Janet said it was not. She had been shown by her mother. The rite was passed down through the generations, from mother to daughter, long before the men of God decided what was right and what was wrong.

'My mother then shared her troubles with me. She told me about the way in which she had been abused by Lady Girnington. She confessed that she had been deboched by the colonel in our home. She told me of the threats that had been made by our aunt. She revealed that she had been interviewed by the session following the delation of Margaret Rammage and how she feared for us all. She believed that if she did not do something, Rosina and I might also be accused. She had to act or see her daughters destroyed.

'I wept when I heard what had happened. I cursed Lady Girnington and the Laird of Clachdean. I still pleaded with her to stop the ritual before it was too late. But they would not.'

'Fresh blood and roasted flesh were mixed with other ingredients Janet had gathered in the woods. I know not what they were. She heated the mixture in a cauldron over the fire. As she stirred, she said a rhyme, a spell, a charm. I cannot remember the words. They were incomprehensible, in a language I could not understand. My mother drank the concoction from a cup. She looked as if she was about to vomit, but Janet comforted her, ensuring that she took the whole draught. She sank into slumber. I could tell she was dreaming as her eyes rolled beneath the lids. When she awoke, perhaps half an hour later, she was sick in the bowl Janet had waiting for her. As she came out of the trance there was a look of triumph on her face. She described to us what she had seen – a vision of Lady Girnington hung for her crimes; the Laird of Clachdean dead, his body food for the crows.'

MacKenzie felt unease move through him like a black bird against a blue sky.

Euphame continued: 'She knew what she had to do. She embraced me. Janet asked her what else she saw. But she did not answer. I pleaded with her never to carry out such a rite again as we might all burn as witches if we were caught. She replied that she knew what she was doing. The path was clear at last.

'We left the cottage in the middle of the night. As we walked back through the woods, she bade me speak no more of what I had seen, especially to Rosina. All would be well. But I did not think it would. Sure enough, two days late she was found drowned.'

Euphame paused to look into MacKenzie's eyes. 'Two days later she was dead,' she repeated. 'I know what she saw in her dream. She saw herself drowned in the Devil's Pool. She thought that she must sacrifice herself. She believed that by taking her life she would save her daughters and kill her enemies.' She hesitated before adding: 'She has been proved right.'

MacKenzie looked at the clock on the mantelpiece. He reflected that Lady Girnington was now dead. The feeling of unease continued to swell within him. There was a hint of nausea.

'Some might say that she was a witch,' she said.

MacKenzie turned his head and realised that he was looking at the portrait of Grissell. For an instant he was sure that he saw a slight smile on her lips. But when he looked again she stared seriously at him. 'Then they would be wrong,' he said. 'She was no witch, just a woman driven by despair to save her children. She planned everything: her own death, the letter she sent to me, the latterwill and testament. This was not witchcraft but an elaborate trap set by a clever, but desperate woman. And she nearly failed. You might have died in the Tolbooth or on the stake. She did not foresee how the hysteria would spread. She should have sought help before attempting such a plan. She could have asked me to intervene. Do not think harshly of her, Euphame. She had nowhere else to turn. I assure you there are no witches.'

Euphame stood up: 'I believe you, John. I do. But in the night I see the faces of my accusers Cant, Rankine and Muschet. I hear the sound of Kincaid's footsteps in the steeple, his order to strip me and hold me down, the indignity of having each inch of my body pierced by such a man. I wish I was able to cast them into Hell as they deserve!'

'I think you do right in leaving Scotland, Euphame. Seek the light, my dear. You will find better days.'

She gave him her hand. 'I must leave...'

He showed her out onto the stairs then went to the window. He looked down on the High Street of Edinburgh. Crowds were going about their business. It was market day in the Lawnmarket.

He saw Euphame ascend into the coach. The affair had not ended well. Lives had been destroyed. The vile ideas of that book – Thou shalt not suffer a witch to live – he heard the words spoken by Andrew Cant – well named, he thought drily. Man would do better when all priests, Protestant and Catholic, were despatched into the flames of Hell! And there he saw it reappearing before his mind's eye; at first just a black speck in the distance. It swelled until a dark chasm opened up before him. He looked into the void and felt himself fall.

HISTORICAL NOTE
The Scottish Witch-hunt

LITTLE IS HEARD of witch-hunting in Scotland before the Reformation of 1560. Soon after, however, a Witchcraft Act (1563) was passed by the Scottish Parliament. The Scottish witch-hunt had begun. By the late seventeenth century the frenzy of persecution was spent; the major hunt of 1661–62 marking the peak. There were intermittent cases after this, but with diminished intensity. The 1563 statute was repealed in 1736.

In Scotland, the witch-hunt was closely associated with the Protestant Reformation which gave rise to a revolutionary Church committed to controlling the lives of Scots more vigorously than ever before. The reformers sought to create a godly state, cleansed of the stain of witchcraft. Many of the witch-hunters were ministers of the kirk or smaller lairds who were radical Protestants.

The backdrop to the witch-hunt was a time of crisis in Scottish history: political, social and spiritual. During the early-modern period from c.1550 to 1700, society was in a state of flux. Change caused anxiety and fear, unleashing frenzies of witch-hunting which could be based in a locality, such as Easter Ross in 1577 or North Berwick in 1590–91, or on a national scale as in the hunts of 1597, 1628–30, 1649 or 1661–62. It has been estimated that the Scottish witch-hunt was ten times more deadly than the English one in terms of executions per head of population. Probably more than a thousand men and women were executed for witchcraft in Scotland during the sixteenth and seventeenth centuries.

Although a substantial number of those accused were men, the vast majority of the executed were women. The witch-hunt partly reflected the deep unease of a puritanical church towards women, especially female sexuality.

The witch-hunt could not have occurred without a widespread belief in magic, charming and divination, and the acceptance of Satan as a real presence in the life of the people.

Witch-hunting declined when the revolutionary zeal of the Scottish Reformation ran out of steam in the late seventeenth century. Scotland began to turn its back on persecution and look towards the more tolerant and commercial age of the Enlightenment.

If you want to learn more about the Scottish witch-hunt, the following works are recommended:

J Goodare (ed.) *The Scottish Witch-hunt in Context*. Manchester, 2002
PG Maxwell-Stuart, *The Great Scottish Witch-hunt*. Stroud, 2007
G Sinclair, *Satan's Invisible World Discovered*. Edinburgh, 1685

Death of a Chief

Douglas Watt

ISBN 978-1906817-31-2 PBK £6.99

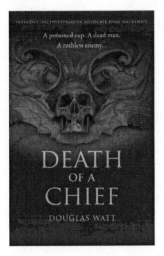

'It seems your father has been poisoned, sir.'
Hector's lips trembled slightly. 'Then it is murder, Mr Stirling?'
'Murder... or suicide.'

The year is 1686. Sir Lachlan MacLean, chief of a proud but poverty-striken Highland clan, has met with a macabre death in his Edinburgh lodgings. With a history of bad debts, family quarrels, and some very shady associates, Sir Lachlan had many enemies. But while motives are not hard to find, evidence is another thing entirely. It falls to lawyer John MacKenzie and his scribe Davie Scougall to investigate the mystery surrounding the death of the chief, but among the endless possibilities, can Reason prevail in a time of witchcraft, superstition and religious turmoil?

This thrilling tale of suspense plays out against a wonderfully realised backdrop of pre-Enlightenment Scotland – a country on the brink of financial ruin, ruled from London, a country divided politically by religion and geography. The first in the series featuring investigative advocate John MacKenzie, *Death of a Chief* comes from a time long before police detectives existed.

Move over Rebus. There's a new – or should that be old – detective in town. I-ON EDINBURGH

The Price of Scotland

Douglas Watt

ISBN 978-1906307-09-7 PBK £8.99

The catastrophic failure of the Company of Scotland to establish a colony at Darien in Central America is one of the best known episodes in late 17th century Scottish history. The effort resulted in significant loss of life and money, and was a key issue in the negotiations that led to the Union of 1707.

What led so many Scots to invest such a vast part of the nation's wealth in one company in 1696?

Why did a relatively poor nation think it could take on the powers of the day in world trade?

What was 'The Price of Scotland'?

In this powerful and insightful study of the Company of Scotland, Douglas Watt offers a new perspective on the events that led to the creation of the United Kingdom.

Exceptionally well-written, it reads like a novel... if you're not Scottish and live here – read it. If you're Scottish read it anyway. It's a very, very good book. I-ON

Bad Catholics

James Green

ISBN 978-1906817-47-3 PBK £6.99

It's a short step from the paths of righteousness...

Jimmy started off as a good Catholic altar boy. Growing up in Irish London meant walking between poverty and temptation, and what he learnt on the street wasn't taught by his Church. As a cop, though some called him corrupt and violent, his record was spotless and his arrest rates were high.

It's a long time since he left the Force and disappeared, and now Jimmy is trying to go straight. But his past is about to catch up with him. When one of the volunteers at the homeless shelter where he works is brutally murdered, a bent copper tips off a powerful crime lord that Jimmy is back in town. However, Jimmy has his own motives for staying put... and can he find the killer before the gangs find him?

The first in the thrilling new Jimmy Costello series.

Stealing God

James Green

ISBN 978-1906817-47-2 PBK £6.99

Jimmy Costello, last seen at the epicentre of a murder investigation and a gangland turf war, is now a student priest in Rome. Driven to atone for his past sins, Jimmy is trying to leave the hardbitten cop behind him, but the Church has a use for the old Jimmy.

When a visiting Archbishop dies in mysterious circumstances, Jimmy is hand-picked to look into the case. With local copper Inspector Ricci, Jimmy follows the trail from the streets of the Holy City via Glasgow and back to Rome, where they stumble on dark forces that threaten everything Jimmy hopes for. But who is really behind their investigation – and are they supposed to uncover the truth, or is their mission altogether more sinister?

An explosive sequel to *Bad Catholics*, the first in the Jimmy Costello series.

Yesterday's Sins

James Green

ISBN 978-1906817-39-8 PBK £9.99

Deliver us from evil...

Why would anyone put a bomb in the car of a retired USAF Major who writes cookery books in a small Danish town? Charlie Bronski has a past and it looks like it's catching up with him.

Charlie recognises the bomb attempt as professional and he should know because it used to be his line of work. When Charlie asks for help from the people who provided him with his new life and identity they ask him for a favour. It shouldn't be too hard, just to kill a middle-aged widower who's doing a placement as a Catholic priest. Name of Costello, Jimmy Costello.

A race against time begins. Can he get Costello before somebody gets him?

The third in the compelling Jimmy Costello series.

An intelligent and well-written thriller.
THE HERALD

Eye for an Eye

Frank Muir

ISBN 978-1906307-53-0 PBK £6.99

One psychopath. One killer. The Stabber.

Six victims. Six wife abusers. Each stabbed to death through their left eye.

The cobbled lanes and back streets of St Andrews provide the setting for these brutal killings. But six unsolved murders and mounting censure from the media force Detective Inspector Andy Gilchrist off the case. Driven by his fear of failure, desperate to redeem his career and reputation, Gilchrist vows to catch The Stabber alone.

Digging deeper into the world of a psychopath, Gilchrist fears he is up against the worst kind of murderer – a serial killer on the verge of mental collapse. Can Gilchrist unravel the crazed mind of the killer?

Eye for an Eye is the first in the DI Gilchrist series.

Rebus did it for Edinburgh. Laidlaw did it for Glasgow. Gilchrist might just be the bloke to put St Andrews on the crime fiction map.
THE DAILY RECORD

Hand for a Hand

Frank Muir

ISBN 978-1906817-51-0 PBK £6.99

An amputated hand is found in a bunker, its lifeless fingers clutching a note addressed to DCI Andy Gilchrist. The note bears only one word: Murder.

When other body parts with messages attached are discovered, Gilchrist finds himself living every policeman's worst nightmare – with a sadistic killer out for revenge. Forced to confront the ghosts of his past, Gilchrist must solve the cryptic clues and find the murderer before the next victim, whose life means more to Gilchrist that his own, is served up piece by slaughtered piece.

Hand for a Hand is the second in Frank Muir's DI Gilchrist series.

A bright new recruit to the swelling army of Scots crime writers.
QUINTIN JARDINE

The English Spy

Donald Smith

ISBN 978-190522-282-7 PBK £8.99

He was a spy among us, but not known as such, otherwise the mob of Edinburgh would pull him to pieces. JOHN CLERK OF PENICUIK

Union between England and Scotland hangs in the balance. Propagandist, spy and novelist-to-be Daniel Defoe is caught up in the murky essence of 18th-century Edinburgh – cobblestones, courtesans and kirkyards. Expecting a godly society in the capital of Presbyterianism, Defoe engages with a beautiful Jacobite agent, and uncovers a nest of vipers.

Subtly crafted... and a rattling good yarn. STEWART CONN

Delves into the City of Literature, and comes out dark side up. MARC LAMBERT

Excellent... a brisk narrative and a vivid sense of time and place. THE HERALD

Between Ourselves

Donald Smith

ISBN 978-1906307-92-9 PBK £8.99

Amongst the dirt and smoke of 18th century Edinburgh, Robert Burns ponders his next move. Frustrated with the Edinburgh literati and the tight purse of his publisher, Burns finds distraction in the capital's dark underbelly. Midnight assignations with working girls and bawdy rhymes for his tavern friends are interrupted when he is unexpectedly called to a mysterious meeting with a dangerous man. But then Burns falls in love, perhaps the only real love in a lifetime of casual romances, with beautiful Nancy, the inspiration for 'Ae Fond Kiss'.

Donald Smith has written the real life love affair of Nancy and Burns into a tantalising tale of passion and betrayal, binding historical fact and fiction together to create an intimate portrait of Burns the man.

The Fundamentals of New Caledonia

David Nicol
ISBN 978-0946487-93-6 HBK £16.99

David Nicol takes one of the great 'what if?' moments of Scottish history, the disastrous Darien venture, and pulls the reader into this bungling, back-stabbing episode through the experiences of a time-travelling Edinburgh lad press-ganged into the service of the Scots Trading Company.

The time-travel element, together with a sophisticated linguistic interaction between contemporary and late 17th-century Scots, signals that this is no simple reconstruction of a historical incident.

The economic and social problems faced by the citizens of 'New Caledonia', battered by powerful international forces and plagued by conflict between public need and private greed, are still around 300 years on.
JAMES ROBERTSON, author *The Fanatic* and *Joseph Knight*

A breathtaking book, sublimely streaming with adrenalin and inventiveness... Incidentally, in a work of remarkable intellectual and imaginative scope, David Nicol has achieved some of the most deliciously erotic sequences ever written in Scots.
SCOTTISH BOOK COLLECTOR

Lord James

Catherine Hermary-Vieille
ISBN 978-1906817-54-1 HBK £20

Told from his final days in a Danish dungeon, James Bothwell's tragic story unfolds, centring on his intense relationship with Mary Queen of Scots. Set against the backdrop of French and Scottish history, in a climate of revenge, ruthless killings and religious strife, James finds himself divided between his loyalties and his conscience.

The life of the fierce warrior and passionate lover is followed from his troubled childhood to the events of his final betrayal. Yet it is his meeting with the beautiful Mary Stuart that would ultimately secure his fate. Whilst Scotland, England and France grapple for power, a tragic destiny awaits the lovers, with consequences that would alter their country forever.

This story is one of devotion, desire, and a love that was to divide Scotland, spill blood, and haunt Bothwell to his dying day.

The Prisoner of St Kilda

Margaret Macaulay

ISBN 978-1906817-65-7 PBK £8.99

The true story of this lady is as frightfully romantic as if it had been the fiction of a gloomy fancy.
JAMES BOSWELL, 1785

Married to a Scottish law lord, Lady Grange threatened to expose her husband's secret connections to the Jacobites in an attempt to force him to leave his London mistress. But the stakes were higher than she could ever have imagined. Her husband's powerful co-conspirators exacted a ruthless revenge. She was carried off to the Western Isles, doomed to thirteen bitter years of captivity. Death was her only release.

Based on contemporary documents and Lady Grange's own letters, *The Prisoner of St Kilda* looks beyond the legends to tell for the first time the true story of an extraordinary woman.

It's a stunning story and Margaret Macaulay has done it full justice.
THE HERALD

Women of Scotland

David R Ross

ISBN 978-1906817-57-2 PBK £9.99

In a mix of historical fact and folklore, 'biker-historian' David R Ross journeys across Scotland to tell the stories of some of Scotland's finest women. From the legend of Scota over 3,000 years ago to the Bruce women, Black Agnes and the real Lady Macbeth, through to Kay Matheson – who helped liberate the Stone of Destiny from Westminster Abbey – and Wendy Wood in the 20th century, these proud and passionate women shaped the Scotland of today.

Leading his readers to the sites where the past meets the present, this is a captivating insight into some remarkable tales of the Scottish people that have previously been neglected, a celebration of and tribute to the women of Scotland.

Women of Scotland, it is you who will bear and nurture our future generations. Instil in them a pride in their blood that will inspire the generations yet to come, so that our land will regain its place, and remain strong and free, defiant and proud, for the Scots yet unborn.
DAVID R ROSS

Luath Press Limited

committed to publishing well written books worth reading

LUATH PRESS takes its name from Robert Burns, whose little collie Luath (*Gael.*, swift or nimble) tripped up Jean Armour at a wedding and gave him the chance to speak to the woman who was to be his wife and the abiding love of his life. Burns called one of the 'Twa Dogs' Luath after Cuchullin's hunting dog in Ossian's *Fingal*. Luath Press was established in 1981 in the heart of Burns country, and is now based a few steps up the road from Burns' first lodgings on Edinburgh's Royal Mile. Luath offers you distinctive writing with a hint of unexpected pleasures.

Most bookshops in the UK, the US, Canada, Australia, New Zealand and parts of Europe, either carry our books in stock or can order them for you. To order direct from us, please send a £sterling cheque, postal order, international money order or your credit card details (number, address of cardholder and expiry date) to us at the address below. Please add post and packing as follows: UK – £1.00 per delivery address; overseas surface mail – £2.50 per delivery address; overseas airmail – £3.50 for the first book to each delivery address, plus £1.00 for each additional book by airmail to the same address. If your order is a gift, we will happily enclose your card or message at no extra charge.

Luath Press Limited
543/2 Castlehill
The Royal Mile
Edinburgh EH1 2ND
Scotland
Telephone: +44 (0)131 225 4326 (24 hours)
Fax: +44 (0)131 225 4324
email: sales@luath. co.uk
Website: www. luath.co.uk